BAD ANGEL

Also by Helen Benedict

FICTION

A WORLD LIKE THIS

NONFICTION

VIRGIN OR VAMP: HOW THE PRESS COVERS SEX CRIMES
PORTRAITS IN PRINT
RECOVERY: HOW TO SURVIVE SEXUAL ASSAULT FOR WOMEN, MEN,
TEENAGERS, AND THEIR FAMILIES

BAD ANGEL

HELEN BENEDICT

A DUTTON BOOK

DUTTON
Published by the Penguin Group
Penguin Books USA Inc., 375 Hudson Street, New York, New York 10014, U.S.A.
Penguin Books Ltd, 27 Wrights Lane, London W8 5TZ, England
Penguin Books Australia Ltd, Ringwood, Victoria, Australia
Penguin Books Canada Ltd, 10 Alcorn Avenue, Toronto, Ontario, Canada M4V 3B2
Penguin Books (N.Z.) Ltd, 182–190 Wairau Road, Auckland 10, New Zealand

Penguin Books Ltd, Registered Offices: Harmondsworth, Middlesex, England

First published by Dutton, an imprint of Dutton Signet,
a division of Penguin Books USA Inc.
Distributed in Canada by McClelland & Stewart Inc.

First Printing, March, 1996
10 9 8 7 6 5 4 3 2 1

Sandy Reyes merengue from *The Making of a Transitional Community: Migration,
Development, and Cultural Changes in the Dominican Republic* by Eugenia
Georges (New York: Columbia University Press, 1990).

 REGISTERED TRADEMARK—MARCA REGISTRADA

LIBRARY OF CONGRESS CATALOGING-IN-PUBLICATION DATA
Benedict, Helen.
    Bad angel / Helen Benedict.
      p.   cm.
    ISBN 0-525-94100-2
    I. Title.
    PS3552.E5397B3   1996
    813'.54—dc20   95-36833
                                                                   CIP

Printed in the United States of America
Set in Garamond Light

PUBLISHER'S NOTE
This is a work of fiction. Names, characters, places, and incidents are either the
products of the author's imagination, or are used fictitiously, and any resemblance
to actual persons, living or dead, events, or locales is entirely coincidental.

To Emma, *mi cielito*

ACKNOWLEDGMENTS

As always with a novel, many people besides the author are behind the scenes. I therefore owe my deepest gratitude to Jocelyn Climent and Betsy Hernández for their willingness to answer my impertinent questions, and to Sandra Allen Gonzalez, Maria Lamadrid, Augustus Puleo, Kate Taylor, and especially to Janet Rodriguez for their suggestions, faith, and encouragement. I also wish to thank the students of the West Side Academy for their inspiring poetry, Judge Judith Sheindlin for letting me witness the drama and tragedy of family court, the subway cleaners at the 207th Street terminal for their moving stories of abandoned children, and Rosemary Ahern for her superb and sensitive editing.

Finally, my thanks go to my beloved family: Simon and his exacting ear, Emma and her miraculous existence, and, above all, to Stephen O'Connor for giving me the inspiration, love, and comradeship that enabled me to create this story.

What is so real as the cry of a child?
                      —Sylvia Plath, "Kindness"

PART ONE

Bianca

Mami's praying again. Soon as I get in I see her mumbling at this little altar she's made in the corner of our bedroom, pulling at her fingers till the knuckles crack. "Mami, what's wrong?" I ask her, but she just snaps at me. "Bianca, you go play with the baby. You don't see her all day. Go play and quit bothering me."

She won't say nothing else, then she gets ready for work and, zip, she's gone for the night. That's what it's been like since the baby come. Mami, she stays here looking after it in the daytime, then soon as I get home we eat, she puts on those ugly-ass work clothes, gives me ten million chores to do, and she's out the door fast as a roach. Ever since that thing was born it's been like my old life with Mami was ripped away, nothing but a piece of paper torn off a notepad. We used to be so tight, like sisters almost. She used to like fixing my hair, saying I'm so pretty she be thanking the Lord every day just for giving her me. Now all she does is yell at me and tell me to clean up and wash the diapers and put away the dishes and make the bed and change the baby, over and over till I wanna jump out the window. She looks so skinny and old, her cheekbones sticking out like wings in her long face and her eyes tired and dark, and she kneels at that altar of hers day and night, mumbling at her wooden statue of la Virgen María she's painted this gold color that's gone all rusty so it looks like blood. When Mami acts like that, praying and moaning and carrying on like some kinda santa loca, with all those candles flickering around her and making weird shadows on the wall, I just wanna shrink her up and push her down the drain.

The baby don't love me neither, I can tell. It stares at me with these big eyes and this old man face, crying and crying. Why's it have to stare at me like that, what's it think I got, horns? Mami, she tells me the baby be trying to get to know me, that it's learning I'm its mother, but I think it's spooky.

It isn't just Mami, though—every part of my life's turned different now. Like, when I found out I had a baby to grow I didn't see no reason to keep going to my dump of a school. All I wanted was to stay at home and start my life with Juan, right? But after he left, Mami and this counselor made me come to this place for pregnant girls instead. They say they want to keep me there so I can get my education. I think they just wanna hide me away. We're s'posed to bring the babies to class so they can teach us how to feed them and play with them and stuff, but I think it's dumb. I mean, I been round Tía Yolanda's babies my whole life, so what's the point? Mami, she be pushing me to stay in school and do good enough so I'll graduate and get a better job than hers cleaning subway cars, but if I do, it won't be for her. I don't wanna waste *my* life away working underground like a rat, getting my brain poisoned with chemicals and my ears deafened by those subway trains screeching and shrieking like hell's having a party. Anyhow, why don't those social workers at the school do something to make the fathers stick around, huh, insteada preaching at us girls all the time? I mean look at Juan. Soon as the baby come he just said, "I got things to do," and away he goes. So how come it's us girls gotta listen to all that shit about how we gotta work and be responsible and be good mothers? What about those bastards I'd like to know?

And another thing—I don't like mixing with the girls in this school. Those girls are trash. Every day, practically, two or more of them get into a fight. You'd think they'd know better with babies inside them to protect, but not those ho's, oh no. Yesterday I saw these two girls tearing each other's faces up with their fingernails like wildcats. They file their nails long and sharp and put layers and layers of nail polish on them to make them hard like knives. It was sick! Two big pregnant girls, bellies like beach balls, fighting and screaming. Most of those girls don't even know where their boyfriend is. And they never got married like me. They shoulda had more self-respect.

Juan married me before I had the baby and our wedding, it was something. Just as good as any of those fancy weddings on our street I used to watch when I was a little kid. Mami and Tía Yolanda, they told me they had to work hard to get Father O'Hearney to marry us in the Church of the Ascension 'cause he didn't approve. He thought we were too young, and of course he didn't know about the baby. But when I stood at the top of those big steps for those people I'd known all my life to see, right above the white statue of Jesus holding out his stumps 'cause somebody always be stealing his hands, I felt so proud I coulda floated up to heaven. I wasn't too swelled up yet so the baby didn't show, and I looked so fresh in my white, white dress with gauze ruffles going round an' round me like an ice-cream cone. White looks real good on me, see, 'cause I got this long black hair and these big dark eyes that drive the boys crazy—even when I was eleven, boys was always wanting to put their hands on me. I set my hair in ringlets for the wedding, pulled it up high on my head with a ribbon and let the long part fall behind so my hair was gleaming this blue-black on my white dress, clean and shiny like a new paint-brush. It was pretty! I got it all down in my wedding album, which Juan's never even seen. I still do my hair like that sometimes 'cause I like how it swings when I run, how it feels when it brushes my bare back in the summer. It tickles so sweet and gentle it give me a private feeling all over, like I'm beautiful and strong and no one can mess with me. When Juan met me he thought I was sixteen, not twelve. He said I looked good enough to be one of those girls on TV in the Coke ads. When I look in the mirror I think that might be true 'cept my top lip's too short. Every night I pull at it to make it longer. The baby looks like me when it's not crying.

Juan looked real fresh for the wedding, too. He was wearing this white tuxedo he rented from a store on Amster-dam, and it fitted him real tight and sleek like a superhero suit. I told him the two of us looked better than those wed-ding pictures you see in camera stores, but he just nodded and gave his friends the eye when I said that, like he was afraid they'd throw tomatoes at him. I got his ring on my fin-ger to this day, a real wedding ring with a knot in the middle to show his love.

The baby's screaming again. What is wrong with that thing? I go over to her playpen and look at her, bunching up her little fists like she wants to punch me. I pick her up and stick her bobo in her mouth till she quiets down, and take her to the changing table. She's so scrawny she don't even have a butt. I wipe her and put her in a clean dia-per, then make her a bottle and give it to her in the living room. Mami don't like me to feed her in here 'cause she's trying to keep it nice for visitors, but since we don't get none I don't see the point. After my brothers moved out, Mami saved up her money and she tried to make this room look like a palace. Everything's red—red curtains, red rug, red velvet chairs, and a red couch with gold brocade round the edges—and all of it's covered in this thick yellow plastic that crackles when you sit on it. All 'cept the shelf by the window, where she's got our photos glued down under glass, fading away in the sun like we're all long dead and in a museum. She never, ever takes the plastic off, even when guests do come, so I don't know who she's saving all that velvet for, 'cept maybe the Angel when he comes to take her to heaven. Clara and my other friends, they say this room looks like a whorehouse. Anyhow, since Mami ain't home, I'm gonna sit right here on the couch and give the baby her bottle, drips, mess and all.

I like it when the baby's sucking the bottle like this, or sleeping. Then she's quiet and not bothering me and I can feel how soft and little she is. I like how she smells so sweet, like a morning in a doughnut store, and how her fuzzy hair tickles my nose when I kiss her. Little baby, what am I gonna do about you? I'm fourteen years old and my life is over. I look out the window at my friends, laughing and bugging out on the street, and there's this huge, empty hole hanging between me and them. I'm sorry little thing, I know it ain't your fault, but why did you have to come into this world?

I'll tell you one thing I know about this baby, though. It's something I been thinking about watching those ho's scratch each other's eyes out at school. I'll die before I let my baby grow up trash like them. She's gonna get an education and make something of herself, like I was trying to do before she was born. When Juan comes back from Santo Domingo, we'll find us our own apartment like he promised so I don't have to listen to none of that nagging from Mami no more, and we'll buy the baby pretty clothes and teach her how to mind her mami and papi. When he comes back I'm gonna dress her in a little white bonnet and white socks with lace on them, and I'll put on my pink hair ribbon with my hair up and swinging the way I like it, and I'll take her out in the stroller, strutting the streets and feeling the boys looking, and I'll know I'm a pretty mami and a married woman and they better not fuck with me 'cause I got a husband.

And, another thing. If my daughter gets pregnant before she's married, I'll kill her.

Teresa

La Virgen de la Altagracia, thank You for sending my little angel granddaughter into my arms, mi cielito, and thank You for my children being alive, all but my Hernán, rest his soul, and thank You for Your patience for a woman whose life is wearing her down like the old sole of a shoe. I clean those subway cars at night, which is dirty work not fit for a woman it is so hard on the arms and the back, and I never keep my temper and my words pure, but Virgen, You know the love I hold in my heart and how I try. So, if You could listen up a minute, I would be so happy. I need Your help bad. You sent me that lady today and I don't know what it means. I only know I am scared.

I hope I didn't talk too much and confuse the lady, but soon as I saw her I thought help might be coming for me and my Bianca, and my tongue it just loosed itself, the words they kept spinning out like they was a rope I was throwing to the lady to save us from drowning. You know how it is, my money going first on Bianca's fancy wedding, and now on baby formula and clothes to keep little Rosalba looking pretty and clean—I want her to have a good start in life, and maybe if she looks nice her mother will love her more, pobrecita. But the landlord, he raised the rent, and he sent round those malandros last week to get the four months back rent I owe, and they said they would throw us out if I don't pay by the end of the month—I know he is just looking for an excuse to get us out so he can sell this building, his heart is so black. I feel trapped, Virgen, running round and round like a rat in a garbage can. So when that lady came I thought maybe You was answering my prayers.

It was funny how it happened. I was home with Rosalba, having a rest 'cause she was asleep and Bianca was at school, when I hear this knock on the door. "¿Quién es?" I said, 'cause I know a knock can mean danger. If it is that landlord's men again, I said to myself, I am not gonna open till I call the police. Then I hear this Americana voice saying, "My name is Sarah Goldin and I'm a reporter from *New York News*. May I come in and speak with you?"

I didn't believe it 'cause what would a reporter want with me? Then I thought, "Mi Dios, something's happened to one of my kids," and I got so scared remembering how it felt when the police told me about Hernán. Right in front of my eyes I saw those pictures I see almost every day in the newspapers, those ones that show the grieving mothers weeping over photographs of their dead children. I been there, Virgen, though no newspaper bothered with me when my son died—he was just another junkie to them, shot in the drug wars uptown—but it made my heart jump so hard I thought I was gonna faint. I looked through the peephole, my chest pounding inside, but all I could see was the face of this little white woman standing there all alone. She held up some card I couldn't make out and said it was her press pass, so I decided to open. She looked too small to hurt even an abuelita like me.

"What happened?" I asked her in English soon as I opened the door. "You got bad news for me?"

The lady looked surprised. "No, no, don't worry," she said. "I'm doing a story on tenement landlords in New York, and I have some questions about the owner of this building. Could I talk with you a minute?"

"Shh," I said, waving her in. She was as short as me, I noticed, with a skinny top half and a wide bottom half like I seen on a lot of American women. "Don't talk so loud," I told her. "The neighbors, they got ears like bats." And I closed the door behind her.

At first I was ashamed to show her my home. I can see how bad it looks when fresh eyes come, the peeling paint and the stains of my children's hands on the walls, but this lady, she was okay and she never turned up her long white nose at me. I took her into the living room so she could see the best I got, and I made her sit down on my biggest chair. This woman's face, it was small and kind, with pretty gray eyes and a thin mouth, and she was dressed in a smart brown pantsuit which was the exact same color as her hair. I could tell it musta cost her a lot of money, 'cause it was so silky and soft, but it made her look like a piece of furniture. I gave her some coffee and watched her while she took out her notebook and pen. Then she began asking me her questions and before I knew it, I was telling her all about my life. I just laid it out, maybe 'cause there's been so much on my mind lately, or 'cause she seemed to want to just sit there listening, her big eyes watching me like I was the most important thing. Virgencita, I told that doña things I never even told Bianca, and only You know why.

I told her all about my family and how I first came over here. "Papi, he had been un dominican-york for two years already when he sent for Mamá and us kids to come over," I said. "He left in 1962, the year after Trujillo was assassinated, you know?" The lady nodded, her straight brown hair flapping round her face like a curtain. "Papi thought he could give us everything once that evil man was gone. He thought he could come over here, a free man, and make us all rich. Dios querido, what he didn't know." The lady wrote all this down but she didn't say nothing so I kept going. I hope I did right to trust a white woman I didn't even know.

I told her how it was for me when I first got here; how the people, they was all speaking in these harsh, ugly voices, how the buildings looked so dark and dirty, and how I felt tiny and lost like a bird let out of its cage, small and bright and all wrong in this big, gray place. "I was only four-teen when I come here, like my daughter Bianca is now, bless la diablita mia," I said to the lady. "I was a village girl. I'd been to Santo Domingo only once in my short life—what did I know about a big city like New York?" I told her how I missed the sound of trees rustling outside my window, the leaves thick and wet and the flowers loud like summer dresses, the smell of guayabas and the steamy air before the rains. I was so confused then, with nothing but soot and sirens and garbage and miles and miles of streets and walls all around me. When I walked out with my mother and my sisters I couldn't tell one street from another, our building from our cousins' building. It all looked the same to me, gi-ant and terrible and cold, like a city the devil made in hell. The only place me and my family felt at home was in church, even if the Irish priest he didn't speak Spanish. I started going every day just to be someplace where I didn't feel like a stranger, just to be someplace where the flowers and the candles, Your gentle face, Virgencita, and the whis-pering prayers made me feel safe.

I remember how at nights, when Papi got home from work, he would gather us six kids around him—three big girls and three little boys—and he would tell us how this one would own a string of bodegas, and that one would build a fine house outside Santo Domingo, and this one would go back to our village at home and be the richest man there and show all those campesinos who used to laugh at him just how important the Rodríguez family could be. I would stand next to his knee, the middle of the sisters, a child people often forgot, and to me he would seem like a man of thunder, his wishes were so strong. Yes, yes, Papi, I would think, I will help you make it all come alive. "And look at me now," I said to this reporter, "I got no husband, a deserted daughter, a fatherless grandchild, and a crooked landlord trying to throw me out on the street like I am nothing but a bum." Forgive me for saying such things to a stranger, Virgen—perhaps I ought to have more self-respect—but I thank You Papi is not here to see me now.

The lady stopped writing and looked at me, her eyes wide and sad, and that is when this thing happened that I think is Your sign. I was just gonna tell her about how Papi, he lost his job and everything turned bad so sudden, when Rosalba started crying. The lady looked real surprised. "Is that your baby?" she said.

I laughed. "At my age? You teasing me. No, she is my granddaughter. You wanna see?"

The woman nodded, tucking her hair behind her ears, so I went to get Rosalba outta the bedroom. She was looking pink and mussed, like babies do when they been sleeping, so pretty you wanna eat her. I picked her up and kissed her little head, blessing her like I always do when she first wakes. "Come, niña, meet a real, live reporter," and I took her to the lady. "This is my Rosalba," I said, the pride swelling my heart. Rosalba, she is so beautiful, mi muñeca, everybody says so. She got these round, dark eyes like Bianca's, and a perfect little kissing mouth. That Juan was a handsome bastard, and with Bianca such a beauty, Rosalba couldn't turn out no other way. Forgive me, Virgencita, but I love to show her off.

The lady smiled. "¡Qué linda!" she says in a bad accent. "How old is she?"

"Nine weeks. She is growing fast."

The reporter peeks into Rosalba's face. "¿Qué pasa, Rosalba? Does she prefer English or Spanish?"

"My daughter, she speaks English to her. I use both. It don't matter. You want to hold her while I make a bottle?"

The lady backs away then like she is scared, but I don't pay no attention. I seen that in childless women before. What they think, the baby's gonna bite? "Take her," I say, and I give the woman Rosalba and leave the room. I know it was You guiding my actions, Virgen, 'cause when I come back I see the strangest thing. The lady, she is sitting on the chair with my Rosalba, not even minding her expensive silk shirt getting covered with baby slobber, and she is kissing and cooing over that child like she was born to love her. I stand there and stare, 'cause a vision's coming down on me so strong I can't move. There's this strange woman loving up this baby like she'd die for her right now, and there's this baby who nobody but me in the world wants, and suddenly I see it. This lady is gonna take my Rosalba away. I know it. It is destiny. And I don't want it to happen.

"You like babies?" I say, needing to interrupt 'cause this vision, it is tearing at my heart. The lady jumps like I already caught her stealing, and nods. "You got children?" I ask, though I know the answer. The woman looks away from me and her mouth gets tight and old with pain.

"No, but I . . . I've been trying to have one for years." Her voice shakes a little. "Nothing seems to work."

I take Rosalba back safe in my own arms and give her the bottle. "Ah, that is too bad. Some girls, they get pregnant soon as a boy looks at them, others, they hope and pray to God but nothing. I had three and every one of them turned out bad. Life never works out right, hunh?" I watch this lady's face like it is a movie screen.

"I guess not," she says, her eyes turning away from me quickly. Then she looks around the room. "Where's your daughter? At school?"

"Yes." I sigh. "My troublemaker. She gives me worries all the time now."

"Does she look after Rosalba?"

"Maybe a little, but I do most. She is too busy picking out clothes and fixing her hair, you know? Listen, lady, she is only fourteen, a little girl, my youngest, and such a pretty thing the boys won't leave her alone. They won't let her be the child she is. She is growing up too fast." The reporter shakes her head and looks over at Rosalba, who is making these tiny gurgle sounds babies do when they drink. "My Bianca, she didn't want to keep this baby," I find myself telling her then. "I told her don't worry, any child of yours is a child of mine. I told her I will help raise the baby. What else can a mother do, hunh?"

The woman shrugs her thin shoulders like she don't know what to say. "Well, Rosalba's a beautiful baby," she says then. "You're lucky to have her. She's smart, too, I can tell. Her eyes are so alert." And then the lady gives me this smile so sweet something makes me say,

"Don't give up yet, Miss Goldin. If you want it bad enough, the good Lord, He will help you out."

She looks down, embarrassed, and suddenly I notice she is old. She might have these expensive clothes like in the magazines, and good makeup to hide her age, but underneath I guess she is almost as old as me. You can see these little scratchy lines round her eyes and chin, and her neck looks scrawny. I feel pity for her then, 'cause she seems a good soul, and the vision comes back even stronger, but this time with a voice. This voice, it says in my head, "If you let her take Rosalba, then she is happy, the baby's got a rich life, Bianca is free to do good in school, and you can quit that night work that's killing your body with pain." Then I think, Teresa Rodríguez, ¿tu estás loca? Is that the devil speaking in your ear? I love that baby like my own, mi cielito lindo, mi vida. And I cross myself quick to drive that devil voice away.

I wait for the lady to finish writing some things on her notepad, then I say, "Touch the baby again, miss. It will bring you luck for having your own child." And You know what happens? This little woman blushes but she reaches her hand right out and strokes Rosalba's tiny hot head, and I swear it, I can see the magic flow. I know something is gonna come from this, and that is what is making me scared. I pray to You, la Virgen de la Altagracia, make that something good.

"Now," la doña says, picking up her pen again, "we better get on with the interview, okay? I'm supposed to talk to as many tenants as I can, but at this rate . . ." She smiles.

"Miss Goldin," I say, "I make you a deal. I will pray for you to get your baby, and you write an article to get my landlord in jail for me, right? He is so evil, coming round here and scaring me and my neighbors half to death, you wouldn't believe. Maybe if you do this thing, then you get lucky and I get a break, hunh? What you think?"

The reporter opens her eyes wide, so big and light they are like windows, and she nods and shakes my hand. "Okay, tell me all about him Mrs. Rodríguez, and we've got a deal."

So, Virgencita, this is my prayer today: Help that lady save my apartment so we don't get kicked out into the street like a couple of homeless. And give her a baby, but don't give her mine. Amen.

Bianca

My ex–best friend Clara came round to see me this morning, which was a big surprise since we quit talking after this fight we had over Juan, and I could kill her for what she started. I'm lying on my bed with the baby next to me, trying to grab a moment to just think, when in she comes like a tornado. Seems like I can never just *be* no more. The baby's always yelling, or Mami's bothering me, or somebody be interrupting and telling me I got some million things to do. That baby, she only been around a couple months, but it seems like forever since she was inside of me and I had some peace. Not like it is for Juan, that bastard, soaking up the sun in Santo Domingo like nothing he do matters. For me there is never any peace. Like this morning. I was just lying there remembering being pregnant, thinking, I don't know how that big thing ever fit inside of me, when Clara has to bug in, messing with my mind and nearly killing that baby right there in the bedroom.

The best thing about being pregnant was I got time to be quiet and think. I used to stay home a lot just so I could listen to the radio or look out the window and dream. Mami was on the day shift then, so I'd have our place all to myself. I'd be feeling so good, the baby turning round inside of me making my stomach jump, my legs fat and lazy. I liked that, dreaming 'bout the cute little thing it'd be and the clothes I'd buy it and how all my friends'd be jealous 'cause I'd have a beautiful baby to love and they were still just kids. Sometimes I'd hold up the little white sleeping dresses Mami and me bought together, and those tiny shoes look like they're made for dolls, and I'd feel warm and happy inside and I'd start crying from nothing in particular, just a lotta feeling. I'd think about Juan and how he'd be so proud of me when he comes back, having his child so beautiful, and how we'd be a mami and papi together. I'd think about if it was a boy what I'd call it, or a girl and how I'd dress her in those tiny pink dresses I seen in the windows on Amsterdam that look so cute. Or I'd just think about nothing, just drift. I like my dreaming time. It's all I got left since none of it came true.

Anyhow, I was in the middle of all this thinking when I hear the doorbell go. I don't get too many visits these days— ever since I got pregnant, my friends be finding other things to do—so I figure it's somebody for Mami and roll over to look at the baby lying next to me on her belly with her little butt in the air. She's like a doll when she's asleep, her legs and arms so skinny in her nightie, and that teeny nose of hers pressed flat against the sheet. I named the baby Rosalba. Rosalba Tonia Rodríguez Díaz. I gave her that name 'cause I want her to grow up pretty, like a rose. Like me. Then I hear Mami say, "She is in the bedroom," and before I know what's happening, the tornado walks in.

"What you doing here?" I ask her, real suspicious. Last time I saw Clara she tried to cut me 'cause she said I took Juan away from her. I was two months pregnant already but I had to beat her good to prove he was mine. I get up from the bed, embarrassed 'cause I'm in my baby-doll nightie and my hair looks like the springs in a mattress. I give her the evil eye just to let her know she can't mess with me.

"I just came here to see the baby," Clara says, all fake-innocent like she's still my best friend.

"Keep your stinking hands off of her. She's mine and none of your fucking business, bitch."

"Bianca, don't go talking to your friends like that," Mami says, sticking her nose in where it don't belong. "Show Clara the baby."

So Clara begins acting sugary sweet, and I have to sit there taking it while she coos and slobbers over the baby and talks about sleep and bottles and other crappy stuff, sucking up to Mami like I was born yesterday. I watch from the corner of the bed. I know better than to trust that ho.

Well it happened, just like I thought. Soon as Mami's outta the room Clara starts getting at me. "You got pregnant on purpose 'cause you wanted my man," she says, her face all hot and her eyes flashing white. "That's the only way you could keep him. He knows you a ho!"

"You liar!" I scream. "Juan never even liked you. Soon as he saw me he wanted to marry me. You just a fuck to him." I didn't like to say it, but it was true. He told me himself he never had any respect for Clara. For one thing, she's a boca grande and you can't trust her with nothing. For another, she ain't as pretty as me, nowhere near. And how dumb can she get saying I got pregnant on purpose! Listen, if I told that boy to be careful once, I told him a hundred times, but do those bastards give a damn? No way. I washed after each time and I used that foam stuff kills sperm but I guess God wanted this baby to come and it's His choice and not Clara's to question. But that ho wouldn't understand nothing like that, she's too dumb. So let her crawl off home with a baby in her belly and watch her friends disappear and her life go to hell and see what it's like.

Well, we got so mad we started fighting pretty bad. Clara

grabbed my hair and was pulling on it so my roots screamed out, and I was shoving at her face, trying to get her off of me. The baby woke up on the bed from all the noise and started crying, but I couldn't give her no notice 'cause I had to take care of that Clara first. Twice I've beat on her now, but she keeps coming back for more. She just won't believe Juan don't give a fuck about her. I gotta teach her, that's all.

So we're in the middle of this fight, Clara trying to get my face with her nails, when I push her hard and she loses her balance and lands on the bed, bang, and the next thing I know I hear this squeal and I see the baby falling. I try to catch her but I can't get at her 'cause that dumb Clara's in the way and the baby's on the other side of the two beds me and Mami got squeezed up next to each other, and everything's a mess—I don't know how it happened, honest, 'cept maybe she bounced off the edge when Clara fell on the bed. "Shit!" I scream, "the baby!" and I scramble over Clara like she's no more'n a pillow and I find the baby lying on the floor with her arm all twisted up under her, looking real weird, crying so hard her face goes blue. Mami runs in and sees the baby and screams, and she smacks me hard in the mouth, yelling about us being baby murderers. That shuts Clara up. She runs outta here, fast.

Mami picks up the baby, real gentle, and she won't even look at me. "She okay?" I ask, and I'm sobbing, too, my hand on my lip where Mami whacked me so hard it's bleeding. "¡Demonia!" Mami hisses at me, but she won't say another word. She wraps the baby's arm tight against its body with a blanket, grabs her purse and runs out the door. I guess she's taking the baby to St. Luke's. All I know is, one minute I'm in bed kissing its little head, and the next I'm standing alone in the apartment with my lip bleeding and my knees shaking, swearing I'm gonna kill that Clara next time I see her, and wondering how things can turn so bad so fast. I hope that baby's okay. I hope nothing got broke.

Later, while Mami's still at the hospital with the baby, I
go into the living room to write Juan one of my letters. It's
the only thing I can think to do to drive my worries away.
When he was still here and things got bad at home, I could
just walk down the block to his place and yell his name outside his window, and he'd come down to be with me. If it
was sunny, we'd go over to Riverside Park and make out on
one of the benches, or lean against that thick stone wall
looking down at the trees below. He'd pull me to him and
put his hand up my shirt where no one could see. Juan's so
fresh, every time I look in our wedding album I can see it—
with his wide shoulders and thick black hair, those big,
hazel eyes with long eyelashes like a girl, and his arms so
strong and smooth. His family is all boys since his mother
passed away, so his brothers and his father were out mosta
the time and we could go home and make love in his bed.
When we were alone in his apartment, it felt like a palace.

I wasn't no slut, though, whatever that Clara says. I didn't
let Juan make love with me for a long time after we started
going together. I told him I had plenty of other boys who'd
marry me first, which was kinda true, and I held out for
weeks and weeks. But then he said Clara had done it and
he'd go back to her if I didn't, 'cause she proved she loved
him more by doing it when he wanted. And one night we
were drinking some beer his brothers left and I was getting
this woozy, loving feeling, so I said okay. But he was the first
one and he's still the only one, 'cause I was saving myself for
someone I love, so that's proof I wasn't no ho or nothing.

When Juan makes love to me, I feel like a princess. His
skin is so silky, like my wedding dress, and he smells so
sweet with that aftershave he uses. He makes me feel cloudy
and sleepy like I'm drifting in the air. I like the way he runs
his hands over me and kisses me on my belly and says he
loves me. He makes me feel safe. He didn't wanna leave me,
I know it, even if he did say those things 'bout living his own

life first. I know he loves me. It's just that his tíos needed him home and his dad made him go back, I understand.

Anyhow, since I can't go down the block to find him no more, I figure maybe writing to him'll make me feel like he's still here. I'm good at writing, my teachers say so. I've always gotten these great report cards, 'cept when I cut school. My teachers tell me I'm real smart, specially at my favorite subjects, writing and math, and I can tell it's true 'cause I always know when they're lying. You know, like when they tell us all we gotta do is work hard to get someplace in life? What bullshit! Look at Mami and Tía Yolanda. They be working hard all their lives and where's it got them? Landed with a bunch of kids in a tiny apartment and no man, that's where. Lately things been so tight round here we been eating nothing but rice and beans, and Mami says I can't have no more new clothes till after Christmas—and she's got a good job compared to most. Listen, I know we live a lot better'n some folk. We got a nice street, not one of those places in the South Bronx Mami said my tíos used to live, with burned-out buildings and empty black windows where they sell drugs all over the place. I mean we got these skinny little trees marching down our block, and gray stone buildings with fancy designs carved into the brick, and even a few awnings sticking out over the doorways like hotels. We're right near Broadway, too, so our street's got some class even if the crack dealers won't go away and there was a Puerto Rican maricón beaten to death on our corner a few weeks ago. But I see the white people who live on our block, I think mosta them are students, and I see them disappear every summer and come back all tan from vacation, and I see them wearing shabby clothes 'cause they think it looks cool, not 'cause they have to, and I see them hanging with their friends in those restaurants on Broadway where I can't even afford a Coke—and I know they ain't working hard. But those people'll get much more outta life than

Teresa Rodríguez or Bianca Díaz, I can tell you that. If you're not born rich and white in this world you're screwed from day one, and when those teachers try to tell me different, I just think, you're gonna burn in hell for telling those lies, mister, you're gonna burn in hell.

So, like I was saying, I'm sitting on the floor in the living room trying to write Juan this letter. It takes me a long time 'cause I want it to sound just right, not whiny, not mad, not too cold—I wanna make him miss me. I start a few times before I can get the first line. "Dear Juan: How are you? Is it real hot down there?" I wonder what it's like in the DR. Mami tells me about it sometimes, but every time I ask her to take me there she says no. She says it's warm and beautiful, but there's too much violence. "Why's it better here?" I ask her. "It gets so cold and everything's so hard, and there's plenty violence here, Mami. Why can't we go live on a sugarcane place like you did when you was a kid?" She shakes her head and says no, the DR's no good. "No freedom, too many shootings," she says. "And, mi hijita, it is too much money to go for just a visit," and she won't tell me no more about it. "You are an American, be grateful." Then she tells me to shut up, as usual.

I think of the next line: "Is your tío paying you good?" then I scratch that out—it sounds like nagging. I look around, trying to think what to say. It's late and the living room looks dark and shadowy and lonely. I wish my brothers still lived here, like when I was little. I'm ten years younger than even my youngest brother Luis, and Hernán was two years older'n him, so they both left a long time ago, but I remember how it was with all of us here together. They used to play with me and tickle me and chase me round. I was like their doll, I guess, but I always had plenty of people to fill up my life. This place seems so empty now, even with the baby screaming. Mami says it's the Lord's way that the children grow up and leave, but I wish Luis'd come back sometimes to see us. It's like he never really cared about me, he just played with me and forgot me.

I go back to my letter. I'm not getting anywhere with this. Outside I can hear the neighbor's stereo—he puts his speakers in the window and turns them facing the street, which is okay 'cept when you're trying to sleep—and he's playing salsa. It makes me feel romantic. There's so much I wanna tell Juan. I wanna write him about how lonely it is here, about how I miss his soft skin and his arms holding me the way nobody's done since he left. I wanna tell him how Clara beat on me but hurt me even worse 'cause she's not my friend anymore and I don't have nobody to talk to 'bout Mami Mean and his baby, who's tiring me to death. I wanna tell him how at night I cry a lot 'cause I feel so stuck here and the baby grows so slowly and needs so much, and how she fell off the bed today and I feel so bad about it. And I wanna tell him how I'm scared, when I'm alone with her and angry 'cause I'm having no fun and everything's going wrong, how I'm scared I'm gonna do something to that baby that'll hurt her even worse.

Teresa

Mi Dios, what a terrible time! What with running to the hospital 'cause of the stupid thing those girls did to my Rosalba, pobrecita, and punishing Bianca to teach her not to act like some kinda delincuenta—I got no time even to breathe. La Virgen de la Altagracia, please forgive my Bianca and that Clara for behaving like animals and hurting little Rosalba and scaring the life outta me. What is it with these girls, fighting like tigres? That is not the way my mother taught us to behave, not the way I taught my daughter. This city is so evil it turns even the girls into hoodlums.

Every night on my way to work I worry about the trouble I am leaving behind in my house. Before all this grief with Bianca and the landlord I would enjoy the ride just for looking at the faces of the people around me—all those faces the good Lord, He put in the world—but now I got no mind left for nothing but worry. When I worked the day shift, I used to like to sit facing west, so when the train came up outta the ground on its way to 125th Street I could catch a glimpse of the river between the projects and get a little sky in my life. The light would only last for a moment before the train went back underground, but it always made me think of home, just the sun and the sky, which I don't get too much of in my apartment. But when I look out now, all I can see is my tired face reflected in the window, the bags under my eyes sagging like plums and my mouth hard and bitter. Virgencita, could that dragged-out looking woman be me?

I don't get more than two hours sleep these days, not with working the night shift and having to be awake to get Bianca off to school and the baby fed. I take naps whenever Rosalba does to keep up my health, but my life it feels chopped into pieces like a stale pie feeding too many people, and it never seems like I am all the way awake. I wish we'd found Bianca a school with child care so I coulda kept the day shift, but the only one I heard of was too far away and I didn't want mi hijita taking trains to Brooklyn with that baby in her arms for muggers or rapists to attack, not in this city full of perverts. Now I feel trapped in a mist with this no sleep, like the early morning damp back home just before the rains, when the air is so wet your hair frizzes up and your lungs feel squeezed outta breath. I look at Bianca through this mist and it don't seem like I can see her. Not clear enough to know I am doing right by her, anyhow. That is why I am sitting here on this orange subway seat with chewing gum stuck on the edge, thanking You, Virgen, for protecting Rosalba, who twisted her little muscles, so thin like elastic, but nothing worse, and asking You to help me know how to do right by Bianca. I beat her good 'cause she gotta learn you don't leave babies lying around to get hurt like that, a baby is not a toy, but in my heart I feel bad for her. I wanna teach her right, but instead I only see hate in her eyes for her Mami she used to love. I think of the time she was tiny, sitting on my lap to look at the TV, giggling when I kissed her neck and sucking her little thumb when she lay in my arms, rubbing the sleeve of my dress between

her pudgy fingers. Now she makes me so mad, with her
pouty face rude and sulking, so sorry for herself like she is
the only one who suffers in this world.

I gotta change to the A train now. I hate the elevators at
168th, so hot and crowded like you're taking a trip to hell. I
hold my nose 'cause a homeless is stinking up the place.
Least my terminal at 207th is decent and clean. It is one of
the best places to work this job. The barns where they store
the trains, they too cold in winter, too hot in summer, and
you gotta walk right on the tracks to clean a train, that third
rail lying there like a death trap. Working the terminals I get
to stay safe on the platform, and even if it is like a pizza
oven in the summer time, it is warm in the winter and I got
my friends and the routine. The worst thing is we never get
to sit down, 'cept for fifteen minutes on the coffee break and
thirty for lunch. The rest of the time we gotta stand all day,
eight hours on our feet and that's if we don't work overtime.
Our supervisor, who is this man from India or Pakistan, I
don't know which, he is okay, he don't drive us too hard,
but he won't let us cleaners sit down together. "You can talk
between trains," he says, "just don't socialize. No coffee and
cake." We joke around. Well, it is a life. It is not the life I expected for myself, not the life my Papi he expected for me,
but it is a decent life. I been here ten years and I got seniority to pick my place of work and my hours. Not everybody is
so lucky, I know it, so I am not gonna complain.

But looking at all the other people around me on this
train, I can't help thinking of the family I once had that is all
gone now, scattered like seeds over the earth, lost and gone.
If Bianca had family like I did, like most of these people
here probably got, she would be learning to watch out for
others insteada this me, me, me I see in her day and night,
wearing me out till I am an old woman before my time.
When I was a girl her age, and more and more of my family
were coming over from Santo Domingo to find work, we

lived all in two rooms and nobody could say only me, me, me 'cause we had to watch out for each other. It was hard times but I liked it, me and my sisters and brothers and Mamá and Papi and mis primos and los tíos all in two rooms. I liked the filled-up apartment, the laughing at night and the sharing of meals. I liked the feeling of a village in our home, of family that was safe and full of love protecting me from Americanos and their cruel looks and this strange, cold city of evil. Now my family, it is all gone, so Bianca has never had that feeling since she was tiny, she has never had that village of family to remember. All she knows is her Mami, her crazy tía, and little Rosalba. That is no kind of family to make a girl strong.

The reason my family all got scattered and lost is because of the Rodríguez curse. Mamá, she always used to say this curse started when a few years after my family moved here from la República, Papi and my brothers, they stopped going to church. The curse, she said, was the Lord's punishment for us leaving our natural born home and religion, and acting no better than money-hungry gringos who love the dollar more than they love God. The first sign of the curse was when the hotel where Papi and my oldest brother worked went bankrupt and they both lost their jobs in one day. Then the garment factory us girls worked in closed down 'cause of a fire, and suddenly all of us old enough to work was out of a job at once. When things begin to go bad they turn to worse so fast it is like water running out of a bucket. Papi dropped dead of a heart attack from worry, and suddenly Mamá was all alone with six kids and no income and it broke her heart. I remember this Sandy Reyes merengue she used to sing at night while she cooked a dinner she prayed would stretch enough to fill all the stomachs. She would stand at the stove, her big stomach swelling out under her apron from all her babies, her arms strong and thick from a life of work in the sugarcane fields, and she would open her tired old face and sing:

Aquí la vida no vale
una guayaba podrida
si un tigre no te mata
*te mata la factoria.**

You would think that was enough for one family to bear, but no, that curse went on. Once those jobs fell apart, my family did, too. My oldest sister, she married a Mexican and moved to L.A., and she took Mamá with her so the poor woman had to die in a place where she had no family to warm her last days and to pray over her bones when she was gone. That I find hard to forgive, it was such a selfish thing to do. Then my little brothers, they got into running numbers on Amsterdam and they thought they were gonna get rich but all they got was busted, and they ended up, one in jail, which Bianca don't even know, and the other, he was deported and told never come back to this country again, never. And my youngest brother, the baby of the family I used to love and cuddle, he just disappeared. I don't know what happened to him and I never could find out though I looked and looked. I think he got killed by somebody he owed money to maybe, or some enemy he made. And mis primos and los tíos, they all went their own ways, too busy scrambling for the dollar to think of family. So the next thing I know, it is me and my little sister Yolanda, my whole family gone like smoke, with only me and her left to make alive Papi's dream.

Mamá and me and my sisters, we used to pray so hard to end this curse on our family. We thought if we prayed

*"Here life is not worth/a rotten guava/If a hoodlum doesn't kill you/the factory will."

enough, the Lord, He would take pity on us and forgive our men and take the curse away. We used to go to our church on the corner, the one I went to every day to fill up my loneliness, and we used to kneel down together at Your altar, Virgen, in a pretty little chapel on the side. I would pray so hard, the hope swelling my heart like water in a sponge. This church, it had a beautiful statue of You, painted so delicate and real, its eyes big and sad and black like pools of tears. My sisters, they gave up the Church after a while, sucked in by the curse too quick to look where they were going, but Mamá and me kept praying, and after my big sister stole her away I went by myself. When I looked up at Your lovely face You seemed to be smiling down on me with a promise—once I heard You say, "Teresa, pray hard and you will be saved." I am praying hard, Virgen, all my life I been praying hard. But this curse, it goes on, helped by the evil streets of this city and the temptation to make money easy and fast. My tíos fell for it, my brothers and sons, too. La Virgen de la Altagracia, please don't let my daughter get sucked in as well.

I don't tell Bianca these stories. I don't want her to know the curse on our family. I keep hoping she will get out of the bad luck 'cause I know she is smart. But I look at her now, fighting her friends over that boy and feeling nothing but sorry for herself, and I am scared. All I got to hope for is that this reporter doña will come with the help she promised and get my landlord in jail and his thugs off my back, so at least we can be safe in our home. I know it is a skinny hope, no stronger than a wish on a chicken bone, but I want Bianca to stay in school, I don't want her ending up like me, working her childhood away till she is a worn-out old abuela by the age of forty-five. And I don't want her turning out like my sons, running away from hard work just to end up dead or lost. I want her and Rosalba, mi lechuza, I want them to have a life.

It is time to get to work. My bucket and mop, they waiting for me there on the platform like a baby waits on its mamá. Forgive me and Bianca our sins, Virgencita, and don't forget that reporter lady. Bless her with a child like I promised, and make her help us out before this Rodríguez curse, it takes everything I love away.

Bianca

I'm lying here in bed again and I'm not gonna move for nobody, no matter what happens. I got Mami in a whole lotta trouble at school. I didn't mean to, it just kinda happened, but she asked for it, treating me like I'm no more than a dog. She thinks I don't feel nothing for that baby, she thinks I'm just some kinda animal, so let her find out what it's like being hated so bad.

Y'know, when she came back from the hospital with Rosalba she never gave me one chance to say a word? She just put the baby down in the playpen, picked up that belt she used to hit my brothers with, and beat me so hard it felt like fire. She had me on the kitchen floor curled up tight and she wouldn't stop hitting and hitting on me, yelling how she was gonna teach me to be responsible about that baby if it kills her. When she got tired she locked herself in the bathroom and I could hear her crying. She never hit me like that before. I remember her beating on my brothers sometimes, but never me.

I stayed down there on the kitchen floor a long time, crying and wanting to die just to make her sorry, till I saw a roach coming at my face. When I sat up it felt like the skin on my back was burned all over hot with an iron. I crawled into the bedroom to see if the baby was okay. She was asleep in the playpen and I didn't see no bandages on her, so I could tell her arm wasn't broken or nothing. I thought I was gonna feel mad at her for causing me all this trouble but she was so little and thin, with her round cheeks and her red mouth, small and curly like a flower, that my anger it just dripped away. I leaned over to kiss her cheek—I like the way her skin bounces back under my lips—and I sniffed her tiny ears. Y'know baby's ears are so soft they fold under your fingers like petals? The baby woke up then and when she saw me she smiled, a real smile, not one of those gas grins, and she looked just like Juan. She made this cooing noise and reached up her sticky little hand. I cried some more then 'cause I felt sorry for what I'd done to her and 'cause I felt sorry for what Mami'd done to me. I put my face on the baby's belly and rubbed my tears off on her nightie, and she giggled. "I'm never gonna treat you like Mami treats me, little baby," I said to her. Never, never, never.

Anyhow, it happened 'cause of what my teacher, Miss Mandel, was saying. She's the one teaching us baby care and nutrition and all that crap. She was yakking about discipline and why it was bad to hit kids and her words just got to me, I couldn't help it, and I began crying in class like a dummy, everybody staring at me. After class she called me over and asked if I wanted to tell her what's wrong. I don't know why I did it. I mean, I don't believe in telling people your family problems. That's private stuff, it's none of their business, specially nosy white teachers. But I was burning up inside from knowing Mami was wrong and from feeling so bad about the baby. I was so mad and sad I just told Miss Mandel right out that Mami beat me on the back with that belt.

"Do you want to tell me more about it, Bianca?" the teacher said, looking all worried and using a voice like you use for a three-year-old. She's new and she still takes things serious. The more worried she looked the more I was telling her all the bad things Mami does, and it got so I began mixing the things she's done with the things I just thought sounded bad, and the next thing I know Miss Mandel's saying, "What's your address, dear?" and she be telling me she's gonna come over on Sunday and see Mami for a talk.

Now I'm waiting to see if the shit'll hit the fan. Mami, she been awake for hours, as usual, praying at that altar in the corner where she's got la Virgen María surrounded with flowers and candles on this white cloth like a statue on a wedding cake. I ain't said one word to Mami since she hit me that night and I'm not gonna start now, no matter what. If that teacher comes it'll serve Mami's damn ass right.

"¡Vaga! Get up outta that bed and put some clothes on. It is time for church," Mami says in that snappy voice she be using on me all the time these days. She's all dressed up in her Sunday suit, the dark pink one with the narrow skirt and her matching high heels. Her hair's up in a knot and she's got that jittery look on her face she gets when she wants to impress people. Mami's too proud, that's her problem, with her whorehouse living room and the plastic covers and this suit that looks like she going to the president's wedding. She thinks too much about people looking up to her. Maybe that's why she got no friends. "And wash that sassy smile off your face!" she yells, putting her hands on her hips and staring at me like I'm no more'n a speck of dirt. I turn over in the bed, pull the white bedspread over my head, and I don't move. You don't know it, Mami, I say to her in my secret self, but you digging your grave. Then the doorbell goes.

"¡Estúpida! You get up right now!" Mami yells on her way to answer it. I hope it's my teacher. That'll scare the bitch.

The baby's lying in the playpen, quiet for once, staring at the window and sucking her bobo, so I don't need to do nothing but wait and see what happens. I put my arms under my head and look up at the ceiling. It needs painting. We got this bathroom light in the middle of it, a plain glass square looking all dusty and buggy with a lightbulb behind it, and the ceiling round it's peeling and showing this ugly green underneath. I remember when we painted six years ago and we made this room a pretty light pink so it would look like a real feminine bedroom. The rest of the apartment we left white 'cause it was the only color the landlord would pay for, he's so cheap. But now the paint looks yellow, with cracks all over. Hernán came to help with the painting—that was a year before he got shot up on 145th Street for getting mixed up in some drug deal. Tía Yolanda's boyfriend was there, too, the father of Jonny, her new baby. (That boyfriend's already history, like all her others.) Anyhow, I was only eight but I can remember the smell of the paint and how my brother played the radio loud and let me take puffs on his cigarette when Mami wasn't looking. I didn't know Hernán that good—he was twelve years older than me and he wasn't home much—but Mami and me cried for three months after he died 'cause he was her favorite son and her firstborn and the nearest thing I ever had to a papi. But it was cool that painting time, having some family round I could feel like I belonged to.

I wonder if Juan got my letter. If he comes back I'll have a daddy for Rosalba and somebody to run to with all my troubles. Mami's always moaning 'bout how we got no family left, and it's true. Tía Yolanda spends most of her time kicking out boyfriends and bailing her kids outta trouble, my other brother Luis never comes home 'cept to ask for money—he didn't even come to my wedding. Papi, he went away when I was two, so I don't remember him. And I never met Abuelita or Abuelo 'cause they both died of broken hearts before I was born, Mami says, and she looks at me funny when she says it like she expects me to kill her the

same way. Why won't Juan come back and help us out? He's
never even seen his own child, that bastard.

"Bianca!" I hear Mami calling. "We got a visitor!" I get up
slowly and put on my same old raggedy jeans and T-shirt I
always wear at home. I'm not even gonna brush my hair. I
don't wanna help Mami impress nobody if she goes on beating on me and calling me names. She's gotta learn to show
me some respect.

I hear the door close and before I even make it out the
bedroom, Mami starts babbling. "Come in, lady, come in. I
hope you not here 'cause my Bianca is in some kinda trouble? Bianca, she is a good girl, miss, least most of the time—
you know how it is with the teenagers. And the baby, she is
a lotta work. . . ." She goes on and on, her bony face all nervous, the shadows under her eyes looking like somebody
punched her, and her pink lipstick mouth talking and talking—she makes me wanna die of shame. I go out in the
hallway, which is real dark and depressing 'cause the paint
is so old, and there's Miss Mandel, just like I thought. I can
see right away she can't stand the way Mami's acting, neither. I can tell by her uptight face and the way she says,
"Yes, yes, Mrs. Rodríguez," like she's already dying to get
outta here. Miss Mandel's one of those skinny-ass white
ladies, tall as a streetlight, with crumpled old shoes and a
skirt gone all limp and no color in her clothes. Ratty hair,
too, gray and dry and sticking out in patches. She's probably
butting in my business 'cause she's got no man to keep her
busy. I never noticed it before, but standing in our hallway
looking down her nose at Mami and acting all impatient
with her, she looks like a witch.

We're still in the hall listening to Mami babbling when
Miss Mandel interrupts her, looks right at me, and says, "So,
Bianca, how are you doing?"

I shrug and stare at my feet. I'm beginning to feel real
stupid about this whole thing. "Okay," I say.

"May I sit down, Mrs. Rodríguez?" the teacher says then. "I have something serious to discuss with you. Bianca, perhaps you could leave us alone for a few minutes?" "Go play with Rosalba," Mami says, shooing me away like I'm a pigeon. "This way, miss."

I try to hear what they're saying while I'm in the bedroom but the baby's whining 'cause she wants to be picked up and I can't hear a thing. "Shhh," I tell her, "can't you ever be quiet?" Finally I hear Mami calling, so I carry the baby in with me. Mami's looking worried, her face all scrunched up and shadowy, and the teacher's sitting up stiff on the couch like she's holding a flag at the head of a parade.

"Come, sit down," Miss Mandel says, patting the seat next to her. "I want to ask you a few questions." She smiles at me but her eyes don't smile with her and I can't tell if I'm in trouble or not. I sit as far away from her as I can. "Your mother has been telling me a little of your . . . background. May I ask what kind of birth control you're using?" Just like that she stares at me and asks. What a nerve! I tell her I'm a married woman, thank you, and I don't go sleeping 'round with boys like some kinda ho, and I have a right to have a baby with my husband if I want, and anyhow it's none of her fucking business.

"Watch your mouth, Bianca!" Mami snaps at me, and the teacher raises her skimpy little eyebrows and says, "What husband?" So I'm satisfied 'cause I can hand the baby over to Mami and take out my wedding album and show her Juan's picture. But all the teacher does when she sees it is smile this sad little smile makes me wanna slug her, then she tells me the name of a clinic to go get on the pill, like I haven't heard the same damn thing a million times at school. I don't wanna take none of that poison fucks up your hormones, and whose gonna pay for it I'd like to know? Our Lord made women to have babies, and when I've had enough—when

I'm older and I've got my family together—then maybe I'll get my tubes tied like Tía Yolanda did.

My tía is the gutsiest woman I know. And the skinniest. The last time she was pregnant she only weighed ninety-nine pounds, and she's five foot two, same as me. Mami says it's drugs, but I think it's just natural. She had four babies by two different men, both of them in jail now, and when she was in the hospital with Jonny, the last one, she made them tie her tubes. The doctors tried to stop her doing it. They said she's still young, and she might find a husband and want more babies. She laughed in their face. "More babies?" she said. "I already got four with no fathers. You can't trust no man to use birth control. It's my body—do it!" And they did. She's got all boys and they all be running with the wrong crowd 'cept baby Jonny, and he will, too, sure as anything, soon as he gets the chance. He was only four pounds when he was born and already he looks like a tugboat.

Tía Yolanda, she's tough. She made those doctors do what she wanted. I wanna be like her, 'cept for one thing— she's too bitter. She tells me you can't trust men, any men. She tells me Juan ain't never coming back, that soon as a man smells a baby he runs. I don't believe her. Maybe she can't keep a man 'cause she's too bony and she got a mouth, and even if she don't take drugs I know she drinks too much. But I'm pretty and boys like me, so it's different. I can keep anybody I want.

Anyhow, Miss Mandel gets up from the couch at last and tells us she's gonna come back every month to see how me and the baby are doing. Can't she tell we don't want her? Before she goes out the door she says in her white-ass way, "I'm glad to see that you keep an orderly house, but if I hear of any more physical harm done to Bianca I will have to alert the authorities."

Mami just swallows her pride then, I see it right in front of my eyes. It goes into her throat, sticks for a moment, and slides on down. "Yes, miss, I know," she says. "No more trouble, I promise. Thank you for coming." Thank you! Shit. When the teacher's gone Mami gives me a long, mean look, like I turned into a rat. "Bianca," she says at last, and her voice is so quiet it scares me. "You make trouble again and you know what is gonna happen? They gonna take you away and put you in a Home."

"I don't care," I say, kicking the wall. "It's better'n being here with you."

"Those Homes, y'know what they do, estúpida? They like prisons. No going out, no boyfriends, no seeing friends. You gotta pull together with me, Biancita. We gotta be family together, we gotta look after Rosalba and get you through school. So no more of that lying, mi hijita. You listening?"

I shrug and turn away. She don't know nothing about those Homes, she can't fool me. Mami looks at me a while longer—I can feel her eyes on my back—and then she goes into the bedroom, kneels down in her tight pink skirt in front of that altar, the baby in her arms, and starts her praying, asking the Lord to forgive me for what I've done in a loud voice so I can hear, and to forgive her in a softer voice but I can hear anyhow. I hope the Lord don't go forgiving her too fast. She got no right to hit me like that, almost killing me there on the floor. A mother's s'posed to love her daughter, not beat on her like that. It's not right and I know it. But she didn't ask me forgiveness, I notice. She only asked God, and excuse me, but He ain't the one she hurt.

Teresa

This Rodríguez curse, it is back again. Everywhere I look I got Trouble grinning in my face, his teeth as long and pointed and mean as a tigre's. My landlord, he is back on my case. He sent those delincuentes round this morning when Bianca was at school, and what they did, Virgen, I hope You never forgive. Three big white boys with scars on their faces and arms the size of buses, they came busting through my door like the lock was made of butter. I think they musta picked it, 'cause I know they are all right outta jail, but they did it so fast and quiet I didn't even know they was in the house till they jumped up right next to me like ghosts when I was washing the dishes. I screamed when I saw them and dropped a plate, smashing two of my best glasses.

"You got the rent you owe?" they growled at me, their mouths sounding like they was full of broken teeth.

"I can give you one month," I said to them, 'cause I wanted them to know they don't scare me even if I am only as big as one of their arms, "but the other three months, it comes later, after my next paycheck."

"The rest comes now, bitch," they said, and they pushed me down on a chair like I was no more than some cat to kick outta the way. Then they went tearing up my home like it was a party, looking for any little thing that glittered they could take. They got all my rings 'cept my wedding ring, which I still wear so I look respectable. They got my one and only gold chain my husband José gave me before I kicked him out, and they got all the earrings me and Bianca own, mosta which aren't even real gold, those estúpidos. That was it for jewelry—it's not like Bianca and me, we got drawers full of treasure. So they took the TV and they even tore out my telephone. There's a hole in my wall now, wires hanging out of it like dead spiders. Then those ladrónes, they looked around, sneering their fat lips and they said, "That all you got in here?"

"You should be ashamed," I told them, "stealing from a woman who done nothing but hard, honest work her whole life. I am gonna call the cops on you."

"Shut up," they said, and words I wouldn't wanna soil my lips with even remembering. "You call the cops, bitch, and they'll get you evicted for living someplace you ain't paying the rent." Then they kicked over a table with my family pictures on it, breaking the glass. "We'll be back," they shouted at me, and they left. I stayed on that couch, glass and mess lying around me like I been in an earthquake, shaking for fifteen whole minutes before I could move to clean up. Why You let them do these things to me, Virgen? And where is that Goldin woman You sent round here to help me out? She has gotta expose that landlord in her newspaper and get him in jail. I know what he is doing is against the law.

So I got all this trouble, and that is headache enough, but the curse, it isn't finished yet. Bianca, she is turning against me, my own hijita. Just when I need her so bad to help me through all these worries with the landlord, she gets some devil in her blood and tells the teacher those lies. What's that foolish woman know, the difference between teaching Bianca a lesson and doing abuse? I pray to You, help us outta this safe before that girl gets the both of us thrown in jail.

I saw a thing on the subway the other day which made me think of my Bianca, her troubles and her future. It is no accident the subway is under the ground near hell. I was inside the train, mopping the floor next to my friend Big Al, when I hear a shriek like a pig having its throat cut on the farm back home. "What the hell is that?" Big Al says, and his hearing isn't too good 'cause he been working down here in this terrible noise for fifteen years now, so Virgen, You know how loud that scream must have been. I look around, and what do I see running up and down the car behind us? A half-naked child, yelling his little head off.

"Holy shit," Big Al says, and we both drop our mops at the same time and run into that car fast. That little boy, he wasn't no more than three years old, and some trash mamá, she stripped him of everything but his T-shirt and abandoned him on that train like he was no more'n a piece of throwed-away lunch. The poor baby, he couldn't say a word, just yell like a wild monkey, running up and down with his little butt bared to the world. "Why didn't nobody on the train help him?" Big Al says, and he picks this boy up like a natural father and comforts him. It is hard to believe but the passengers, they just sat there watching this kid, stop after stop, nobody doing a thing.

So me and Al, we took the little boy upstairs, covered him up with my sweatshirt, and bought him some Chinese food. I never seen a kid eat so much, so fast. Then we called the cops and they took him to the hospital. That is the last I heard of him, but it shook me so deep. I watch my Bianca with little Rosalba and I wonder, would she do that? Would she leave mi nieta on the train like that, or in a church like I heard some girls do? She is no more than a child herself, not ready to be a mother—who knows what she would do? La Virgen de la Altagracia, give me the strength to deal with this Bianca troublemaking so I can keep both my babies safe.

I have not done so good with my kids so far, Virgen, I admit it. I tried, but each one, they somehow slipped through my fingers when I wasn't looking. It seems like soon as I was busy with one in diapers, the one I wasn't watching got swallowed up by the devil. Maybe I am not as bad as that cuero who abandoned that poor boy on the subway, but I know I am not perfect. I lost my firstborn to those drug wars uptown, and between You and me, if Hernán hadn't died of a bullet he woulda died of SIDA: he had the no-good blood of his father in him, or maybe of his lazy tíos, and I couldn't do nothing to stop him. Then my other son, my little Luis, he followed his big brother like Hernán threw magic dust in his eyes. I prayed to You, Virgen, I prayed every day to save my sons, but the evils of the city are too much for the men, You know how it is, and my strength was not enough to fight it. Now I have not seen my Luis in three years. Last time he came here his eyes were crazy with that crack and he tried to steal from his own mamita, so I threw him out. "Don't you never come back till you got not even one drop of that evil drug in your blood" I told him. I had to do it to protect my Bianca. She was my only little girl and I didn't want her sweet innocence ruined with the evil that boy was bringing to my house. So Virgencita, You see, I have not been the mother I hoped to be. And I want so bad to do better.

Maybe I wouldn't be losing my temper with Bianca so much if this night shift it wasn't wearing me down. I don't mind the ride home from work at dawn, watching the sky come up pink over the projects, the streetlights dimming under that morning glow like the Lord, He touched it with His glory, but I mind a whole lot being so tired after eight hours on my feet that my head feels like a big bucket of bricks just wobbling there on my neck, waiting to fall on down and crush my toes. It is hard to keep ahold of yourself when you are that tired with work and worry. I don't know how long I can keep this night shift thing going, not with Bianca and my Rosalba to look after. I am scared I might get sick or have an accident, or do some terrible thing in my anger I will live forever to regret.

So, la Virgen de la Altagracia, I am asking You to please help me. I bought You new candles, which I got lit in these pretty little silver holders all round my altar, a flame for each one of my no-good sons, one for my sister Yolanda, one for Bianca, one for Rosalba, and a whole bunch for my lost tíos, Mamá, and Papi, and all the other sad souls in this cursed family. And I got a big special one with gold patterns on it for You Yourself—I hope You like it, 'cause I need Your help bad. I ask You again, like I been asking you so much of my life—please stop this curse. Bianca and Rosalba, they gotta have a better fate than my sons and that baby on the train. Send me help before it is too late. Send me that Goldin woman to save my home from my landlord, culebro, send me some way to find money, send some love into Bianca's heart, send me a sign—send me anything, Virgen, so long as it helps.

Bianca

There's this weird boy on our block, Roberto Valdes, real short and tubby with big ears who Juan used to laugh at. He keeps asking me out! I tell him I'm married, but he says that don't matter to him. He says he been watching me for weeks walking down the street pushing that stroller, looking so fine, and he wants to take me to the movies. He says he'll pay, though I'd like to know what with. I laugh at him and tell him to stop saying those lies. He's okay, kinda quiet, but I ain't interested. The one I got my eye on is this fly friend of his, Orlando. He's a mad cutie.

Mami says I shouldn't have nothing to do with older boys like Orlando. She says he be bad news 'cause he's got a new red Z-car he goes screeching with round the block, and that means he deals. What's she know? I think she's just jealous 'cause he got more money than she's ever gonna have. And why should I listen to her dis my boyfriends—she didn't do so good keeping Papi round here, did she? Anyhow I like it when Orlando parks that car out on the street and opens the hatchback and lets that music fly. He makes the whole block into a party. I hang out the window to watch him and the other guys dancing to the music, and I want so bad to go down and join them. But then Mami sees me and starts the yelling and says Juan would kill me if I run with other boys, and he'd be *right*. Can you believe it? She just don't want me to have no more babies for her to look after, I'm no fool.

Tía Yolanda says different. She came round the other day when Mami was out and we had a long talk about it. I like talking with her so long as she isn't high. She came round wearing this ugly old outfit—real tight blue jeans with silver studs all over them, these white tassels on the seams, and a tiny yellow top showing off her ribs. She be even skinnier than Mami, and that's saying something; the two of them are like a coupla twigs, specially when they tie their hair up in ponytails so they look like little girls with an aging disease. Anyhow, she opened a bottle of beer for me and her to share, and we leaned against the window talking girl talk while her baby boy Jonny toddled around the playpen, poking at Rosalba like he was visiting a monkey at the zoo. Tía Yolanda smelled of perfume and beer and it made me feel good, I don't know why. Maybe it's just 'cause I know my tía, she likes me, and I can relax with her like I never can with Mami 'cause she don't nag at me or try to make me someone I don't wanna be.

Anyhow, Tía Yolanda, she told me Juan ain't never coming back. She said this boy Orlando has money and I should go with him while he still has it, forget my troubles, and have a good time. "Find yourself a new love, Bianca," she said, taking a swallow of beer from her bottle. "Don't be waiting on a boy like a squirrel begging for a crumb. You should have more self-respect." I guess she's right, but now I don't know. When I hang out the window and watch Orlando and think of being in that car and the other girls looking at me, their eyes all sharp and jealous—specially Clara—I like it. But then I think of Juan and our love and I feel bad, like I'd be betraying something beautiful. Still, Orlando is real cool. He ain't as cute as Juan—he's got this long face and a mustache so skimpy it looks like an eyebrow, and he's kinda yellow—but he wears these fresh shades and his clothes are always up with the fashion and he has this way of standing like nothing in the world could ever bother him, his head up high and strong like he's king of the street. Maybe I'll let him take me out once, just to see, but I swear my heart'll be faithful to Juan.

Mami's calling me from the kitchen. "Stop looking out that window, niña, and get in here! Can't you hear Rosalba, she is crying? She needs changing." Mami must say that twenty times a day. What's she think I am, some kinda robot? I go in the bedroom and pick the baby up outta the playpen—she likes to lie there feeling the net sides with her fingers—and dump her on a towel on the bed. Her legs are getting plump. I give one thigh a squeeze. It's real soft so I squeeze a little harder just to feel it squish between my fingers. Her skin feels kinda like dough but springier. The baby yells and Mami comes running in. "What you doing, demonia?" She pushes me away and smooths the baby's head, crooning, "Pobrecita, mi lechuza," till the baby stops screaming. Then she turns on me. "What you do to the baby made her cry like this?"

"I didn't do nothing. That brat yells at everything."

"If you didn't do nothing what is that mark on her leg, hunh?"

"What mark?" I say, opening my eyes wide and innocent.

Suddenly Mami slaps me in the face, pop in the mouth when I'm not looking. "Don't you lie to me, tremenda! You hurt Rosalba again and I'll strap you so you never sit down!" I'm crying, my lip swelling fat under my fingers. I wanna scream back at Mami but I'm too scared. She's soothing the baby again, crooning at it like she used to do with me. "Pobrecita, mi vida," and the baby's looking up at her, its eyes all helpless and dumb. I go out the room and slam the door.

I wanna keep walking away from here forever and never come back, never, never, no matter what. So I go downstairs and I cross our street and I go up to Orlando, who's polishing up his car while the music plays, and even though I never do things like this and it makes me nervous as hell, I look right at him and I say, "Hi."

He looks up, blinking and real surprised. "Yo, Bianca. What happened to your mouth? You been in a catfight?"

I cover my mouth quick with my hand. "It's nothin'." I lean my butt up against his shiny red car. "This car go fast?"

He runs his eyes over me, up and down. "Not as fast as my heart beats looking at you, babe."

I feel myself blushing, so I stare at the ground. My feet look real far away.

"You wanna come riding with me sometime?" he says, and he comes right up close to me and leans down near my ear.

I smile, even though it hurts my lip. I'm gonna show Mami now.

Roberto

Hell, it's noisy in here. I be trying to write me a letter but I got my little sisters and brother running round my feet like a bunch of yapping puppies, and my aunt Maria mumbling to herself in the corner in her Spanish I don't understand, and a car alarm screeching out in the street and some radio thumping outside the window, all of it going crash, bang, scream, shriek in my ear. . . . I could get me more peace and quiet sitting in the middle of Grand Central Station during a fire alarm.

"Juanita, shut the fuck up!" I shout at my sister, but it don't do no good. She be too busy chasing Carmen with the Barbie she's torn the arms off of. I sit back and watch them a while, 'cause even though they be wild, they kinda cute, too. I look at them tearing round the coffee table, picking up our ratty old pillows and whacking each other over the head with them. One pillow goes flying right past my aunt's ear, but she be so deep in her knitting, her fat legs spread out beneath her skirt, she don't even move. Then Juanita—she's seven, the oldest and the baddest—she grabs ahold of

Diego's action figures and starts ripping the weapons outta their hands and flinging them round the room, too.

"Berto, Berto, make her stop!" Diego screams, and he runs over to me. He's four, real short and chubby with a face round as a penny, and his big sisters don't never stop giving him a hard time. I look at my aunt for some help but she got her little black eyes fixed on her knitting and she ain't moving a toe, so I gotta take care of it myself. I wish we still had our TV to keep them all quiet, but my dad sold it for drug money so all we got is each other.

"Juanita, you know better'n that," I say, and I make her gimme back the dolls. "I'm gonna keep them right here in my pocket till you two stop fighting over them like a coupla alley cats." It makes me feel dumb but I am always sticking my hands in my pocket for a pencil or something and coming out with a fistful of tiny soldiers instead. I bet everybody at school think I still be playing like a six-year-old.

After Diego stops crying about that, he and Carmen, she's five, they sit down on our old couch to look at the book I got them at the newspaper store. It's only some old "Sesame Street" magazine, but it's the best I could do with my lunch money. Nobody buys them books no more, not since my moms died, but I don't want them to grow up ignorant with nothing in their future but welfare and dealing like mosta the kids in this hood. Sometimes I walk down the street and I see my homies, the guys I used to play Rambo and G.I. Joe with when I was little like Diego, I see them flashing that crack money round and I think, You all gonna end up dead before I even finish school, you stupid mothafuckas.

I turn back to the paper I got spread out on the table. I push away the plates of chicken and rice we had for supper and pick up my pencil again, keeping one hand over my ear to block out the noise. The light ain't too good in here 'cause there's only one lamp, this heavy marble deal all green and gold in the corner with the bulb gone that we ain't got the money to replace till my aunt's welfare check comes through next week. The ceiling light's all we got, a bare bulb poking outta the painted-over light fixture way up over our heads. Still, I can see good enough to write if I bend over close.

I take a quick look at Juanita to make sure she ain't up to mischief—that one you gotta watch night and day, else she'll have the house torn to pieces in a minute. But she be sitting on one of our big old armchairs, and she looks real little and cute curled up in it all of a sudden. She's drawing on her shoe with a marker but I can't be bothered with that. I know it's hard for the kids to find much to do in here 'cause our apartment ain't too big and every bit of it's filled up with stuff. We can't even move in the living room it's so crammed with furniture and mess: my moms never would let us throw a thing away no matter how raggedy it got. She said throwing away good things is sinful, but if you keep them and reuse them and don't make waste in the world, that's closer to God's way. So we got the green couch and matching arm-chairs with the stuffing coming out, those red wooden dining chairs my moms wanted to go with the table we never got, and our big, clunky coffee table covered with my sisters' dolls and Diego's plastic dinosaurs and weapons. Even the walls in here look crowded, with my old posters of Michael Jordan, and my moms's pictures of her home back in the DR, and her crosses and those paintings of Jesus dripping down his blood for our sins. The entire wall over the couch be filled up with that big old painting Dad bought someplace of an African woman with tits like a shelf, 'cause he wanted to show my moms he thought African-Americans like him got better heritage than Dominicans like her. I swear, if I wasn't so used to it, this room'd give me nightmares.

I'm just getting my pencil ready to write my first words when Diego climbs up onto my lap. "What you writing? Can

I see?" he says, looking at my paper. "They ain't nothing here. Make me a plane, Berto, huh?"

I kiss the top of his little head and give his pudgy belly a squeeze. "Get down you little brat," I tell him. "I be trying to write a letter. I can't even think in here."

I shouldn't have said that 'cause soon as she hears it, Juanita stops drawing on her sneakers and comes on over to snoop. "Who you writing to?" she says. "Is it a girrrl?" She makes her voice sound all snotty like she be talking something dirty, and she screws up her pretty, almond-shaped eyes in that look she gets when she wants to make trouble. She looks so much like my moms sometimes it makes my guts ache.

"None of your business." I push her away. I am running outta patience here. Soon I ain't gonna want to write this letter no more. The feeling will be shoved outta me by all these interruptions. "Jesus Christ, can't you all leave me alone for one second!" I shout.

"Roberto, watch your mouth," Aunt Maria says suddenly from her chair, like a statue come to life. "We got enough bad influence round here from your papi." She crosses herself and we all go quiet for a moment, like somebody dragged in a body. My aunt finally sighs, puts away her knitting, and gets up from her chair with a moan. "Come on, bedtime," she says, and muttering under her breath she pushes the little ones outta the room. They always do what she says, when she bothers to say anything. I watch them with a smile. Look at those two girls, so sassy already in their tight leggings and pink shirts, and that Diego fulla the devil. I gotta get them away from here safe before this street sucks them down like it sucked my moms, and before my dad comes back. I hope that fucka never gets outta jail.

I brush some yellow rice off the paper and pick up my pencil. Slowly, with a whole lotta pauses when I rest my head in my hands trying to think of the words, I write out my letter in my finest script.

Dear Bianca:

I hope it don't bother you getting this letter, but I been needing to tell you this so long. I know you don't notice me much, you be watching Orlando and his dope car all the time, but I want you to know how I feel about you. I seen you with Juan and even back then I liked your pretty smooth skin and those shining big eyes, Bianca, you look like an angel to me. And now when I see you wheeling that baby down the block, a real little mama, my heart swells up cause I wish that was my baby and my wife.

I don't got no car like Orlando but my heart is good. Juan didn't know how lucky he was. I would look after you and the baby, I would treat her like my own. I know I'm no hunk to look at, and I know you said no when I asked you before, but you'll never be sorry if you give me a chance. I can see you feel alone, like me. I can see you and me both need love. We could leave behind all our troubles together, we could talk late in the night and tell our secrets. We could make our own family where people can't hurt us and make those tears spill. You hear me, Bianca?

Come on out with me, girl. I'll be waiting under your window for a sign. Give me a chance and you'll see I'm better than Juan and Orlando. They not interested in you, only in your pretty shape. It's the person you are that I care about.

The One Who Loves You.
Roberto.

Bianca

Mami's cleaning house—she's always cleaning when she ain't yelling—and I'm trying to decide what to wear for my date with Orlando tonight. Nobody knows about it 'cept Tía Yolanda. I'm taking the baby over to her place after Mami leaves for work, and Orlando and me gonna drive off in that fly car together and have ourselves some fun. My tía agreed to take the baby 'cause she wants me to forget Juan. She says to quit waiting on the mail for his letter like a puppy waiting for a kick. "He ain't never gonna write back to you, girl, you better face it," she said, sticking her hands on her skinny hips and looking at me with the same big, deep eyes Mami got. Still, it's only been a coupla weeks since the last one I wrote, so what does she know.

I think maybe I'll wear my tight black top with my red skirt. I like black and red together, but I don't have any panty hose left. They all got runs in them or the elastic broke at the top when I was trying to stretch them round my pregnant belly. I sneak a look in Mami's drawer while she's in the kitchen. She's about my size, 'cept round the middle, so I take a pair of black panty hose and hide them in my drawer for later. She won't need them cleaning subway cars.

"Bianca, what you doing?" I swear that woman can see through walls.

"Nothing. I'm changing the baby." I walk over to the playpen, where the baby's lying on her stomach, sucking her bobo. Sometimes when I'm mad at her, I take the bobo away just to watch her cry. I can make her cry and stop her crying by pulling that thing in and out, just like a light switch. I'm not mad today, though. I just wanna show Juan he ain't the only fish in the sea.

"Bianca, come in here and help me out." Mami's got that whiny edge to her voice again, the one that means she's getting dangerous, so I move quick. "You wash these pots here, I gotta get ready for work." She frowns and hands me the rubber gloves—for someone who mops up rat turds all night she sure is fussy about her hands. "Rosalba okay?"

"Yeah." I shrug and start scrubbing the big frying pan. It weighs a ton. I hate washing pots.

"The baby, she needs you to play with her more," Mami says, pouring lotion onto her fingers. "Then maybe you would like her better, you know? She needs playing with, Bianca, to make her happy."

"Happy?" I roll my eyes. "You crazy?"

"Why you say I'm crazy? Babies gotta be happy like everybody else." She stands there, rubbing in that lotion, her forehead all wrinkled with bad temper, her narrow face mean and worried, and I can feel myself getting mad at her already.

"What do babies know 'bout happy?" I say. "All they do is cry."

"No no, Bianca, you wrong. Babies are born happy. It is life that kills it in them." Sometimes Mami gets like this, saying all these heavy little wisdom things, and I hate that almost as much as I hate cleaning pots. Anyhow, I think it's

Mami that's wrong. I don't remember my baby being born happy; I remember her face red and blotchy and scared. When they showed her to me in the hospital I wanted to scream, What's that ugly thing got to do with me? My baby's pretty. Somebody made a mistake! But all the nurses be putting on these fake smiles and telling me I should be so proud. Then, when we got home, the baby just looked out at us with those black eyes like she expected us to murder her and I said to Mami, "I think this baby's got the evil eye. I can't look at it." Mami said don't be stupid, all babies look like that when they're new. I don't think so. I think the baby knows the only person wanted her is God.

I don't say anything for a while, just scrub that frying pan, watching Mami sticking up there like a broom waiting for an answer, and this hot feeling comes up in my throat again. "Well, you make her happy! She don't even like me!" I shout, smashing the pan down in the sink.

"Don't you talk like that!" Mami snaps. "It is your own fault, pinching her all the time. You don't treat her like a mother should, how can she be happy?"

"That's a lie!" I yell, and the soap suds go flying off my hands. "I don't pinch her. She just cries whenever she sees me. She hates me!"

Then I'm crying again. I don't know why, I just am. It happens every day. Mami comes up to me where I'm standing at the sink and I flinch, thinking she's gonna hit me, but she puts her arms round me instead and holds my head on her shoulder, patting my hair. It's been so long since Mami put her arms round me they feel strange, like they belong to somebody I don't know. "She don't hate you, cuquita, she too little to hate. It is gonna be easier when she is older, you wait and see. Mi vida, no te preocupes que todo saldrá bien."

"I don't pinch her, I don't."

Mami holds me a while, stroking my hair, till I calm

down. Then, just when I'm beginning to feel good, liking her arms round me like the old days, she says, "I gotta go to work now, Bianca. You be good, you hear?"

I push Mami off me and turn my head away. She don't really care at all.

After she leaves, looking like some kinda construction worker in those big clumping work boots and that dumb baseball hat with the MTA symbol on it they make her wear, I take out my red skirt and put it on the bed. Course the baby begins crying right then—it's like she knows to start screaming soon as you get busy with something. I bring her to the living room and sit on the couch to give her a bottle, resting my cheek on her head. The baby, she bothers me a lot, but I like the way her head feels soft and hot. Sometimes she don't look real to me, she be too little, like a doll, but always she feels real, warm and solid and heavy. Juan would be so proud. Today she's wearing pink pajamas and she looks like a little sausage—I think she's growing outta all her clothes. I tap my foot. "Hurry up, I gotta go," but she sucks away lazily, her eyes closed, all drunk and blissed-out on the formula. Wish I could get happy so easy.

When the baby finishes at last, I burp her and put her back in the playpen. See, I'm not a bad mother. Sure I get mad sometimes, but so does everybody, right? I know how to look after that baby, how to give her what she needs. She never gets diaper rash, she never goes hungry round me. So what's Mami complaining for? I wish she had a real crib, though, so I don't have to bend over so far to pick her up— that baby's getting heavy. We didn't have the money for a crib and a playpen, so we just use the playpen for everything. It's one of those plastic folding ones, expensive. I don't see why Mami wouldn't use the old things she used with us, but she said she gave them to Tía Yolanda for her babies and, anyhow, she wanted my baby to have something new so she wouldn't feel like used goods. What would a baby know? But no, Mami wants to spend her money on this thing, and it's her money, she keeps reminding me, so do we get something different to eat than beans and rice, or a night at the movies for a change? Nope, the baby gets the playpen and I get a backache.

She's crying again but I'm gonna ignore her so I can finish getting dressed. What's she want now, anyhow, does she just like bothering me? "Shut up!" I yell at her, "you ain't the only person in the world, brat," and I put on my clothes. I like dressing fancy. There's this mirror on the back of the closet door, and I can watch myself change. I get out of my jeans and T-shirt and put on the red skirt and my black lace top and Mami's panty hose—my legs look long and slim in my little flat shoes, sleek like a model's. I use the makeup me and Mami share to cover where my mouth's bruised from when she hit me, and I stand back and check myself out. I look pretty good. Nobody'd know I had a baby to look at me. I put on some of that perfume Mami got for Christmas from Tío Alfredo back in the DR—just a little so she won't notice it gone—and that deep red lipstick makes me look so sexy, and I brush out my hair, teasing out the bangs over my eyes, and I pin it up so it's swinging down my back the way Juan used to like it. Then I pick up the baby, change her to stop her crying, and rock her back and forth, back and forth, humming a song Mami used to sing to me and listening till I hear Orlando honking his horn in the street.

Downstairs, he is leaning against his car, his hair slicked back and his eyes hiding behind those cool shades. He whistles when he sees me. I get in the front with the baby on my lap and tell him where Tía Yolanda lives uptown, and he drives there so fast, screeching his brakes and making everyone stare, that I'm afraid the baby'll shoot through the window. "I got a baby here in case you didn't notice," I yell at him above the music, but I can't even tell if he hears. "Slow

down!" When we get to Tía Yolanda's house I'm real relieved to hand that baby over in one piece.

"You be back for the baby by ten now," Yolanda says,
bouncing Rosalba in her arms. "You don't come back, I'm
calling the cops."

"Ah, mamita, don't you worry your pretty head," Orlando
tells her, pinching her cheek. My tía, she smiles, liking the
way he be flirting with her. No wonder she got four babies.
But now I'm free and I don't care. No baby crying in my ear,
no Mami nagging, the summer wind blowing through my
hair and the music blaring—I feel like I'm eighteen years old
and fine. Orlando looks so fresh beside me, his shades shining in the headlights and his red mouth smiling. He's driving
me to Fort Tryon Park to watch the sunset. He says he's got
a picnic in the back and a blanket to lie on, and we're sharing a bottle of rum while he drives. He's poured it into a
Coke can so the cops won't catch him. I'm kinda disap-
pointed—I wanted to go downtown and see a movie in
Times Square and eat in a restaurant where people'd look at
me and I'd feel beautiful, and I'm worried I won't know
what to say to Orlando. He's twenty-two and he seems so,
like, old all of a sudden that I'm afraid he'll make me feel
stupid. And I don't know him like I knew Juan. But the air is
warm and it's a pretty night and I haven't felt this good since
the baby was born.

Y'know, it's been so long since I been in a car I feel like
I'm flying. The last time I got driven anywhere was on my
way to have the baby in the hospital, and that wasn't exactly
a whole lotta laughs. I coulda had her at St. Luke's, but
Mami wanted Roosevelt 'cause she knows a nurse who
works there, so insteada doing it the easy way and going
right next door we had to take a cab downtown. It happened at night. The water broke when I was in bed. This
gush came wooshing down my legs, making a big puddle
on the sheets, but it felt good after the first shock. Then the

pains began and, Jesus Christ, I thought they'd kill me. It was like someone took a big ax and was trying to push it right through my middle. I screamed and cried and Mami said hush but I didn't care, I just held on to her and yelled, trying to keep my mind on the noise I was making insteada the pain. Mami threw her coat round me and got me outta the house somehow and pushed me down to Broadway so she could find a cab. I screamed all the way till the windows went shooting up and people stared, but I didn't care so long as God would promise to strike me dead on the spot. Each bump in the cab made another pain come, like a claw inside me digging, pulling my guts out. "For Chrissakes, lady, can't you make her be quiet?" the cabdriver said. "¡Mama huevos! You have a baby!" I said back at him in between the pains, and Mami smiled.

When we got to the hospital they put me on a bed and left me there like I was a sack of old laundry. "Mami!" I shouted, and I saw the nurses look at each other and shake their heads.

"How old are you, honey?" one of them asked, a big Jamaican woman with a soft, rolling voice, who looked like she'd had nine children of her own. She seemed okay so I told her, when I could talk between the pains. "So young, so young," she muttered, and I told her to shut the fuck up and get my mother.

God it lasted a long time. I felt like I was there for ten years, the pains getting worse and worse and faster and faster, that claw digging and that ax cutting me in half. It was real bad when the doctor examined me 'cause she made the pains come harder, but she said the baby'd come out soon. Mami was with me by then, holding my hand, and I was glad when this new nurse came in and told me how to breathe and how to lie on the bed to help the baby come. The breathing didn't make the pain go away, but it did give me something else to think about. I was sure I was gonna die, as sure as I knew my name. Something was going wrong, no human being could live through this. Mami prayed beside me, holding my hand and kissing it. I squeezed her fingers so hard I left bruises round her knuckles—she showed me after. I lay there, screaming and pushing, my body ripping open, and I said good-bye to the earth and to Juan and to Mami, who right then I loved more'n anybody in the world, and I prayed to die so it'd be over. They never even gave me drugs. Maybe they think it's good for you or something, maybe they think they'll stop girls like me from having babies if they make us suffer. Maybe they just like to torture women, I don't know, but they wouldn't even give me a mothafucking aspirin. When it was all over I couldn't believe I wasn't in the grave. Afterward, Tía Yolanda was like, "Don't you worry, soon as you want another kid, you'll forget the pain," but I know that was bullshit. "Mami?" I said later, "did every baby you had hurt you this bad?" She just smiled and shrugged, then she said, "Every pain I had for you was worth it, mi vida. Children bring you a second life, gracias a Dios," and she kissed me. Wish I could feel that way about Rosalba.

"Yo, Bianca." Orlando's voice breaks into my thoughts. "What're you looking so down about?"

"Nothing. Just thinking."

"Thinking? What you wanna do that for?" He laughs like he's funny. We're getting near the park now and it seems to me that it's kinda dark for a picnic. I look at Orlando, who's singing along to his tape.

"Where we going?"

"I told you. I know this place with a view of the river. It's real romantic."

"But it's too late to be this deep in the park. How we gonna see any sunset through all these trees?"

"You don't want my picnic?"

"Course I do. But I don't wanna get jumped, neither."

"Chill, baby, it ain't gonna be dark yet, it's gonna be

pink and pretty. Anyhow, I got friends hang there. It's safe, trust me."

I don't like it when boys show off to me but I'm thinking maybe it'll be easier with a bunch of his friends, so long as they don't act too old and snooty, so I don't say nothing. I just look out the open window instead, at the buildings zipping by and the streetlights shining yellow and the trees all big and black in the dark and the graffiti on the walls and the garbage clogging up the street and the drivers in the other cars singing to themselves and picking their noses. I like it in this car. I like my hair flying in the wind and the music playing loud and the car zipping through the streets low and fast and red, and I specially like the way people stare at me and Orlando, thinking, Wow, catch a look at those two, they must be movie stars. I lie my head back on the seat and look up through the sunroof at the purple sky and the skinny slice of moon like a smile. I wish we could keep driving like this forever, on and on, away from Mami being angry and my street being always the same and Juan being gone and Clara being an enemy and the baby being a pain in the ass and me being sad and bored and lonely. . . . I'm gonna let this wind blow through my hair and right through my brain till it wipes everything I hate clean away.

When we get deeper into the park it's like Orlando said. I can see the big streetlights and the guys hanging out under them, sitting on their cars and motorcycles with their girls and the booze, and I relax a little. The rum's buzzing in my head and I feel high and loose and easy. Orlando zooms right up to his friends in his car and screeches the brakes when he parks. The guys holler at him, and when I get outta the car I see them look me over and it feels weird. I mean, I got nothing against being admired, but this makes me feel like a new jacket or something, just something Orlando brought along to show off. I look away from their eyes and he gives me another drink. I take a few swallows of the rum but suddenly I don't like it so much. I hand the bottle back and tug down my red skirt. "You wait here a minute, okay?" he says, and pats me on the head. "I got some business to do. I'll be right back."

"Orlando . . . ," I start, but he's already walking over to his friends. I watch him for a while, waiting for him to bring me over and introduce me, but the minutes tick by and he just leaves me standing by the car like a shopping bag. I wonder if he's embarrassed 'cause I'm so young. The other girls look older than me, and not too friendly, neither. I stare at them and I feel bad 'cause these girls, they are ho's. You can tell from their makeup and the way they wear their hair slicked and shiny and piled high on their heads like pretzels. Girls on my street don't dress like that. I get back in the car and look around inside for something to do. I open the glove compartment. A shiny black gun is lying there, staring at me. I slam the door shut quick, get outta the car, and walk over to Orlando. I shoulda listened to Mami, not Yolanda. "I wanna get outta here," I tell him, yanking his sleeve.

He looks annoyed. "I told you to wait by the car," and that's when I notice he's stuffing this wad of money in his pocket. Well I ain't no fool, I know exactly what he's doing and it makes me steaming mad. I didn't go out for no dope-dealing expedition, I went out for a date! I look around, scared now, waiting to see if any cops be zooming in from the trees, but just then Orlando says good-bye to his friends and winks, jerking his head at me like I'm a moron. Him and his friends are putting me in a bad mood. I'm not going out with Orlando no more after this, I don't care about his fancy Z-car and his gun. He's an asshole.

We get back in the car and he screeches outta the parking lot like he's in a cop car chase or something. I'm getting sick and tired of this. "Can't you slow down, you gonna get us killed!" I say, but he just smiles and turns the music up loud. It fills the air around us, making the park seem like the middle of the stinky, sweaty city, and I get even madder. Juan and me used to like the park quiet, we liked listening to the birds when we kissed under the trees. Orlando acts like it's all there just for him.

He drives through the park and stops on a hill where we can see the river and the lights sparkling over in New Jersey. It's way too late for the sunset, but even though the sky is lit up orange from the city lights and the moon is bright so it's not too dark, its smile suddenly looks upside-down like a frown and this place is giving me the creeps. "Let's have that picnic," Orlando says, and he gets out and begins dragging the blanket and stuff outta the back. I just sit there. What's the point of dressing up and getting all excited if we're just gonna sit in the dark listening out for muggers? "Come on, pouty mouth, what's eatin' you?" he says, opening the car door and taking my arm.

I slap his hand off me. "Leave me alone. I wanna go home."

He looks upset a second, then he smiles. "Come on baby, don't act like that. I got this picnic for us, and the blanket's out and the moon's hanging there so pretty—I arranged it all for you, babe."

I smile a little 'cause he's kinda funny, and I get outta the car. "I don't like it here," I say, but I'm a little nicer about it this time. No point ruining the whole date. I'll just be easy till he gets me home, then I'll tell him to fuck himself and his dealing and find his "babe" someplace else. Bianca Díaz is not the kinda girl hangs out with gangbangers, and he's gonna find that out fast.

We sit on the blanket and he opens this fat paper bag, but all he brings out is another bottle of rum. "Where's the food?" I say, "I'm starving to death," but he just hands me the bottle. I shake my head. "I don't want no more. It'll make me puke." He shrugs and takes a swallow, then screws the cap on and puts the bottle down carefully on the grass. I notice how he does that for some reason, laying it down like it's a golden egg might roll away.

"So, Bianca," he says, "what's the story with you and Juan? You was the prettiest couple on the street."

None of your fucking business, is what I wanna say, 'cause I still feel like Juan and me, we're something private, but I guess Orlando's just trying to be friendly so I answer. "His dad made him go back to Santo Domingo. I don't know, I think he didn't want his little boy married already, y'know?"

"He coming back?"

"Course he is! We was together two years, y'know, it wasn't no fly-by-night thing."

Orlando leans back on his elbows and looks at me, or at least I think he does—I can't see his eyes behind those shades. "How old are you?" he says, sounding like some kinda big brother.

"What d'you think?" I grab a bunch of grass and pull it up, tearing it to pieces on my lap. I wish I wasn't here. I wish I wasn't here so bad I feel like the shell of me's sitting here in the dark with this asshole, while the real me is home safe in bed next to Mami.

"Sixteen?" He cocks his head on one side. "Fifteen? You sure are pretty, anyhow. You remind me of Sylvia."

"Who's Sylvia?" I say, making her name sound dumb in my mouth.

"My old girlfriend, don't you remember? She lived in number 201 till her family moved to the Bronx. I don't see her no more."

"Why not?" I put some grass in my mouth and chew it. It tastes disgusting though, so I spit it out.

Orlando shrugs and takes off his shades. His eyes surprise me. His face looks shocked and young without them, and all his tough macho stuff kinda melts away—he looks like a scared kid in a fake mustache. No wonder he wears

shades. "I don't know," he says. "Ask her," and he moves
over to me and puts his arm round me. Oh no, I think, now
I have to kiss him. He smells of rum and something else,
maybe weed, and I don't even know why I thought he was
so fresh. I turn my head away and say, "Orlando, I don't feel
like this now. I feel sick to my stomach. I wanna go home."

"Come on, baby, chill." He moves even closer and starts
kissing my neck, which usually I like, but this time it makes
me pull my shoulder up like a spider's crawling on me. I
push him off with both hands and try to get up, but suddenly he rolls over on me and the next thing I know I'm
pinned under him and he's heavy and long and he's holding
my hands down with his. I push and push against him but I
can't move him one inch. His saliva's drooling down on me
like his mouth is watering before he eats, and his mustache
is wet and gooey. I've had boys do this before, I know the
scene, so I just say, "Cut it out, Orlando, I'm serious. I won't
go with you again if you act like this."

That usually does the trick, but he's not listening, he's just
grinning and putting his knee between my legs. "Why you
holding out, baby?" he grunts. "The whole street know what
you did with Juan—you got a big bundle of proof waiting at
home for you right now." He laughs, lets go of one of my
hands, and begins to tug my panty hose down. I can hear
him ripping them and I know Mami's gonna kill me if I tear
them, so I shout at him to stop and I try to push him off of
me with my free hand, but he just lies on me like a big dead
sack of sand and all I can do is move about half an inch. I'm
getting scared now but I'm not gonna show him that, so I
just say again, "Cut it out, Orlando, you hurting me!"

"Don't be acting like that, girl," he says, panting in my
ear, and I hear Mami's panty hose rip. "You know you want
it bad."

"Get off of me!" I shout again, but he don't seem to understand I mean it. I can't get my breath he's so heavy and

the rocks under me are cutting into my back and his clothes are tearing my skin and his face is big and stinky and I feel trapped and scared and he's trying to get inside me, and it hurts so much I can't breathe, but no matter what I say, no matter what I do, he won't stop.

PART TWO

Roberto

The street say Bianca's sick. I been waiting under her window four days now, but I ain't seen no sign of her. They say her moms beat her good for something, though what she coulda done I don't know. Orlando ain't hanging outside her house so much—I heard they went out together but I guess he don't care if she be sick. If she had a daddy he'd kick the shit outta that fucka for just looking at her. Orlando got some other girl now and he ain't bothering. He as bad as Juan.

I got my letter here, but I still been too shy to send it. S'pose she laughs at it or shows it to her friends? I just stand outside her window, thinking it, hoping she'll get the vibes. I know my love is strong enough to get through the walls and the curtains and up the stairs and the elevator shaft and go right into her heart, like an arrow of strength. The other guys laugh at me, standing here in fronta her house with the garbage bags like some kinda guardian angel, but they don't know nothing about love.

Every day I wait here an hour before school and an hour after, hoping for a glimpse of Bianca's sweet face. I see Mrs.

Rodríguez coming in and outta their building, looking all worried and scrawny like a scarecrow, bumping that baby up and down the stoop in her stroller, but I ain't seen Bianca since she come down that day with a cut mouth. It makes me sad she ain't walking that baby herself, all slim and sassy like she was. A girl like her shouldn't be locked up like that, it ain't healthy. I know something's wrong in her life, and I know whatever it be I can make it better. I know what it's like having a moms too sad to care and a life so hard and bitter. I been through it, too, my dad beating on me and my moms, her crying all day, too sick and hurt to help us kids out. Bianca and me, we could talk together, we could help each other let go of the pain. I wanna make her feel she got somebody who cares, somebody other than a moms who slugs her and locks her up and a mothafucka like Orlando who takes her out one day and dumps her the next.

So I stand here every day, talking to Bianca in my head. I be telling her how we gonna escape from here together, how I'm gonna finish school and get me a job as an engineer and buy her a house to put our babies in and to keep Carmen and Juanita and Diego safe in, too. I wanna get us all away from this hood, away from the crack dealers taking over our space, the bullets flying like bugs, and that coke king who sits so proud in that fake French restaurant cross the street like he owns our lives. I saw somebody shot last night in fronta his place, right round our corner on Amsterdam. I saw the body lying in the gutter like a giant rat, the street all quiet and dark before the cops came. This ain't no place for a pretty girl with a sensitive mind like Bianca. It ain't no place for little kids like her baby and Diego or my sisters, either. I don't care what white people say, we ain't never gonna get used to living like this, with gangbangers shooting up old ladies on the corner and no future to give us hope 'cause this city don't give us no respect. What do those white people think—that we don't mind living like this 'cause we so used

to it we don't know no better? But who could get used to it
'cept animals? Do they think we be too dumb to notice the
difference 'tween West End Avenue, with its big, quiet buildings and its doormen in those uniforms like soldiers; and Amsterdam Avenue, with its bodegos stinking of cat piss, and
junkies and dealers and tired-out angry folk yelling at each
other on every corner? Every time I see some dude going by
in his stretch limo, or some white lady on the bus with fifteen
bags of new clothes, it reminds me of the difference. It's like
two separate countries only two blocks apart: grand buildings you gotta pay a million to live in west of Broadway, full
of rich, white folk; and run-down, crowded tenements on the
streets east of Broadway, full of Hispanics and Black folk
fighting for a crumb.

Anyhow, that's why I gotta get away from this hood with
Bianca and my family. I wanna take them away and keep
them safe, where they won't feel scared and bitter every day
comparing what they don't got to everything white folks do
got, like my dad used to do. And I swear right here on my
mother's bones that I ain't never gonna raise a hand to
Bianca like he did to my moms. He used to beat her in the
face so bad she couldn't see, then he'd turn it on me or
Juanita, even Carmen when she was no more'n three. That
was drink and bitterness, and then crack, but I don't need to
tell Bianca that. It's everywhere.

So when she comes down from that prison up there, I'm
gonna walk up to her on the street, nice and easy, and just
say, "Hey," like I do it every day, "when you coming out
with me, girl? You know I been waiting." That's what I'll say.
And she ain't gonna blow me away this time. She gonna
smile that pretty smile of hers and take my arm, we'll walk
to the park and look over the river, we'll talk about all the
things that bug us in this world and that will be the beginning of goodness in our lives. I got respect for Bianca, no
matter what the street say, I know her and me think alike.

Lotsa girls round here have babies and no husbands and no one's calling them names. That Clara, she just jealous.

Bianca, can you hear me? Are my love vibes getting through? Look out that window and show me your pretty face. Then you'll know, sweet girl, you'll know I'm the one for you.

Teresa

What is going on round here? I come home from work, my bones so tired they feel like flames of pain, and I find my sinning daughter Bianca curled up in bed like a stone, neglecting Rosalba, who is wet and soiled and screaming and nobody minding her little body, pobrecita, and I find the dishes still dirty, and my panty hose gone and my perfume used and the house a mess, and it is like I have a devil for a daughter born to make a hard life even harder. Forgive me for punishing her so bad, Virgen, but I gotta teach her to mind other people and get outta her own selfish little whore-head! I work all night long and I get no thanks but a stone so cold she won't even speak, she won't touch the baby, she won't clean up. She won't even move.

La Virgen de la Altagracia, are you sending me these troubles as a punishment? As if I don't get enough with Bianca, those thugs from the landlord, they come back all over again and tell me if I don't pay the rest of my rent soon they gonna break down my door this time and trash my place even worse. I gave them the money for one more month, which was a hard thing to find, but I still owe them two months back rent and they are not gonna let me forget it. "You don't scare me, you no better'n a bunch of thieves," I told them, but I was trembling inside 'cause I know they just want me outta the building. Those malandros they just shrugged their fat shoulders and told me they'll give me one more month 'cause I paid some, but if I don't come up with the money by then they gonna throw me and my girls out on the street. Where is this reporter lady and her newspaper stories to put that sucio in jail? You send her over here like some kinda messenger to give me hope, then she disappears. Virgencita, all I am asking for is the chance to look after my children in peace.

I told Big Al at work about my troubles with Bianca. He has three girls of his own, and since I made only boys till her I figured maybe he could tell me something to help. I didn't tell him about Bianca hurting the baby, that I am too ashamed of, but I had to talk about my troubles somehow. "Take it easy," he shouted over the train noise, twitching this thick mustache he grows close up under his nose. "You gotta remember, Teresa, teenage girls ain't nothing but kids with boobs and a superiority complex. They think they know more'n God Himself, so you just gotta wait it out."

"I try," I told him, wringing out my mop into my yellow bucket. "I try to be patient. But it is like she is a needle under my skin, y'know? I wanna help her out but she won't quit this digging into my heart."

Al moved his thick glasses round on his face and looked down on me—I only come up to his shoulder. He is a big man, dark as a tunnel, and he is maybe the kindest person I ever met. When I was new at work he showed me how the girls, they snip off some of the mop strings to make the things lighter so it don't ache so bad pushing them round all day. And if I don't make it all the way down a car he covers for me every time. I do the same for him now 'cause his sight behind those lenses isn't so good, so I go over his spots sometimes with the cleaner. The trains come in and outta here so fast we gotta run on and off them quick as a mouse, so it is hard for older folks like Al and me to keep up unless we look out for each other.

"Listen," he said once he got his glasses right, "just carry on giving Bianca that TLC. It's the best you can do. She don't mean to hurt you, she just wants to make her own independent self."

"You think so?" I said, hoping his words are true. "You don't think she hates me?"

"Course not, Teresa." He stopped talking 'cause a train was coming in across the tracks, its breaks screaming. "What makes you think a crazy thing like that? You her mother, you everything to her. She just be trying out her freedom a little, that's all. It's only natural."

We had to end the conversation then 'cause the train came in our side and it was time to get to work—we never get to talk more'n a few sentences at a time with those cars coming in and outta the station every few minutes—but I hope Al is right. Give me the patience to do like he says, Virgen, so everything will turn out okay for me and my kids. Bianca says Miss Mandel, that teacher, she is coming again soon, and all I got to show her is a girl who won't go to school, a baby looking lost and sad with no mother love, and me, nothing but an old abuela, worn out as a rag. Help my girls get a happy life, Virgencita, the both of them. You know they are Your children, too.

Bianca

"Bianca? Get up, vaga!" Mami's standing over my bed like a black cloud, bothering me again. "This is the day you said your teacher is coming, right? If you don't get outta that bed and dressed and acting normal, they gonna take you away and put you in that Home." I shut my eyes and, deep down where she can't see, I don't give a shit. When I think of being taken away from this hellhole I feel a lightness in my heart and I don't care, it feels good. If I was gone from here I wouldn't have to be worrying about her nagging at me, and that baby whining in my ear, and that coño and the hurt he caused me. So when Mami talks to me I just curl up tighter in my bed till my ears are blocked up and I can't hear a thing anybody says. I pretend it's a spaceship and I'm flying far, far away. If Mami beats on me again I won't feel it 'cause I'm not here. And if I get another baby from this I'll kill it and I'll kill myself. In my life God has already put me in hell, so what difference does it make what I do?

When Mami leaves the room, after she tries to pull the bedcovers off of me, I come out from under the sheets and stare up at the ceiling and its buggy light shade again. I wish

I could take a clock and spin the time backward, like I seen in those old movies on TV. I wish I could go back to the time when Mami loved me, and when the baby wasn't around with all her loud crying and spitting up and messing the floor and stinking up the apartment with her diapers, and when I'd never met that evil coño out in the street sticking his thing into girls to hurt them. I miss those times when Mami would hang with me, playing with makeup or teaching me cooking or telling me stories about her life back in the DR. My favorite one is about when Mami was a little girl, like ten or so, and she used to help cut down the sugarcane. "We used this big knife, curved like a fingernail," she told me, "and I got so good at it my muscles, they were like ropes. But Papi, he always used to tease me, 'cause when I brought home my stalks of sugarcane, thick and straight and tall as me, the tops were always chewed off. 'Who been eating our sugarcane, pajarilla?' he would say, and he'd make me breathe in his face so he could smell the sugar. I liked to strip off the tops and suck on the cane inside—the sweetness, it spilled out into my mouth like syrup. I never could get enough. So Papi, his pet name for me was boca-azúcar, sugar-mouth." I love thinking about Mami being a little girl with a sticky mouth, giggling 'cause her papi caught her out. It makes me feel like I know Abuelo and our old home. I wish he had lived till I was alive. He sounded like such a good man.

But Mami never tells me those stories anymore. She says she don't have the time, and I can feel myself already forgetting them. My whole past life with her, the life we had before the baby, seems more and more like some far-off dream. Sometimes I lie here in bed, watching Mami clean up, or brush out her long hair, or do some ordinary everyday thing like that, and I just want our old times back so bad. I feel this love for her bubbling up inside of me like a fountain, and it's just dying to come outta my mouth. I lie there wanting to tell her my thoughts, wanting just to say, Mami, I love you, hug me till I feel better, but then I remember the last time she beat on me, or she slaps me away from the baby, and the fountain falls back down to a little bubble, and pop, the words are gone.

I'm just thinking these things when Mami comes back in and starts her yelling again, like she wants to prove my point. "I told you to get up, niña! That teacher, she gonna be here in ten minutes!" Mami sure don't sound like no sugar-mouth now. I can't stand her nagging voice, so I get back in my spaceship and fly away. She yanks at my arm but I'm inside inches and inches of metal now and she can't reach me. She prays some more and yells some more, but I still don't move, so finally she gives up and changes the baby instead. She dresses her in a pink dress with ruffles and little white booties that musta cost a fortune, and all the time the baby's whining in this screechy voice and Mami's cursing me. I hear the doorbell ring and Mami sets her mouth up tight and sends me a look she wants to freeze my blood, but I'm in my spaceship so I can't see.

Now I can hear their voices in the living room, that skinny-ass and Mami Mean, plotting. Mami tells her I'm sick with the flu but the baby's fine. Miss Mandel says I been absent for four days—what kinda flu is that? Mami says I had to stay home to look after the baby 'cause she been working overtime. Lies. There's quiet for a while and I'm so curious I wanna go in and see the looks on their faces, but then Miss Mandel asks to hold the baby and says, "She looks just like Bianca, doesn't she?"

"Yeah, she is real pretty." Mami sounds proud, like she made the baby herself.

"Where do you let her play?"

"Uh, on the rug and in the playpen. Y'know babies, how they like that?" I can tell from Mami's voice that she thinks she's said something wrong.

"She certainly looks well and nicely cared for. Do you take her out for fresh air?"

"Oh yes, señora. Every day Bianca takes her out." More lies. Mami must be crossing herself.

There's silence for a while, but then I hear one of them stand up. You can tell when anyone moves in that room 'cause those plastic covers snap like firecrackers. "Can I talk with Bianca, now, alone?" Miss Mandel says.

"Oh yes, of course. She is in the bedroom, sleeping. She been so tired since she got sick."

"Indeed?" I can hear the teacher don't believe Mami and suddenly that makes me real mad, this stranger woman poking her nose into our business and making judgments about our private life. I don't like the way she talks to Mami like she's the boss and Mami's some kinda servant, so I sit up and put on my sickest, tiredest face.

"Hello, dear," Miss Mandel says, sticking her head into the bedroom. "How are you feeling?"

I shrug and pick at the bedspread.

"Can I come in?"

"If you want." Miss Mandel tiptoes into the room and I see her eyes taking in the playpen, our two beds, and Mami's weird altar in the corner covered in candles and her Virgen María statue with the rusty dress that looks all covered in blood. I wonder if she notices our peeling paint.

"Are you all right, dear? Have things been okay with your mother?"

I shrug again. "Yeah. I just been sick like Mami said. You don't have to keep coming here, y'know."

Miss Mandel gives me this sorry look like she's trying to help out some kitten got thrown in the river, and it makes me madder'n ever. I don't want her white-ass pity.

"I just came to check up on you, dear. I was concerned about you when you didn't come to school for so long."

"Well now you see, okay?" I grab a tissue and pretend to blow my nose.

"Are you coming back tomorrow?"

"Yeah, yeah. I'm feeling better all the time. I wanna go back to sleep now." And I turn my back on her and lie down.

She sighs. "Very well, Bianca. See you soon," and she goes back to the living room. I hear Mami get up off the couch and mumble something, and then I hear Miss Mandel ask her if she been fighting with me lately. I don't wanna hear that. I don't wanna hear no more about trouble and right and wrong and being a mother and all that crap, so I put my head back under the covers and my spaceship spins far, far away where nobody, not Miss Mandel, not Mami, not that red-car asshole, not even God himself can find me. And I stay there all day.

Teresa

La Virgen de la Altagracia, You been a mother, You
know a mother's troubles, and I got them bad. You see this
soft white cloth I use for scrubbing graffiti off the trains?
Snowy and as clean as a baby's soul, right? That is my
Rosalba. She don't deserve this trouble in her sweet new life.
Forgive me for saying so, but it is not right to make her suffer. You gotta help me.

Bianca, she is hurting the baby. This a hard thing to say
about my own hijita, but I think she been pinching her like
she did that day I caught her and slapped her good. Almost
every day now I find these bruises, little round marks like
somebody been pressing pennies into my poor Rosalba's
skin, and no matter how I yell at Bianca, how I punish her,
she won't stop. What am I gonna do? Give Bianca some love
for that baby, Virgen, so she will quit this hurting. I don't
know where she got that cold heart, but I see her look at the
baby with no more feeling than if she was looking at a shoe,
and it makes me think of that child Big Al and me found on
the train. You know I love Rosalba just as much as my own
children. What is wrong with Bianca that she don't feel it, too?

You know what I believe it is? I believe Bianca, she is jealous 'cause she thinks I love Rosalba better than her. Estúpida, jealous of her own child! She has become like a creature of the dark, mi hija, spitting at me and going into long, silent sulks—I can't make her talk to me, I can't make her go outta the house, I can't make her do nothing but mope around feeling sorry for herself. Why must the baby suffer 'cause of this, Virgencita? I don't mean to question the good Lord's ways, but I don't understand why a little baby gotta pay for the rot in this world.

This morning I took the baby over to the church and talked to Father O'Hearney about what is happening. He told me the Lord's way is to protect the innocent, but I gotta do my part, too. "Mrs. Rodríguez," he says to me, his Irish accent tangling up my name, "if you can't stop Bianca hurting that baby, you have to send the girl away."

I know Father O'Hearney, he is right, but how am I gonna do that? If I was back home I would send Bianca to Tía Sandra or Mamá, rest her soul, to keep my girl close by but safe till she got over this hate, and nobody would think I did wrong. But here, where would she go? I got no family to turn to 'cept Yolanda, and she is no more fit to look after Bianca than El Diablo himself. I can't send Bianca to Juan's family back in the Island—they would treat her bad, another hungry mouth they don't need. That boy, desgraciado, he wanted nothing but to get into her pants, a little girl and a virgen when he got her, then off he goes leaving his package behind! Me and his father, we had to force him to marry Bianca 'cause he didn't even have that much respect—that sucio, he is lucky his father sent him home or my hands would be around his neck! No, I can't send mi hijita to a family with no love. Bianca, she is the last child I got. To send her away to strangers is to rip out my soul. You must understand, Virgencita. They took your child, too.

Maybe I am just gonna have to quit this job so I can be

with Rosalba all the time and protect her from her mother. I will have to go on welfare, like those women I always swore and prayed I would never have to be like. How I am gonna feed my girls and pay the rent I do not know, but I got no choice. I can't trust Bianca alone with that baby no more'n I could trust a witch.

Virgen, I can't talk to nobody but You about all these worries, not even Big Al. I tell him most things, but I can't tell him about the evil my Bianca is doing to the baby, I can't get her into that kinda trouble. I can't tell him my money problems, either, 'cause I am too ashamed. My pay I was always so proud of, it is not enough anymore, not with two kids, not here in this city, not by myself with this crooked landlord—this money thing, already it is so embarrassing that when Al asks me out to eat I have to say no. I can't even buy myself a sandwich some weeks, I gotta just bring something from home in a bag like a schoolkid. But now, on welfare? Now we gonna be real poor, as poor as when Mamá and Papi first came over from la República. Bianca, she will suffer, too, ashamed of her Mami collecting checks and food stamps like some welfare woman in the supermarket. I always protected her from that, I always kept us above that scraping and crawling. But it is her own sweet fault, la niña estúpida.

La Virgen de la Altagracia, I got one last thing to say to You while I scrub away here among the cleaner fumes and homeless napping on the chairs. Bring that reporter doña back here with some help. I been asking and asking for this in my prayers, but You don't seem to hear me, so I am asking again. Maybe if You bring her here, and if she can get that criminal hoodlum landlord off my back with her articles in the newspaper, maybe this welfare thing won't be too much to bear. You gotta help me, 'cause if You don't, something is gonna crack, and Virgencita, I think that thing is gonna be my heart.

Roberto

My aunt Maria is mad as hell at me. She caught me hanging on Bianca's stoop the other day when I was s'posed to be home watching the kids so she could go marketing, and she yelled at me in fronta the whole damn street. A man don't like being humiliated that way, she oughta know that. All I be asking for is two little hours to myself each day—she got the rest. I'm in school, or I'm working for pay or I'm at home watching those cute devils run around my feet—what's she want, a saint? All I be asking for is two little hours to wait here on Bianca. I got needs and desires like any man. Don't she got no respect for love? So I looked in my aunt's grumpy fat face, with mustache hairs springing out over her lip like wires, and I told her if she ever, ever messes with me like that again, I'm kicking her and her husband outta my house.

Her and my uncle moved in after my moms died and Dad got put in jail. First they tried to get all of us to move in with them up in Washington Heights but I said no, even though I was tempted to hide us all away in case our dad got out and came looking for us. I do wanna get my family away from this hood, but not just to go someplace worse. And if we leave we might lose our apartment forever and be homeless the minute Aunt Maria and Uncle Carlos get sick of having us around. I wasn't born yesterday, I know nobody in their right mind ever gives up an apartment in New York, 'less they have their own house to move to someplace better. "Aunt Maria?" I told her, "I know you my mother's sister, I know you and Uncle Carlos being kind to all of us, but you live up there in a hood that's even worse than this for drugs, in one room with one bed—how you expect the four of us to move in there with you?" I gotta give my aunt credit 'cause she listened, though sometimes I think maybe she just wanted someplace bigger to move for herself. So she and my uncle left that poky hole they spent their whole life in, where they raised their kids all crammed up together like beans in a can, and moved in with us. And now she thinks she can boss me like I'm five years old.

Still, even though she says no more'n ten words a day, I'm glad Aunt Maria be here for the little ones. They need some kinda mother love, and I can't do it all. It's only been a year since our moms died, and they still cry for her most every night. Even though she wasn't with us much—her body was but her mind wasn't 'cause she got into that junk and spent her life living in fear of my dad and of missing out on the next high—even though she was like a ghost when she was alive, she did love us. She'd sit on the couch, I remember, her eyes big and sad and sunk into her beaten-up face, and she'd open her arms and let us all cuddle up to her like we was huddled round a pillow. Sometimes she'd just cry, fat tears rolling silent down her cheeks, her throat swallowing, but she kept those arms round us tight as she could. If she hadn't been so sick on those drugs I'm sure she woulda got us all outta there. I remember she tried once when I was real little, before the others were born. She picked me up in my pajamas, with a bag on her back, and

ran outta the house, but Dad caught her before she even
reached the end of the block. . . . I can't stand to think about
that. Anyhow, now, insteada our silent moms we got her
silent sister, but I guess that's the best we gonna get.

If I had a wife, a wife like Bianca with her smart head
and her pretty ways, she could be like a mother to Diego
and the girls and bring some real love into our house. That's
what I be wishing for under her window, a wife to love me
and the little ones, a wife for me to love. Sometimes, when I
be looking up at Bianca's window for a flash of that pretty
little face, my need for her love be so strong my eyes fill up
with tears. Bianca, I wanna say to her, gimme your woman's
love. Even just one little corner of it would help, 'cause
round my own heart, it's turning cold as ice.

Bianca

I just had the worst dream. It was so horrible I woke up
crying and sweating. I dreamed my stomach was real big,
like I was pregnant, and I felt a tickling and looked down,
and I saw the shape of a little child pressing against the inside of my skin. It was walking away from me, stretching my
belly out like it was rubber, this human shape stretching and
stretching. I didn't feel no pain so it seemed okay at first, but
suddenly the child broke free and it turned around and
stared at me with these glassy, green eyes. It started off
black, then it got yellower and yellower and suddenly I
knew it was that shithead Orlando, laughing at me behind
his greasy little mustache. I woke up screaming, pressing my
belly with my fists like I wanted to kill him and kill any baby
he left inside me.

Now I'm lying here in bed, trying to go back to sleep but
too scared in case the dream starts up again. Rosalba is
squeaking in her sleep next to me like she's having a bad
dream, too—Jesus, won't my nightmares stop even when I'm
awake? I got these little evil munchkin types bothering me

every moment. I just want some time in my life when I can live in peace.

Every night now I have a dream like that, a dream about babies dying, or turning into devils and scaring the hell outta me. It's like some Hollywood horror director got into my mind and is making up his movie plots inside my brain. I know it's gotta do with worrying if that cabrón got me pregnant. Every day that goes by with my period getting later and later, it makes me remember him and his stinky breath and makes me crazier with worry. I wish my body would wash him outta my system and outta my mind. I can't relax like this, I can't let it go. I look at Mami and wish I could tell her what happened so she'd make these dreams stop and my period come, but all she does is fuss with the baby and ignore me. In the old days, maybe I coulda told her what happened, and maybe she would be sorry for me instead of this yelling and hitting on me all the time like I was the one did something bad. If that rusted-old Virgen María Mami thinks so much of, looking so creepy and stiff on her altar like one of those dolls in my horror dreams—if she knew the meanness Mami be doing to me, I'm sure she wouldn't be granting Mami none of her prayers.

The worst thing is that these dreams and feelings are making me even madder at Rosalba. Sometimes it seems like all my troubles are 'cause of her. I mean, if she hadn't come along, maybe Juan woulda stayed here so I never woulda got interested in that bastard and his asshole car. We wouldn't be having these money troubles and Mami wouldn't've started this beating on me and bothering me day and night like I'm some kinda slave who's just in her way. I wouldn't be worrying about a devil-child being inside my belly and I could still be the same Bianca walking tall and fresh with my hair swinging who nobody could touch I didn't love. That's how one side of me is thinking, anyhow. Then there's the other side and it just says, "Listen, estúpida, it ain't that baby's

fault and you know it. She's just a little thing never asked
nobody to be here on this earth, so stop making her pay
for your troubles." And I feel so guilty I hate myself, then
I hate Juan for leaving me and never even answering my
letters, then I hate Rosalba all over again, and round and
round I go till I wanna just scream. Jesus, listen to me. I'm
going nuts.

All I know for sure is I feel this thing burning inside of
me, like something real bad's gonna happen. Sometimes,
and this is what scares me the most, sometimes when the
baby be giving me trouble, like she's refusing to eat or
she's crying or whining, I feel like if I don't do something
to shut her up I'm gonna explode into a million pieces. It's
like there's a hot fire inside me, flaming and crackling and
popping, just dying to get out and do some wrong. This
evil feeling's got me so worried I been praying again like
Mami does. I never did that much since I was real little,
when I used to pray for all the people God forgot. I used
to pray to Santo Domingo, who Mami says is like this special
saint that's s'posed to watch over us Dominicans. I don't know
if I believe that stuff now, but I do still believe you have this
guardian angel that takes care of you, who's like this good
angel who fights off the bad. I remember Mami saying when
you did something bad in your life it's a bad angel taking
over, and maybe if you pray hard enough your good angel
will fight with the bad angel and win. So I've started praying
to my good angel to help out. I don't kneel down like Mami
or any of that crap—I don't go for all that crawling around
like you're no better than a bug. I just ask the angel privately
to help me not get so mad at the baby, and to help Mami
quit worrying so much and quit beating on me and to smile
more. Most of all, I ask my good angel to send my bad angel away so Mami will love me like she used to, and so
we can get a little ray of happiness back into our house. I
been doing this a few times a day now, praying to my good

angel, but I'm scared it's not gonna work. I just get the feeling that with me, with Bianca Rodríguez Diaz, the bad angel's stronger than the good one. So strong, I'm scared he's gonna win.

I can feel la Virgen María's eyes on me while I'm lying in bed, like she can hear every word in my head. I get up and go to the window so I can turn my back on her. I hate the way she stands there on her altar watching me with those shiny white eyes like she be spying on me for Mami. I look out the window to get my mind off of her and see that boy Roberto hanging on my stoop again, the boy who sent me that crazy weird love letter made me blush all over. Every morning I look out it seems he's there, staring up at my apartment like it's a movie screen, and sometimes after school, too. I think he's loco. He's so funny-looking, big ears sticking out and his face round and fat. He stands in his baggy pants and his cap on backward, staring up at my window with his eyes burning and his mouth so serious. It's even creepier than Mami's Virgen—Jesus, I got these staring eyes on me wherever I look! When Clara came round the other day I asked her what Roberto thinks he's doing, 'cause I know they're friends, and she said he be watching out for me. "You both loco," I said, "get outta here."

Clara was afraid to show her ass round here for weeks after what she made happen to the baby, so I was real surprised to see her again. She said the word is I got trouble and she decided to bury the hatchet and come over to help. It was only two days after what that shithead did to me so I was still in bed, the sheets up to my nose, and I just looked at her, knowing she was thinking she's won some kinda revenge, sitting there like a grandma asking me why I'm so sick. I swear inside I'll die before I tell that nosy cuero a thing. She said the street's been talking about Mami spending a lotta time with that Irish priest over there in the church. What's he got she can use? Then Clara said, "When you gonna talk with Roberto? You gonna do something to stop him staring at your house like some voodoo weirdo?" I told her I won't have nothing to do with ugly locos from the street, before I remembered I can't act so proud no more, I'm trash. That coño Orlando said I'm trash, he said the whole street knows I'm nothing but a ho who Juan dumped. "Roberto ain't so crazy," Clara said, "he just different," and she sat there picking this scab on her knee till I wanted to scream. Clara's gotten bigger and plumper than ever since Juan left, and her titties are like balloons. She's looked like a woman since she was ten, almost. No wonder Juan went with her.

"What you so interested in Roberto for?" I said. "How come you pushing him at me like this?"

Clara shrugged. "Roberto and me go way back. When his moms was still alive she and my grandma used to work together. Him and me been friends since I was a little kid." She stopped talking and put her head on one side like a parrot. She straightened her hair since I last saw her and it was sticking out all uneven at the ends; she never did know how to make herself pretty unless I showed her. "Bianca," she said, "is it hard, looking after a baby?"

I turned my face away. I won't talk about that thing. All that baby does is screw up her face and scream when she sees me. It's like she can tell I'm trouble. That baby hates me. She don't giggle anymore when I tickle her belly, she just looks scared. Mami says I tickle her too hard, I'm too rough, I hurt her too much, but I think the baby can smell I'm trash.

Clara sat there for five whole minutes before she said, "I guess you don't wanna talk about it, huh?" I shook my head. "Okay," she said, getting up. "You wanna come over to my house sometime?"

"Maybe," I said. But secretly I was glad she asked me. I want my life to get back to normal.

I move away from the window before Roberto catches sight of me, and start getting dressed. "Bianca!" Mami calls out, coming into the bedroom when I'm zipping up my pants. She's all excited and jumpy, her eyebrows jerking round like they had too much to drink. "La Virgen, she has answered my prayers!"

"What you talking about, Mami?" I hate it when she acts like this; she sounds like some kinda Jehovah's Witness.

"That reporter lady! She has come back! She is gonna do a story about the landlord, she is gonna help us! Come say hello—and act nice!" I don't know what Mami's talking about but I check myself out in the mirror in case there's a photographer, and pick up the baby, who's lying on her back kicking like she wants a fight. The baby's cheeks are so fat now you can't see her neck; I think Mami's been feeding her too much of that baby food. Her hair is getting thicker in a ring round her head like a monk, but she still don't look like a girl unless you put her in a dress and a hair band. She likes to roll over and prop herself up on her fat elbows and look round at the world, then her cheeks fall away a little and you can see her chin and those big black eyes. People coo over her more'n ever now, ignoring me like I'm just parta the wall. I think she looks stupid, staring all the time and never smiling. She cries whenever I hold her.

I stick the baby on my hip—she weighs a ton—and go into the living room to meet this so-called reporter. Someone could come in here telling any old lies to Mami and she'd believe them, she's so dumb. I've seen these people at my school, I know the scene. They come to do stories on us poor teenage mothers and how terrible it all is and how helpless we are, and they make us sound like these bimbos who don't know nothing about how to help ourselves. There was this one man, he came and asked me a whole lotta questions at school, and when I saw the story in the paper the next day all was left of what I said was one sentence made me sound like a moron. They think 'cause I'm fourteen, I'm ignorant.

So I lean against the door with the baby on my hip, just waiting and watching. The reporter is white, of course. She's real small, no taller than me, and she's got this straight brown hair in a bob round her chin. Her ass is fat. The baby begins crying, like always, so the reporter turns and smiles at me. You can tell she was pretty when she was younger. Her face is shaped like a heart, with big gray eyes and a small chin, but now she's all tired-out looking. "¿Como está usted?" she says to me. Jesus, does she think I'm fresh off the boat? I stare at her without smiling. It don't faze her, though. She's looking at the baby and she's gone all pink in the face. "Qué linda, qué linda," she says, and suddenly I feel like I gotta rescue her.

"Here, you wanna hold her?" And before the woman says a word, I dump Rosalba in her lap, and the baby's so surprised she stops crying. The reporter's shocked, too. She holds her without daring to move. I can see she hasn't held too many babies in her life—she thinks it'll break.

"She's more beautiful than ever," the reporter says to Mami. "How old is she now?"

"Four months. Yes, she gets more pretty every day." I can see Mami puffing up. She loves it when people say good things about the baby, I notice, but she never says a kind word about me.

The baby sits on the lady's lap kicking her legs and waving her arms, making these weird little grunts she does when she's excited. She sounds like a pig. The reporter stares down at her some more, smiling, and she don't even look at me. I'm tired of being treated like I don't matter, like I'm nothing to that baby but its nurse. How come nobody tells *me* the baby's cute? Where'd they think she got her looks from anyhow? I watch the reporter coo over the baby a

while longer and I think, what is it with these people? Am I
invisible or what? I guess it's true what that coño Orlando
said—all you gotta do is have a baby nobody wants, and the
whole world thinks you're trash.

Teresa

La Virgen de la Altagracia, I gotta thank You so bad. I found a new little happiness inside my life, something good to think about for a change, and it feels like a blessing. It turns out Big Al, he has got a thing for me. For ten years we been working together, morning shift, day shift, night shift—he was always changing his shift with me and now I know why. When he heard I had to quit my job he took me behind one of the pillars, where the supervisor couldn't see us, and said, "Teresa, does this mean I ain't gonna see you no more?"

"I don't know." I was surprised 'cause his glasses were all misted up. "Maybe I can come back when things calm down. But my kids, they need me now."

Al cleared his throat and shifted his big boots around. "Can I come see you? Maybe we can catch a movie, huh?"

"Al, you got a wife and kids."

"Me and the wife split, Teresa. Last year. Don't you remember?" He sounded hurt, and then I remembered him telling me about it. It had gone from my mind, crowded out by other troubles. "It's you I think about now," he said then, and smiled this sly grin like he was fifteen, not fifty.

I looked down at my baggy T-shirt, at my orange safety vest and my messed-up blue sweatpants sticking to me with the heat and the splashes from the buckets. The cap I gotta wear with my hair stuffed under it makes me look even uglier, and I swear I have aged ten years since I went on this night shift and quit getting any sleep. "What you see in a worn-out old woman like me?" I asked him, and he took my hand in his, both of us in our thick, white work gloves.

"I see a woman with spirit and a soul," he says. "I see a woman I like." And he asked me if he could come visit next week.

Virgencita, I feel as foolish as a cat chasing a bee, looking to get stung and not even knowing it, but Big Al, he makes me happy. I haven't had so much as one little romance in my life since my husband hit me once too often and I threw him out. That was twelve years ago, twelve years of raising children and cleaning subway cars without a single visit from their father, not even on Christmas to bring the kids presents. For a while he would send something, a few dollars for buying toys, but he soon stopped even that. He climbed into his bottle, and he never came back out. That is why I call myself Mrs. Rodríguez without the Hernández, his name. My family might have its curse, but at least my parents, they were good people, and they tried to make it in this world. José, he just stopped trying. He don't deserve to pass on his name. He don't even deserve to be remembered.

When I met José, back when I was in high school and full of dreams, just like Bianca, he was gonna be a subway driver. We took the civil service exam together, I remember, so proud that we were gonna improve ourselves, not like those lazy puertorriqueños—we were gonna prove us dominicanos knew how to study and work and rise up in the world. José, he got his call before mine—I had to wait three years before I got my job—so he began his training and I began our children, and it was good at first, living with my family before they all started going bad. But already the Rodríguez curse was waiting to jump us. My boys were both in elementary school, little but full of fire, when I got the call from the hospital. Your husband, they said, he has crashed a train. Ten people hurt, no more, gracias a Dios, and none of them too serious because it was a night train and almost empty, but they found alcohol in his blood and he was in big trouble.

After that there was nothing I could do but watch him sink. From a train driver he went to a cleaner, like me, to scrubbing the platforms only, and down and down, each time the drink wrecking his chances. For five more years we went on like this, him sliding down, me doing the earning, which is why I had to stop having babies even though I wanted a girl so bad. Then, ten years after Luis was born I up and had Bianca, and that was the thing done José in. I remember him looking down at her in her crib, his eyes red and his breath so strong with drink I was afraid he would make her drunk just by breathing on her, and I remember him saying, "What's the good of this? A girl to feed just so she can marry and go into some other man's family? You did this to make me feel bad!" And that's when he hit me for the first time. Well, I put up with that only till Bianca was two, and then I threw him out. "I got enough children," I told him, "I don't need a big baby like you to look after, too." And he was shamed enough to take his bottle and go away, leaving us all forever.

Since then I've had my longings, I confess, 'cause I was always a woman who liked men, but the troubles with my sons, and the care of my Bianca and my work, they left me with no time to be feeling sorry for myself. Maybe a loneliness creeps over me once in a while like a fever sweat and I wish for those good times with José, when he was young and handsome with his head up proud and his black eyes flashing when he pulled that train outta the barn. José, he was something then, that whole long train loaded up with passengers, all for him to control. Why he had to wreck his life with drink I will never understand, 'cept his father was the same way so maybe it was in his blood. And his sons, too, drink or drugs, it is all the same—the way of culebras and cowards.

Anyhow, Virgen, this is a long way to say thank You for Big Al. Thank You for giving me a sweet man who is interested in this worn-out abuela, a man who don't drink and who holds down his job and looks after his kids, even with his divorce. And thank You, too, for sending that reporter lady back to me after I waited so long. That doña and me, we had a big talk the day she come, and it left me feeling like she is not gonna be much help, but I think she is gonna be a friend. And a friend like her is not a bad thing for a woman like me to have.

I was so surprised when she turned up. I thought she had dumped me, just another one of my hopes faded away and gone, like José, like my boys, like the life I dreamed I was gonna have. The way things been going round here lately, with Bianca sassing me and pinching poor Rosalba, and me trying to make those welfare checks stretch to a full dinner and living in fear of those malandros coming back to wreck my house—I wake up every morning just wondering what Trouble is gonna bring me today. So after Bianca went running off to school the day that reporter come, like the sulky niña she is, I took my Rosalba back from the lady's arms, told her all about what those thugs did to me, and asked her right out what was happening with her story about my landlord.

She squirmed round in her chair when I asked that, her face scrunched up like she was sitting on a pin, so I knew her answer it wasn't gonna be much good. "I'm sorry about those men stealing from you, that's terrible," she said. "Mrs. Rodríguez, I want to . . ."

"Teresa, call me Teresa." *Why is she afraid to use my first name, I wondered? Does she think she is not good enough to talk to me like an equal?*

"Okay, thank you. I came to tell you I'm sorry I didn't come back earlier. My editor sent me to the Bronx to do a series on landlords up there, so I didn't have time. Now I'm afraid I'm having some problems with your story. I can't find any other tenants to confirm what you told me about those men, so . . ."

"You mean you think I been lying?"

The reporter wriggled round in her chair again, and she turned red. *I didn't wanna be hard on her, but those words of hers made me mad.*

"No, no, of course not," she said quickly. "It's just that it's going to be difficult to get my editor interested in this story unless I can be a lot more specific."

"But what about the stealing? Isn't that bad enough for him, those punks coming in and taking my rings and my TV?"

Miss Goldin frowned. "Maybe if you'd let me use your name, I could—"

"Forget it, lady. If I let you use my name, who knows what that *culebro* will do. I got children to protect. I told you that."

"Are you sure? If you were willing to go on the record . . ."

"Yeah, I'm sure. Look, I owe the man two months rent, okay? If I get in the newspapers complaining about him he is just gonna say I am doing it to get outta paying what I owe. I am not like that, Miss Goldin. I am an honest, hardworking person, even if that *sucio*, he is not."

Miss Goldin sighed. "All right, if you insist." She began picking at the threads of her skirt. "The truth is," she said quietly, "I don't think I'm going to be able to get my editor to let me do this story, Teresa. I realize this sounds awful to you, but your landlord isn't enough of a big-time crook. I mean, he's trying to raise the rent illegally, right? And maybe he's using scare tactics to get some of you out of the building so he can go co-op, but to my editor this is just an everyday story. He wants the really awful guys, you know, the ones who burn down buildings in the night and beat people up. Even the stealing isn't going to impress him very much, especially not after what we found going on in the Bronx. Did you happen to read those stories I wrote?"

I shake my head. "I don't got no time to read that fat paper of yours."

"Oh, okay, of course. Well, the other thing is he's said we've done enough on this subject for now, anyway."

I frown, stroking Rosalba's soft head, and watch all my plans crumble into nothing. It is just what I have learned to expect, hopes dangled out like jewels only to turn into air soon as I grab at them. "Why you bother to come back here then?" I ask her.

The woman squints at me like I am a light too bright to look at. "I just wanted to explain," she says. "I know you were counting on me to help you out. I feel really bad about it, Teresa, and I'd still like to do something for you if you'd let me." She pauses, looking down at her notepad. "Would you like me to get in touch with a tenant's lawyer to help you fight the rent raises? Maybe they could intimidate your landlord into leaving you alone."

"I got no money to pay no lawyers with."

"No, no. You wouldn't have to pay. I have a friend who does this kind of thing for free. There are organizations—"

"I don't want no charity, either, Miss Goldin. I don't take things from people for free."

"No . . ." She starts flapping her hands like a baby bird who don't know how to fly. "It's a social service. The people who work there do it to protect people like you from crooks. Look, Mrs.—Teresa, they can at least stop the man raising his rent above the legal limit and scare him into keeping his thugs off your back. This is a rent-controlled building and that means you have certain rights."

I get up from the couch and walk up and down the room with Rosalba, who is sucking her tiny fists and whimpering like she can smell the rot in my life. Maybe this reporter came back 'cause she wants more of my prayers for her to get a baby; maybe she is out only for herself. Or maybe she is a good person, like I thought—it is hard to tell. "Lady," I say at last, "this makes me feel bad. I don't have no time for lawyers and stuff."

"There's nothing to be afraid of, if that's what's stopping you."

I look away so she don't see the anger on my face. "I am not afraid," I say, my voice hard, "but what about the rent I owe, hunh? If some lawyer finds out, he will kick me outta my home, and then what will I do?"

"Oh, you don't have to worry about that. These people are there to help you, not get you into trouble. Look, think about it, will you? Here's my card. Call me if you want me to do this."

I take the card and bend over Rosalba's stomach to nuzzle her, giving myself time to think. Then I look down at Miss Goldin in her chair and I say, "Lady, I am gonna tell you a truth, okay? You ready?"

She seems surprised, but she nods.

"You a smart woman, yes? You got a good heart and I can tell you care."

"Thank you very much, but . . ."

"No, hold on, let me speak. I can't deal with this lawyer stuff. I don't know how to do it . . . these people you talk about? They will just laugh at me. Anyhow, I don't have time to go hanging round no offices, waiting in lines, waiting in waiting rooms, waiting to wait. I know what those places are like. All they do is waste your time and I don't have no time to waste, Miss Goldin. I got two kids to look after, I got rent to pay, I got a house to run . . . Did I tell you I quit my job?"

"You did? Why?"

"I wanna protect Rosalba. I wanna be where I can see she is safe." The lady looks away from me, her hair hiding her face, and I wonder if I am saying too much. She is always making me say too much. "This world is dangerous for children, Miss Goldin. You don't know."

She sighs, and I see her rest her hand on her belly like my words are reminding her of its emptiness. "What are you going to do for money now you're not working?" she asks me.

"What all the women do, y'know? Welfare, food stamps. Hah! I work all my life for this?" I spread out one of my hands, all knobbly and swollen at the knuckles, and shrug. Miss Goldin's hands, I notice, are still smooth.

"I'm sorry it's come to this, Teresa. You must be upset." Miss Goldin looks back down at those fingers she keeps picking away at her skirt with. She is gonna unravel the whole thing if she isn't careful—she'll have to go home naked. We stay like that a while, me standing in the middle of the room with Rosalba, her sitting with her head hanging down like a scolded kid, the silence getting heavier. "Listen, Teresa," she says at last, "I'll go to the tenants' organization for you if you'd like. Let's see what they can do, okay?"

I sit back down on the couch, sliding Rosalba down on my lap so her little head is resting on my knees and her round angel face is looking up at me. I grab her feet and move them in circles, which makes her giggle. She is real ticklish, and that laugh of hers could melt the heart of a statue. I look over at Miss Goldin, frowning and worried on her chair. This is a good woman, I can tell; my instincts were right, even if her promises turn out no better than a rotten guayaba.

"Okay, lady, thank you," I say at last. "That would be

good." I smile at her the best I can, though I don't feel too smiley inside. "I know la Virgen, She sent you to me for something. I always felt that you were a sign."

Miss Goldin blushes. "I'll need any rent receipts you have, and a copy of your lease."

I nod, put Rosalba on my hip, and get out the shoe box I keep that stuff in. "I didn't get any receipts since six months ago. The landlord stopped giving them to me, but I got the lease and it says right here this is rent-controlled, see?"

"You don't have any canceled checks?"

I shake my head. "I pay cash, Miss Goldin. He won't take no checks."

"Okay." She takes my papers. "That will help, anyway. Thanks." She stands up to go and I can see the hurry on her face to get outta here. "I'll let you know when I find out something, all right?"

I thank her again, walk her to the door, and watch her little back disappear down my stairs. But I know this time not to get my hopes up. Miss Goldin, she is one of those people who makes promises but never gets any real thing done. She means well but it just don't happen. If I have learned any one lesson in my hard life it's that if anything is gonna change round here, it is me who is gonna have to change it. It is like my Mamá used to say: The good Lord, He only helps those who help themselves.

Bianca

Clara's waiting for me on the stoop, but before I go down I look out the window to make sure the coast is clear. I been spending a lotta time with her now that school's out for the summer, but if I see that asshole and his red car I stay in the house and I won't go out, not for nothing. That hurt inside still comes back a lot, like when I think of a boy touching me, or why my period is so late, or that baby's driving me crazy with her screeching—or when I see that sucio Orlando out on the street. I hope he gets arrested and raped in jail. But otherwise it makes me feel better to fool around with Clara. I'd forgotten how funny that bitch can be.

Mami don't like me hanging on the stoop. She says it looks bad and the respectable girls on the street don't do it. I say Clara's respectable and her grandma lets her hang out, but Mami just grunts and says that's all I know about it, and anyhow, Clara, she isn't dominicana and she don't have the same morals as us. "Don't you say that about my friend Clara, she just as good as you," I said to Mami. "Anyhow, I'm a married woman and I can do what I want." But Mami, she's just like, "Bianca, when you sit there eyeing the boys like you do, you don't look married, you look cheap." What she don't know is I don't care what I look like. I got nothing left to lose.

Anyhow, the street looks clear, thank God, so I go on down to meet Clara. Some of the girls from next door are there, too, and they got a radio, so we turn it on loud and I show the little ones some new dance moves I saw on Clara's TV. The younger girls, they like to hang round me 'cause they think they wanna look like me when they get big. They think it's good to look pretty so the boys chase you—that's all they know. Being pretty just brings trouble, I found that out fast. People want you for your face and your body and they don't care about the rest of you, like your mind and your feelings, just like Roberto said in that crazy dumb letter. They just wanna use you and show you off, then throw you away like a pair of old shoes. Like Juan did with all those lies he called promises. So I don't care about being pretty no more—I even stopped pulling my top lip down at night to make it longer. Being pretty just brings heartache. I'd be happier looking like Clara and living my life in peace.

Clara keeps telling me I should give Roberto a try. She says even though he's kinda crazy, he's okay. She says his mother killed herself and his father was a drunk and a crackhead who was always beating on his family till he got put in jail last year, which is why Roberto acts so weird sometimes. "Go on, give him a chance," Clara says. But I'm not letting another boy touch me as long as I live. I know what boys want, whatever lies they be saying, and I'm done with that now. Just thinking about a man's touch makes me wanna stab a knife into somebody. So when Clara talks that talk about Roberto, I tell her to turn it off and think about something else.

I wish school wasn't out. Clara, she'd laugh at me if she heard me say this, but I miss having someplace to go and something to think about other than Mami Mean and that

screechy baby. I miss my favorite teacher, Mr. Jonas. He's
this springy little man with dreadlocks and a deep voice who
looks like a rock star but who teaches math, and he makes it
seem like a game, full of tricks you can catch. He tells me
I'm a natural, that I mustn't waste my life 'cause I got a real
talent for it. It's nice he thinks I'm so special but I'd like to
know what wasting my life's s'posed to mean. What do I
do, wake up every morning and go, like, "I will not waste
my life today?" What's wasting life anyhow? Ironing, shopping, cleaning a house that's only gonna get dirty again—
that's wasting life. Changing a baby ten times a day, saying
"goo goo ga ga" like an idiot for hours—that's wasting life.
But what choice I got? I don't live in a castle with servants.
Certain things gotta get done, it's just the way life is, and by
the time you've finished doing those things there ain't no life
left to waste. I don't even have time to do my homework
most days.

I wonder how Mr. Jonas got to be a teacher. He isn't rich
or white. Did he have a mother or a wife to do all that
everyday shit for him so he could study? I bet that's it. And
what about that wife or mother, did they get to be teachers,
too? Or does he think they're just wasting their lives?

This is my dream, Mr. Jonas, since you're so interested. I
wanna move away from here, far away from Mami and that
baby who hates me so much, far away from this street and
its garbage and the rats and the crack dealers, far away from
Tía Yolanda with her bitter face and from the spying, gossiping, sneaky neighbors and that red-car coño asshole and the
worry he's put another child in my belly. I wanna go to college in linen dresses and white shoes, like those pictures I've
seen in social studies books about the black girls going to
college for the first time in the civil rights times. I wanna go
to college with my books under my arm and my white shoes
and my mind clear of troubles. And I wanna win awards for
being smart and being able to talk out exactly what I wanna

say, in the way I wanna say it, so I can move the world to become a better place, and so I can forget every person who ever hurt me, and so Mami'd be proud of me and never yell at me again. That's my dream, Mr. Jonas. You wanna come and clean house for me so I can get going?

Roberto

I see Bianca noticing me now. Every morning I see her come outta that building in her tight bicycle pants and that little black top she wear, her hair swinging sweet and sassy again, and she walks past me like she don't even see me but I can tell she do by the way she adds that wiggle to her walk like she be speaking to me, saying, Just be patient, Roberto, and I'll be there. When she walks that walk I need to jump up and down I want her so bad. But that ain't all I want, I swear it. I want her for the comfort we can give each other, for her smart head and her pretty ways and her laugh that sparkles like a star. I want her 'cause I know we be right for each other. We could talk about our secret troubles and the world, we could be soul mates, we could heal up my family with love. So I be sending her my love vibes, day and night, to melt up that heart of hers and bring her down to me.

I catch her looking at me from her apartment sometimes, her face flashing by the window like a sunbeam. Clara say she knows I'm here. "Just wait," Clara say, "and she'll be down. She just need to chill out first." Clara say Bianca be getting interested in me now, she asks about me almost

every day, about my family and my life. Bianca should ask
me herself. I'd tell her—I got no more to be ashamed of than
the rest of this damn hood. Yeah I got a crackhead daddy
who beat my moms so bad she jumped in front of a subway
car, but I seen just as bad behind those pretty lace curtains
on our street and those polite smiles and "How you doin's?"
I know there's worse behind those white people's lives, too,
even if they always be saying it's only us got troubles, like it
ain't got nothing to do with their greedy ways.

But I get scared sometimes, I do. I wish I could talk with
Bianca about it. Some days I wake myself up 'cause I been
screaming in my sleep about my daddy before my moms
died. I'm scared about what's gonna happen to Diego and
Carmen and Juanita 'cause there ain't nobody loves them
like I do. But I'm strong. I can push those scared feelings
away when I got to. I'm gonna finish school and get me a
job that makes real, honest money so I can take my sisters
and brother away from this city before one of us ends up a
junkie or dead. This street, it looks okay, kinda pretty with
its old apartment buildings and the church in the middle
so grand like a big, gray cathedral, but this ain't no place
for us. It's getting almost as bad as Aunt Maria's old hood,
or those streets east of Amsterdam where some kid gets
murdered every week. The violence is creeping nearer and
nearer every day. One of my oldest friends from school, he
got gunned down last week in a drive-by just two blocks
east of here, and his brother two weeks before. Seems like
every month now I go to another funeral, the mothers weeping over their sons, dead young faces lying in the coffin,
eyes that seen no more'n eighteen years of life closed forever. The Church of the Ascension on our street—I used
to think of it as a place for weddings and christenings, a
place for confetti and happiness, but ever since those drug
gangs moved in and started recruiting my friends and shooting each other up over turf, it seems like that church be for

nothing but funerals. I need to get me and my family outta here, fast—you, too, Bianca. And we need to get out together.

Bianca, I got a message to send you, so I hope you be listening: You be like the sun is this morning. Sometimes you out shining, spreading your joy all around; other times you hidden behind clouds of sadness. I know I can chase those clouds away if you just gimme the chance. So hold on tight, girl, Roberto's coming to get you, and he's coming real soon.

Teresa

I give You flowers, I give You a lifetime of prayers, I give You all the faith in my tired old heart, so why You do this to me? My house is getting like a war zone, Bianca causing destruction wherever she turns her demonia self. La Virgen, why are You punishing me so?

I was in the bedroom when it happened, getting some nice clothes on in case Big Al comes by, and leaving Bianca to finish feeding Rosalba her breakfast. I hear the baby fussing so I call out, "Bianca, just take her outta the high chair if she's done," and I hear some scraping around like Bianca is having trouble lifting that baby out. "Just pick her up in the air, estúpida, what is the matter with you?" I tell her, and the next thing I know I hear this crash and Rosalba lets out a scream that could freeze your blood. I run in there so fast it is like I have wings, and it was a sight to stop a mother's heart. Rosalba is on the floor, still half in the chair, her mouth open but no sound coming out, and there is blood everywhere. "Did you push her over?" I shout at Bianca, and God forgive her but she nods her head. Rosalba gets her breath back and starts screaming, I am shouting, Bianca is running outta the house crying. It was like a murder scene.

I washed that baby off real gentle and put my hand behind her head to lift her up, hoping her little neck wasn't broke. I know those head wounds bleed a lot so I tried not to panic, but I have never been so scared since I heard about my Hernán getting shot. Then I knocked on my neighbor's door, since I still got no phone, and he called the ambulance for me while I tried to get Rosalba calm—she was yelling her heart out, pobrecita. What a time, Virgen, me praying on my knees to You right there in the ambulance while the EMS lady cleans off Rosalba's blood and checks out her skull and her little bones. I don't understand why You let Bianca do this.

Soon as I got the baby into the hospital, I took out Miss Goldin's card and called her at work for help. "This isn't about the rent, it is about my granddaughter," I told her, "I need your help at the hospital." I knew she couldn't say no, not with that kind heart and the way she looks at mi nieta. I wanted a white lady to help me get the best for Rosalba 'cause I know how these hospitals treat women like me, I know how we get last in line, the worst beds, and the meanest nurses. I remember all that from having my babies, stuck in the corner with the light broke and the tiredest of the night staff jabbing me with needles and telling me to stop my yelling. Even Bianca, when she had the baby, they treated her like that, 'cept for my nurse friend. It still makes me grind my teeth to think of it, those night nurses so angry and mean. I know they are overworked and underpaid, but why do they choose to be nurses in the first place if all they gonna do is bully the patients? So I wanted to do right by my Rosalba and get her the best I could no matter how much crawling I had to do to get it.

That poor baby, mi cielito, lying there so delicate and pale in one of those huge metal cribs they got in the hospitals that look like tiny prisons, her head all swollen up with bandages. I sat next to her, reading from my Bible to give her comfort, looking round at all the other babies in their own prisons, and wondering how Bianca could do such evil. As soon as Miss Goldin walked in I said, "Gracias a Dios, you came. It was a terrible accident. Look at my poor baby." And I told her lies, God forgive me, 'cause I wanted her help but I didn't want none of her blame.

"Rosalba, she was in her high chair, kicking like she do," I said, noticing how pale Miss Goldin was, looking at all the sick babies with tubes in their noses and arms. "Then the leg broke sudden and the chair fell over. It is 'cause I have to buy these things cheap, miss, I can't afford no better. And see what happened!"

Miss Goldin stared at me like she was not so sure about what she was hearing. Her thin nose was pinched and kinda yellow round the edges. "Is Rosalba all right?" she said then.

"I don't know. She hit her head so bad on that floor— blood was everywhere. You have never seen such a thing. Will you talk to the doctors for me? They won't tell me nothing."

Miss Goldin agreed and she went off to find somebody to talk to. The minute I walked into that place, the doctors and nurses were all looking at me like I was a criminal, but I knew it was no use fighting their prejudices. Better to get someone like Miss Goldin to help.

Finally she came back in, looking annoyed and worried. "Christ, they sure give you the runaround," she said, putting her hair back behind her ears like she always do, and rubbing her eyes with a sigh. "Listen, Teresa, don't worry, they say Rosalba's fine. They gave her a few stitches. She has no concussion that they can tell, but they want to keep her in here a while for observation. There's just one problem. . . ." She squints at me like she is real embarrassed, and my heart, it starts speeding up with fear. She can't even look me in the face.

"What is it?"

"Well, it's . . . they want to keep the baby here for a couple of days until one of the doctors checks some things out."

"What's that mean?" I stand up now, feeling this weight hit me round the shoulders like the bad news I been waiting on since I was born.

"Teresa . . . I don't know how to say this." Miss Goldin begins walking back and forth, her short legs waddling and her straight hair swinging over her eyes. "One of the doctors says she suspects abuse, I'm afraid. She says she's noticed little bruises all over the baby and they have records of an earlier accident leading to hospitalization, as well as this one." She looks over at me and I can see she's gone red all down her cheeks and neck.

"This is crazy, this is wrong!" I say. "These people, what they think I am?" I look down at my little Rosalba who I been working so hard to protect, and I think about the trouble Bianca could get in. "How can they say such things?" I tell her. "And how am I gonna pay for all these days in the hospital? I don't have no insurance since I stopped working, I don't have money like this. Mi Dios . . ." I look at the lady, wondering why this Rodríguez curse keeps coming back to wreck up my world, when I notice she is backing out the door like I got a disease. So she thinks I am a baby killer, too?

"I'll come back and see you soon, okay?" she says quickly. "Call me if you need help. I've got to go now." And then she is gone, leaving nothing but the smell of her perfume to help me handle all this hell that's broken loose in my life.

So now I got mi ángelita in the hospital for four days, the bills getting higher and higher, my welfare check disappearing so I never see a cent, and Miss Goldin and the doctors treating me like I am a murderer. What are those doctors gonna do if they decide it is abuse? Put me in jail? Who would look after my girls? Who would pay the bills? And now Bianca, she is so relieved with the baby gone that she is acting sweet and loving like mi hijita again, as if we have no troubles, which just rubs the salt in my wounds even worse. What kinda upside-down world is this?

I guess I gotta face the truth: Bianca and her jealousy, they are too dangerous to ignore. That pinching was bad enough, but this pushing Bianca done coulda killed Rosalba, my little innocent! It is getting so every time I take my eyes away from that baby, Bianca is hurting her or losing her temper in some way. I can see it in Rosalba's face. She has grown afraid of her own mami, she jumps and cries whenever she sees her, and it breaks my heart. Even quitting my job was not enough to protect her—no one body can watch a baby every second. I can't sleep I am so worried about it, I can't eat. And I am afraid that if I do nothing when Rosalba comes back or if they put me in jail, that baby is gonna end up dead or lost like those kids I used to see every day at work, kids no more'n nine or ten riding the trains all day long, scrabbling for leftover food 'cause they got no place to go and nobody to love. I can't let that happen to my Rosalba, my own nieta. So now I am thinking maybe You are right, Virgen, and Father O'Hearney, too; I gotta choose between my two girls if I am gonna protect them. I guess I just didn't wanna see Your message written up as clear as the supermarket lights on Broadway, but I think I understand now, if You will give me the strength. Miss Goldin, she wants to be a mother, but she can't. My Bianca, she don't wanna be a mother, but she is. At least Miss Goldin is a good woman with a serious job and a husband—she is no foster mother in it only for the dollars. If You keep me outta jail, Virgen, I will try to do this thing now and save Rosalba before Bianca hurts her even worse, and before the curse in my family brings that baby down. Maybe this is the way I can keep Bianca by my side and not lose her like I did my sons. Maybe, like I thought that first day I met Miss Goldin, maybe it is destiny.

No part of my heart believes it is right to hand over a child of my own family to a stranger, but my head, it knows I gotta do something to protect my Rosalba from her jealous mother. Help my head teach my heart, Virgencita, for the sake of my girls. Amen.

Bianca

I'm in the bathroom painting my nails. To most people that'd be such an everyday thing to do they wouldn't even think about it, but to me it's a special treat. I haven't had the time to do something like this since the baby was born, but now it's so quiet round here while she's in the hospital I got more time than I know what to do with. It's sad, but a relief at the same time. Mami didn't beat on me after the accident, she says she's too upset to bother. Miss Mandel musta scared her outta doing that stuff to me after all. She just looked at me and said, "You better pray to the Lord for forgiveness, Bianca, if you don't wanna burn in hell," and she shut the bedroom door in my face. Now she just tosses and turns in the bed and cries herself to sleep, but least it's just us again like it used to be.

Listen, I don't mean to say I don't feel bad about what happened. I never wanted to be a bad mami, a bad person, I never wanted to hurt her little head like that, but that baby makes me so crazy it's like I turn into somebody else. I was just trying to get her outta the high chair but it seemed like she was doing everything she could to make it hard for me.

She made her body go all stiff so she was stuck under the tray table thing and I couldn't get her out, then she spat this apple sauce in my eyes and threw her spoon on the floor making this messy splat—she made me so mad I couldn't help it, I couldn't control it. That bad angel just got inside of me and swelled me up with anger till I had to explode. Mami's always calling me "demonia" and I guess she's right. I prayed to my good angel to stop me losing it like that, but my bad angel, he was too strong, just like I thought. So now I been praying to God to heal that baby up, just like Mami said to, right down on my knees like a worm.

I think the Lord answered my prayers a little, 'cause today Mami said the baby's okay, they are just keeping her in the hospital for a couple of days to make sure. But I feel bad for the baby, I do—just thinking about what I did makes me wince and shudder all over—and I feel bad for Mami, too. She loves that baby and I know I hurt her in the heart being so evil. So, last night when Mami got into bed, I climbed in next to her and put my arms round her, like we were kittens in a basket, 'cause I heard her crying, and I whispered to her that I was sorry and that everything's gonna be okay and that I'll never, ever do anything like that again. I even said I love her. She smelled of sweat and that baby powder she uses after the shower—it made me remember when times were good and she'd let me sleep in her bed when I got lonely. She pretended she was asleep when I hugged her, but she did stop that crying. Maybe we can get better while that baby's gone, maybe we can like each other again.

Still, I don't like seeing Mami act like this. She's getting thinner and thinner, like she's shriveling up in fronta my eyes. That yellow sundress she bought at a discount store on Broadway last summer, the one with the cheap-looking blurry white flowers all over it? Even that looks too big for her now, hanging off her like a shower curtain. Sometimes at dinner I watch just to make sure she eats. "Here, Mami, have some of my rice," I tell her, or, "Mami, you want me to get you some bread?" I tell her funny stories about Roberto and she don't even smile. Sometimes, when Tía Yolanda is here, I hang out in the bedroom listening through the wall, hoping to hear Mami let out just one little laugh. How else am I gonna know if she's all right?

At least I got one prayer answered—my period came at last. It was getting so late that I asked Miss Mandel at school where I could get a test, and she sent me to a doctor who said my period was late 'cause I was anxious and getting too thin. The doctor said eat and relax—huh!—and she gave me some pills to take for three days. Now I'm hoping, since I don't have to worry about another baby no more and Rosalba's outta our hair and Mami's quit beating on me, I'm hoping my good angel can take over from the bad angel for a change and keep me outta trouble.

"Bianca?" I hear Miami knocking on the bathroom door.

"Yeah?" I'm holding my hands out, the fingers wide apart to dry my nails.

"Bianca, that loco who hangs out on our stoop, he is at the door for you. He got flowers. You wanna see him?"

I feel myself blush all over. That stupid-fool boy! What a nerve, coming right up here with flowers like he's in some kind of TV commercial. I'm so embarrassed! S'pose it gets round that I let that crazy boy up here? I go down the hall, waving my nails, and there he is standing at the door, shuffling from foot to foot, the flowers so tall they cover his face. He looks unbelievably dumb.

"What're you doing here?" I ask him.

He pushes the flowers at me. "I got you these." His voice squeaks—I guess he's nervous—and I laugh. He just blinks. "Can I come in?"

"You kidding? If you acted normal I might let you in, but you too crazy."

Roberto lowers the flowers down from his face and looks

at me, all serious. I notice his eyes then, real big and this beautiful chestnut brown color. "Listen up a minute, Bianca," he says, and something in his voice makes me have to be still. "Clara say you sad and lonely up here by yourself, so I want you to know you got a friend in me. I know what it's like to be lonely. It ain't right for a pretty girl like you."

"What you know 'bout lonely? Who's lonely? That fucking Clara. Boca grande." He makes me mad, assuming all these things. "You don't even know me."

"I know you more'n you think, Bianca. I know you got trouble with that baby and Juan and your moms."

Hearing him say that name makes me madder than ever. "What's Juan got to do with it?" I yell.

Mami shouts down the hall. "Bianca, you shush. Ask the boy in and close that door. The whole street can hear you screeching." So I gotta let Roberto in.

"You got a vase or something?" he asks, cool as an ice pop. We go to the kitchen where Mami's cleaning up breakfast, and I show him a broken old vase to put the flowers in.

"You do it, I got my nails to dry." I go to the bedroom to get away from Mami, and he follows me and sticks the flowers up on the dressing table me and Mami share, with all the makeup and deodorant and other private things, and I'm even more embarrassed 'cause Roberto's looking at them and at our crowded apartment with the paint peeling and the curtains full of holes, where me and Mami sleep in the same room 'cause there ain't no other room to put me in. I'm so embarrassed I just wanna throw him out.

I sit on the bed, sulky, and tell him to sit if he wants. Roberto looks at the chair but it's covered with underwear, so he crouches on the floor, leaning against the wall and staring at me. "You made up with Clara yet?" he asks.

"None of your business." My nails are dry now so I begin picking at the bedspread. It's white with fluffy knobs all over it and I pick at it a lot. Mami always yells when she sees me doing it—she says I'll make it look like a spider web. There's a long silence, but I ain't gonna help this loco mess with my mind. I glance over at Mami's Virgen María. She is watching us with her teeny painted eyes, and that makes me feel worse than ever.

"You get my letter?" Roberto says at last, all quiet.

"Maybe."

Another silence. I look Roberto over. He seems relaxed, like he's been sitting in my room his whole damn life. What a nerve! He smells nice, though, some kinda aftershave like a pine forest. Better than that hair grease some boys wear.

"I don't see you going out much no more," he says at last.

"Oh, yeah? You think that's your business? Why you watch me all the time, anyhow? I feel like I'm being spied on, like I can't move, and the whole street be teasing me 'bout it. Why d'you want to know so damn much about me?"

Roberto stares down at his hands and suddenly it seems like he's not so sure of himself. I look at the top of his curly head bent over his knees with those big ears sticking out, and I feel kinda bad for him. I think of that crazy love letter he sent me. Poor guy. "Forget it," I say then. "It's a free country, I guess."

"I was just asking," he mutters, looking up at me again. "Wanna go down to the park with me and Clara later to cool off? Better'n sitting in fronta that fan all day." He points to the fan in our window. I hate that fan. It rattles all night and keeps me awake, or else it gives me nightmares that people be shooting in my window, like Mami said the guardia did to Abuelita and Abuelo back in the DR.

I shrug. "Okay. Maybe this evening. Clara and me are going downtown to check out the shoe stores, so I gotta go now." I look at him, thinking about all those days I saw him hanging on my stoop. "What're you doing this summer?" I ask just to make conversation.

"I got me a job at Mr. Aquino's liquor store. Y'know, the man who owns that place down Broadway?"

"Oh yeah? How come he hired you?"

Roberto laughs. "Guess he couldn't find nothing better! Nah, he a good man, he likes me. I'm gonna deliver for him."

I'm impressed—a real job. No boys I know got jobs, other than selling drugs like that red-car asshole. I remember what Clara said about Roberto watching out for his brother and sisters 'cause his dad's in jail. "How old are you anyhow?" I ask.

"Eighteen next month. I'm finishing school next year."

"Twelfth grade?"

Roberto nods proudly and gets up off the floor. "I'll walk you out," he says.

"Okay, if you want." I grab my purse and yell bye-bye to Mami. Then I stop him at the door. "You gotta promise me one thing."

"What?"

"You gotta promise to quit standing outside my house staring at my window like you been doing. It gives me the creeps."

Roberto looks like he's about to say something, then he stops and smiles. "Okay, it's a deal. Anyhow, maybe I won't need to no more."

Teresa

I am pushing mi ángelita slowly down my street, bags of canned beans and sacks of rice making her stroller so heavy it feels like my arms are gonna drop off. This is one of the hottest days we had yet this August, so sticky I gotta fight my way through the air like it is made of syrup. I pass the Baptist church on the left, all done up in fake crazy brick and painted bright red, and the Church of the Ascension in the middle of our block, which looks so rich and old compared to the other. I notice they gone and blinded the statue of Jesús in the front with a new coat of white paint again. Why can't they let Him have His eyes at least, insteada painting them over like He don't wanna see what goes on in the world?

My street looks so peaceful today, but my heart it is at war. I got my Rosalba home from the hospital, safe and sound, and I don't have to worry about jail 'cause that doctor, she got too busy to remember about those bruises she found on mi nieta, and I got my plans for the baby and Miss Goldin, but these things are tearing me apart, like my heart is made of wet paper. La Virgen de la Altagracia, get Miss Goldin over here quick, before I change my mind. I don't wanna worry no more about Rosalba ending up abandoned on some subway when I'm dead and gone, and I can't live the way I am much longer. I can't keep my Bianca from Rosalba, it is too unnatural, it is driving Bianca away from me. She is running to the park and that boy and maybe the streets, and I am so afraid of losing her like I lost my sons. I have given up everything for Rosalba now—my job, my time, my health, and my sleep—I gotta give up my daughter, too?

I stop and rest on somebody's stoop, letting my eyes wander down the block till I get my breath back. This is a pretty street in the summertime. The skinny trees in the sidewalk are trying to reach up to the little piece of sky between the buildings, and the sun is sparkling in the windows. I like the red flag, too, the one the church puts out waving at you like it's desperate to get someone to come inside. You'd never know this place is a crack dealer's heaven to look at it, not unless you live here like me. It is like a puta, this street, with a painted smile and a black heart. I take a deep breath, getting what little air I can outta this syrup, and push the stroller on down to Amsterdam, the bad end of the block where I live. When I get to my building it bothers me all over again that I gotta live in the worst-looking house on the whole street. It hasn't been painted for years, and when it was the landlord chose gray like he wanted to make it look like a prison. Now it is covered with graffiti and the lock is busted with nothing but wires sticking out of a hole. I sneaked some cleaner home from work one time and scrubbed the graffiti off, but those kids next door, they only put it back on the next day. Mi Dios, why do I bother to work so hard just to keep my children in such a miserable world?

When I get to my stoop I see that loco Roberto sitting on the wall again, nodding his head to the radio like some junkie. He is so short and tubby he looks like a tree stump.

You would think my Bianca, she would have better taste. I turn the stroller round and yank it up the stoop, staring at Roberto till he wakes up enough to get up off his butt and help. "I hope the elevator is working," I say to him, but of course it isn't, it only stinks of garbage like always, so I gotta face the stairs.

"Let me do it, Mrs. Rodríguez," he says, and he picks up the stroller and carries it up all those steps to the top floor while I struggle behind him with the bags. Empty beer bottles are scattered on the stairs and I see a crack vial lying in a corner, but at least, I am thinking, this boy has got manners.

"Gracias," I tell him, and shut the door in his face. Bianca, she isn't home, and I don't wanna have to look at Roberto's sad little orphan self right now. That boy is a lost soul and I don't trust him. He acts too strange, like he is touched in the head. I don't want no bad-luck loco hanging round mi hijita.

When he is gone I pick up my Rosalba, who is sleeping from the hot air, and slip her into the playpen. Her cheeks are red from the heat, mi muñeca linda, and her little mouth is folded closed like a kiss. When other mothers see her in the park with me they go, "Oh, she is so beautiful." I know, I say inside, she is my angel flower. But now even that hurts.

I go back to the kitchen and I am just putting away the cans of beans when I hear the doorbell go. Checking through the peephole in case it is those landlord desgraciados again, I see Miss Goldin, looking sweaty in the face. Thank You, Virgen, for bringing her back so quick. "Sit down," I tell her when I let her in. "It is a hot day to be climbing all those stairs. You want some lemonade?" She nods and falls into one of my chairs, panting. "How you doing?" I ask, looking at her this whole new way now I got my plans, but she is too busy drinking down the lemonade to answer. I fill up her glass a second time and sit opposite her. She seems nervous,

the brow of her worn face tired and creased. "You okay?" I
say again to fill the silence.

"Fine, thanks, just hot." She smiles and puts the empty
glass on the floor. She has gained a little weight in the face, I
notice, but it don't make her look any younger. "Is Rosalba
all better now?"

"Yeah. The bandage is gone. She is . . . good. You wanna
see her?" She nods, so I take her to my bedroom which is
dark 'cause I got the curtains drawn to help the baby sleep.
Rosalba, she is stretched out on her side in the playpen, all
floppy, her thick hair sticky with sweat. I hope Miss Goldin
notices how slow and peaceful the baby is breathing, even if
she do look kinda hot. I want her to know this baby is in
good shape. I want her to know that doctor in the hospital, she was crazy. I go to the window and turn up the fan
more, pointing it at Rosalba, but it only seems to blow the
air hotter.

"I bet she's pleased to be home," Miss Goldin says as we
sit down again in the living room.

"Yeah." I sigh and look at my hands, so dry and swollen
with work and worry. I don't have time for empty talk.
"What you come here for, Miss Goldin?"

She stares into her lap. "You don't need to keep calling me Miss Goldin, Teresa, just call me Sarah." She stops,
like she has lost her words. Then she takes a deep breath
and glances at me. "Well, I have some questions I need to
ask you."

For some reason my heart jumps when I hear this. Something in her voice, maybe. All I know is my insides are saying, "Uh-oh."

"Oh, yeah? What is it?" I notice Miss Goldin has gone all
pink in the face, like a little girl who has wet her panties.

"Well, the first thing is . . ." She breaks off and clears her
throat, fiddling away on her lap again, like she is knitting an
invisible shawl. "Look, I don't know how to say this but . . . I

need to find out what happened to Rosalba. I'm sorry to pry, but I don't feel right not knowing."

"You think 'cause you helping with my rent problems it is your business, hunh?" I look at her sharp till she shrinks back in her chair.

"Well, I . . ."

"Uh, forget it." I stand up and pace the room the way I always seem to do round that woman. It helps me think. My sundress is sticking to my sweaty legs and it makes me feel sloppy and messy, but I can't be worrying about that now.

"Okay, I tell you," I say, not looking at her but pacing, pacing, my slippered feet marching up and down the red carpet like I got some important place to go. "It is my sister Yolanda who done it. She is no good, a crackhead. And even when she is off the drug she drinks too much. Yolanda, she was looking after Rosalba and she let the high chair fall." I look over at Miss Goldin to see how she's taking this. "I don't mean to say she is a bad woman, miss. Don't get me wrong. I don't like to speak against my own sister, God forgive me, but this is what I find out about her. I will never let her near Rosalba again."

Miss Goldin watches me telling my lies, her gray eyes resting on me like she's got some right to judge. "Why did you let a crack addict baby-sit?" she says suddenly.

I start pulling at my fingers again like I do when I feel trapped. "I didn't have no choice. I had to go get my welfare check and go food shopping, right? Bianca was out some- place—I never know where that child is no more. So I asked my sister. It is a natural thing to do, hunh?"

"I guess. Look, I'm sorry to poke in your business like this. I . . ."

"Okay, let it be." I pick her empty glass up off the floor. "Miss Goldin, did you talk to that man you know 'bout my rent yet?" You better get something done, I say to her

in my head. You owe me with all your nosiness and your
broken promises.

"Yes," she says, sounding happy we changed the subject.
"He said he can help, but he needs some records to work up
a rent history. Are you sure you have no receipts or notes
from the landlord about raising your rent?"

"He didn't send me no notes, Miss Goldin, he just sent
thugs. I got old receipts like I told you. You can look if you
want." I get the shoe box out again and hand it over.

"Okay, thanks." She puts the box on her lap, pushes her
hair off her face, and looks at me. "Teresa?" she says in this
quiet voice I don't like. "Those two accidents, and the bruises
that doctor mentioned—was it all your sister?"

I stare at her, trying not to get so mad I throw her out.
Who's this woman think she is? "Miss Goldin," I say, "I can't
tell you right now. I gotta think about it. I gotta pray for
some guidance."

"Just tell me the truth!"

I shake my head and fix my eyes on the picture I have
hanging on the wall, my favorite one of You, Virgencita,
holding Your dying son on Your lap. "I gotta pray for guidance," I tell her again. "I am sorry, Miss Goldin. You come
back tomorrow, yes, and we can talk then? I got something I
wanna say to you but I need to pray for help first."

"I don't want to come back tomorrow." She stands up,
holding my box in her hands, and for the first time I see a
fierceness creep into her tired gray eyes. "I came all the way
here to ask you this, Teresa. I'm sorry but I just feel I should
know. And why do you need guidance to tell me the truth?
Isn't your conscience enough?"

I put her lemonade glass down on the table. "Maybe you
not religious, I don't know, but that is between me and the
Lord and nobody else."

She blushes. "I'm sorry," she says.

I shrug and nod, and we both sit back down. We stay

quiet for a while, feeling too bad to look each other in the face. Then I think, what have I got to lose? I might as well tell her everything. Maybe then she will want to help me even more. So I take a deep breath. "Listen," I say to her at last, "I know you a good woman, Miss Goldin, so I will be straight with you. It wasn't my sister did those things, it was just accidents been happening to Rosalba, honest, and a little pinching Bianca does when she gets mad. There is no abuse, I swear, it is just Bianca being jealous. That is the truth, so help me God. Bianca, she is only a child herself, Miss Goldin, but she is mine, and I got no other children left to call my own. I didn't wanna let you know 'cause I love my Bianca and I don't wanna get her into no trouble. I hoped and prayed she would bring herself outta this jealousy she's got about Rosalba. I thought I could teach her to love the baby, but I can't make it work. Even quitting my job hasn't helped. She is just a child, miss, she don't know no better."

I stop to take another breath, too scared to look right at Miss Goldin, and the woman, she just sits there silent, serious and sad and making me feel like I am in court in front of a judge. But I go on talking anyhow, hoping to touch her heart. "After that accident with the high chair I saw things were getting dangerous, and I prayed hard, I prayed so hard. Now la Virgen María, She has showed me what to do. I gotta give up Rosalba, Miss Goldin, can you understand? I gotta protect the baby from Bianca, I gotta separate the two of them, but I can't send my Bianca away, not for nobody. Where could I send her? I am all she's got. She got no place else to go." And I tell Miss Goldin right then that if I keep Bianca and Rosalba together under my roof much longer, I am afraid of what might happen—not only to the baby but to all of us going down the drain so fast with no money and no job and no help in this evil world. "Please take Rosalba, Miss Goldin," I say, the tears filling my eyes with shame. "Take her and save my children for me."

Miss Goldin she goes white when I say this, and I see her hand fly to her heart like she wants to protect it from my words. Am I such a sinner hearts need protecting from me? I try to ignore what she is doing and fix my eyes on Your picture instead, praying inside. Do You hear me, Virgen? Let her understand, let her have some pity. But Miss Goldin, all she does is stand up and stare at me like I am spitting poison.

"Look lady, I know this is kinda sudden," I tell her quick, "but you told me you been trying for a baby for years with no luck, right? Now you can have one, and one you know is beautiful and smart and healthy. There's a lotta women would die for the chance."

She just keeps staring at me, then all of a sudden she says, "Are you crazy? How can you talk like that about your own granddaughter?"

"It's 'cause I love her," I say, and my throat gets thick and achy. I swallow so I can talk. "I want her to have a better life. She is so scared of Bianca, miss, you should see the look on her little face. Every time my daughter walks in the room that baby cries and shrinks up like she's afraid she is gonna get hurt. I can't stand to see it, I can't stand to have her living like that. I wanna protect her."

"You don't mean it," Miss Goldin says, shaking her head. "You're just panicking. Listen, I'll help you out if you want, okay? I can lend you the money to catch up with your rent, if you'll take it. But don't do this to yourself and Bianca."

I wanna say, "No, you don't understand, lady, I been thinking and praying about it for weeks," but I see it isn't gonna help. So I just look at the ground. "Miss Goldin, I don't want your money. Think about what I am saying, hunh? Will you?" But all she will do is shake her head some more, pick up her purse, and say good-bye, real quick like she is scared I am gonna put a curse on her if she stays another second.

"You will come tomorrow?" I say.

"I'll try. I'm very . . . tired."

I nod. "You will come. Adiós." And I hear her run down the stairs like she is escaping a fire.

Little Rosalba, forgive me. I tried to help you through life and took you on like I was your natural mother, but that wasn't the Lord's way, mi cielito. Dios, He has another plan for you, and we must have faith it is a better one. La Virgen de la Altagracia, She will look after you like She looks over all the children, don't you worry your little head. I will pray for you every day, mi Rosita. We won't give up our hope, right? And we will see if I can get you this new mamá.

PART THREE

PART THREE

Bianca

September's almost done and I'm in the ninth grade now. I'm still in this same stupid pregnant school, but Mr. Jonas says I should be proud anyhow 'cause lotsa girls in my situation wouldn't've made it to a high school grade yet. Not me, I tell him, I'm not like those bimbos. I know what counts in this world, and it ain't cutting school just to mess with some baby. I might be making mistakes sometimes and doing dumb things, but one thing Bianca Rodríguez Díaz is not, and that's a fool.

I wonder how old Mr. Jonas is. He looks like maybe he's about twenty-five, but it's hard to say. I don't think he's married. I asked him once if he has any kids, but all he said was to keep quiet and pay attention to my work. I like it when he comes over to help me with my math. When he leans over my desk his dreadlocks fall over his face in this sexy way, and his big eyes peek out all serious and deep. Then he reaches out this muscular arm of his to show me some problem, and I feel kinda hot and funny all over. Sometimes I get so wrapped up watching the muscles in his arm move when he's writing I forget to listen to what he says, and then he gets mad and shouts at me to wake up. Some of the other girls in class, I know they got crushes on him, and they be teasing me all the time 'cause they say he likes me, but I tell them to shut up. I ain't so stupid I'd fall in love with a teacher. I'm done with men, they don't know. It's just that I like his voice, which is real deep, and the way he says I'm too smart to be at home changing diapers my whole life.

Speaking of diapers, it's the baby's half birthday today. Soon as I get home from school Mami says to wish the baby happiness and I just stop and stare at the time that's passed so quick. Y'know, when I was real little, a week or a month seemed like forever. I mean, I couldn't even imagine the end of the week it felt so far away. Now I can't believe it's been six months already since that thing came outta me. All that pain and yelling I did, feeling like my insides were ripping open, and there's no sign of it to look at me now. Sometimes I watch the baby lying on her back sucking her toes or doing some other dumb thing, and she looks so different than the baby born outta me I can't believe she's the same person. She's a being all her own now. Her legs are pudgy and round and she smiles at Mami and giggles at her private thoughts. She don't seem to have anything to do with me. It's like any old person coulda just brought her in and dumped her here, and we wouldn't know the difference. I guess most mothers feel that sometimes, but I think it's worse for me 'cause Mami still won't let me near her. What's she think I'm gonna do to the baby, bite her? Okay, I know I been mean to that baby sometimes, like when I pinched her a little or left her alone when she was crying, or when I pushed her over, though that was only once—but it's not like I do it always. I feel better about her now, least mosta the time. She still bothers me a lot, but that hot, crackling feeling hasn't come in a long time, not since my period started and I quit having to worry about a devil-child inside of me. Now sometimes I wanna just pick that baby up, or cuddle her pudgy hot body, or tickle her little fat feet and hear her giggle. But ever since the baby came back from the hospital Mami been keeping her and me apart like I got some disease. Mami, I wanna say, why you acting like this? I mean, who d'you think had that thing? Who was it went through all those pains and thought she was gonna die, huh? And now look, you won't even let me touch her. But when I try to say these things to Mami she just starts yelling at me or telling me to do the dishes or clean up our room, and I end up so mad I don't feel like saying anything at all. I think sometimes Mami don't realize I got feelings, too. I miss how the baby's head is warm and fluffy when you rub your cheek on it. I miss how, when you wanna cry, holding her rubbery body makes you feel better inside. So y'know what I'm gonna do today? I'm gonna skip my lunch even if the doctor did say I gotta eat more, and after school I'm gonna use that money to buy the baby something real cute like a rattle or a hair band to prove to Mami I still care.

"Bianca," Mami calls, "come and eat, quick. Your dinner is getting cold and I got something to say." I go in the kitchen where Mami's frying up some chicken. Her hair's up on her head in a knot and she's got her yellow apron tied tight around her skinny hips. "You look like a banana in that thing," I say, and I sit down to eat. The baby's in the high chair with baby peaches all over her face like some kinda orange skin disease.

"Biancita," Mami says, turning round and wiping her bony fingers on her apron. I know she's gonna say something heavy 'cause she never uses that name with me otherwise. "Biancita, mi hijita, I don't like to tell you this, but we might have to move to another apartment, mi lechuza. Our landlord, he wants us outta here." And before I've even taken a bite, she sits down at the table and tells me she can't keep up with the rent 'cause of quitting her job and having the two of us to feed, me and the baby, and she says we might have to move in with Tía Yolanda for a while. "Mi cielito," she says, taking me by the face with her scratchy hands. "I know you like it here, this street, this place is your home. But the rent keeps going up and even when I had my job I was having problems to pay. I tried to get that reporter lady to help, but I have heard no word from her and I don't know if she will do anything real. . . . I am sorry, cuquita."

Now this I don't want. My tía, she lives up on 206th Street, and it is terrible up there. I mean, it's okay to go there to visit once in a while, but not to live. There's these drug dealers all over the place, and people getting shot by the gangbangers, and all kinds of shit going down that's even worse than my street. I know, I hear the stories she tells me, and some of the girls at my school are from up there, too. "I don't wanna go, Mami!" I say. "I got my friends here."

Mami sighs. "I know, pobrecita, but we got no choice." Then she says this other thing which is so weird I stare at her like she's turning green in front of my eyes. She says she's gonna send the baby away! She says she wants to send her someplace else to live till we get a home we can afford. She says she's gonna find the baby a nice, safe home, where she can be looked after by some person who cares. "Yolanda, she don't have room for all of us, Bianca. And I gotta go back to work soon so we can get another apartment with no crooked landlords trying to push us out. I can't do that with the baby to look after. And Bianca, I wanna spend more time with you, mi muñeca. I miss you."

"What?" I stare at Mami. "You gonna give the baby to somebody else?"

"Bianca, you listen to me." Mami lays her hands on me again, gentle, like she hasn't done in years. "Calmate niña, and listen to your Mami." I sit still like she has a spell on me—I can feel my mouth hanging open. And she begins saying these words seem like they come right outta my head.

"Bianca, you know how hard our life has been since you had Rosalba, hunh?" I nod. "You know I had to quit my job 'cause you too young to look after her safe—no, don't get mad, I am not blaming you, Biancita. I understand. And you know how much more you and me been fighting?"

"Yes, Mami," I say, and I feel the tears come to my eyes just to hear her say this truth.

"Well, I been praying to la Virgen, and I been asking what to do about it. And, Bianca, She tells me to let Rosalba go to another family so the baby, she can have a chance to be more in life, and so we can have a chance to be happy together."

"But Mami, you love her. How . . ." I look over at the baby, gurgling in her high chair and sucking the peaches off her fat fingers, and I feel so bad for her it aches inside. I mean, there she is, a tiny thing not even big enough to feed her own self, and she's being kicked out into the world like a grown woman. What makes Mami think there's anybody out there for Rosalba better than her?

"Sí, I love her," Mami says. "That is why I gotta do this thing, Bianca. This life is no good for her. We got no money, pretty soon maybe we got no home. I can't stay on this welfare thing, it is killing my soul. But if I go back to work, and I leave her with you . . ." Mami goes silent and looks at me till I squirm, then she lets out this big sigh. "School is going so good for you. . . . I want my Bianca to be something."

"You mean she's gonna go to like a foster home? So we can get her back in a while, like when we got a new place?"

Mami shifts her eyes away from me and I notice how tired she looks, the lines round her mouth folding like a fan. "Maybe," she says. "Maybe we find a foster home, maybe a good mother who will want to keep her. I don't know yet, mi linda, you just gonna have to trust me."

I close my eyes 'cause it all seems like too much. And I think about if the baby was gone, how I could come home

from school and Mami'd be back from work like the old
days, and how she'd be tired but ready to listen to me like
she used to, and how I might even read her from some of
my schoolwork to show her how good I'm doing. I think
about how I'd have Mami all to myself again, and my heart, I
can't help it, it starts singing. Then my eyes fly open 'cause
the baby yells all of a sudden—she's rubbed some of those
stingy peaches in her eyes—and Mami gets up and wipes
the baby's face and picks her up outta the chair and rocks
her till she stops crying. And I think about how I can't even
do that. Every time I touch that baby now she curls her fists
up in a ball and yells. I don't pinch her anymore, honest, but
she remembers. She don't forget or forgive, so what's the
point? I look at her with her eyes squeezed up and the tears
rolling down her fat cheeks and her noise that makes you
wanna run outta the room, and my bad angel comes out and
says, "Good riddance." But at the same time good angel, he
comes flying in saying, "Whoa, hold on there Bianca. She's
only a tiny baby, girl, and she's yours."

"Mami?" I say at last, and I'm thinking how she musta
been planning this whole thing for a while, "you got somebody in mind you gonna give the baby to?"

Mami slides her eyes away from me again like she been
doing a lot lately. "I got some ideas, Biancita, but I don't
wanna tell you them yet, not till I know for sure. The person
I choose, she will be a good woman, don't you worry. You
know I would never give her to nobody we don't like."

I look at Mami's face, which is swollen up with secrets,
and I'm so full of questions I can't sort them out in my mind
but I know it is no use to ask, so all I say is "Can I go out
now?"

Mami sighs. "You never stay home no more, Bianca. You
done your homework?"

"Yeah. Clara's waiting for me downstairs."

"Okay, okay, go. But get back here in half an hour. That Miss Mandel, she is coming again to see you."

"She is? I told her we didn't need her no more. I told her to leave us alone. Can't you tell her to get lost?"

Mami puts her hands out like she's catching the rain. "You the one got her here in the first place, niña, so you better come back, hunh?"

I sigh. "Okay." But I got a sneaking suspicion Mami asked that teacher to come here herself.

"Bianca? Wait a minute," Mami says before I go out the door. "Come here, cuquita." I walk up to her, wondering what weird thing she is gonna say now. "Biancita, I know this thing is sad, mi chula, but you got the rest of your life to have babies in. And I got my baby, and Bianca, it is you." And Mami leans over me with the baby in her arms, and I can hardly believe it but she kisses me. Of course, soon as the baby gets near me, it shrieks and kicks out, hitting me right in the eye. But y'know what? I cry all the way down the stairs, just 'cause I know now Mami's come back to loving me again.

When I come out the front door to the stoop, Roberto is already there, as usual. Now that Mami's quit work and I got more free time, I hang with him and Clara most days after school. We don't do a whole lot, just listen to music, sneak a smoke or a drink sometimes, or watch the city turn dark, but I like it. It makes me feel like I got people to be with, like I did before the baby came. It makes me feel like Bianca again, insteada like somebody who got stolen away.

"Don't you got nothing better to do than hang on my stoop?" I tell Roberto, but he just smiles. I tease him like that all the time. He says he does his schoolwork late at night, after he's helped his aunt put his little brother and sisters to bed. Roberto's the only boy I know who even breathes the word homework. He drives me crazy a lotta the time, but at least he knows better than to get into crack like that red-car maricón and his gang. Those malandros, they deal on the corner of Amsterdam now like it's their territory, and it's got so I don't even cross over to there anymore. I see these skinny white people, they be coming up to buy all day long, looking like they'll fall over dead any minute. It's two different worlds now, the southwest side of the street where the dealers hang, and ours on the north. Mami says the street's getting more dangerous every day 'cause of those dealers. I wish they'd all get busted and rot in jail.

Roberto has his boom box with him, and he asks me if I wanna go down to Riverside Park and listen to some music. "What about Clara?" I say. "Where's she at?"

"I don't know. With some new boyfriend, I think." I believe him, 'cause even though I know now Tía Yolanda was right—all boys lie—Roberto's different. He just don't lie, I can tell. Maybe he's too dumb.

"I gotta ask my mother first." I run back upstairs and find her talking in the living room with Miss Mandel. That woman's gotta be a witch—how else did she sneak in here without me seeing? The baby's sitting on the floor, chewing on one of my shoes—I wish Mami wouldn't let her do that—and I notice Mami shuts her mouth up tight soon as I come in, so I know she been gossiping about me again. I refuse to look at Miss Mandel. Don't adults have any respect? Just 'cause I'm a student in her school don't mean she can go round talking about me like I got no more feelings than a bug. I give the teacher the evil eye. "Mami, can I go to the park with some friends?"

"What friends?" she says, sharp as a tack.

"Y'know, Clara and a couple of girls?" Mami don't like Roberto, I don't know why. You'd think he's the kind of boy would make most mothers drool.

"Okay, but Bianca, I want you back in one hour, you hear? Say hello to Miss Mandel."

I nod at the woman, my body halfway out the door.

"Hello, dear. I hear you got an *A* in your math class last semester. Well done."

"Thanks." I look down at my feet, scuffing the rug. "I gotta go."

"Mr. Jonas is very proud of you. He's planning to enter you in some math competitions this year."

I turn my head to look out the window so she don't see me blush when she says his name. Lady, get the hell outta my business, is what I wanna say, but instead I'm like, "Yeah. I gotta go. Bye," and I run down the stairs, wondering what she and Mami are getting so tight about.

Outside, Roberto is waiting with his boom box and his smile. He's no God's gift to women, but I do kinda like that smile he got. His whole face dimples up, like he's just found out the best secret and can't wait to let you in on it. We walk across Broadway, past those homeless bums filling up the benches on the traffic island, drinking and fighting and sleeping like it's their own private living room, and go down a side street till we get to Riverside Drive. "Wanna go in?" Roberto says, and I nod, so we walk down some steep stone steps into Riverside Park, which is this skinny strip of grass and trees between the Drive and the highway next to the Hudson River. I always liked this park 'cause it's kinda se-cret, hidden behind a wall and way below the street, with the river sparkling on one side like you aren't in a city at all, and the view of New Jersey and cliffs and trees and build-ings across the water. In some places you can't even see the highway so it's like you're in the woods, specially in the spring when the cherry blossoms are out pink and white and red, or the fall, like now, with huge trees full of green and yellow leaves, the little paths winding under them like they can really take you someplace.

A lotta people are out on the grass today barbecuing their dinners 'cause it's one of those September days that don't wanna give up on summer, and it looks like a party with people laughing and kissing and lying around on picnic blankets. It smells real good, too, juicy meat and charcoal. All these families are running round, the grown-ups drinking beer and joking, the little kids screaming and spraying each other with squirt guns and playing Frisbee and stuff, and when I look at them this sharp pain goes right through me like an electric shock. Every time I see a big family like that, specially a happy one, I feel this way. It makes me want a real family so bad, a daddy and little brothers and sisters to play with. All I got is Mami shriveling up with worry, and Tía Yolanda, who's drinking again and never comes round no more. I hear her oldest boy got arrested. I don't wanna move in with her.

"We should do a barbecue like that with Diego and my little sisters sometime," Roberto says, like he's reading my thoughts. "You should see them. They all full of the devil, but so cute. You'd like them, I think."

"Yeah, that'd be cool." I can just see myself, chasing those little girls, their dresses flipping and their voices squealing. Maybe I'd teach them some of the moves I know jumping rope. We walk past the barbecuing families, me still feeling kinda sad and mixed up from my talk with Mami, and that's when Roberto takes my hand. His touch makes me so nervous I try to pull away but he just gives me this look like a kid after a popsicle, so I have to give in. No boy's touched me since that pendejo Orlando, and even the feel of Roberto's fingers makes me sick to my stomach. I shut my eyes for a second and tell myself, Pretend he's Mami, and that helps a little. But I still can't wait to get my hand back.

We walk along this dirt path until we get to a bench under some big old trees, and at last Roberto lets go of me so he can turn on the radio. I can tell he's in a romantic mood, though, and I don't like it. He's okay for a friend, but not for that. He puts the music on kinda quiet, resting the radio on the wall that looks over the highway and the river, and smiles at me again. Most boys, when they take you out, the whole time they be teasing you and showing off, but Roberto, he's different, all calm, sitting there looking at me like he could wait till the moon turns purple. He acts so old sometimes it's creepy. I sit on the bench, fiddling with my fingers, and he moves up next to me. I wish Clara was here.

We sit awhile, not saying much 'cept a few words about the music and school. He asks me how my mother is doing, so I complain my usual complaints, but I don't tell him about moving or giving away the baby. I can't make it that real. Meanwhile he's moving closer and closer on the bench and I know he's gonna put his arm round me and my heart begins banging loud and hard. I scoot away from him, but I see he notices 'cause he stops moving. He leans his elbow on his knees, looking down at the ground between his legs, and he says, "What's eating you, Bianca? What you scared of?"

"Who said I'm scared?"

Roberto sits back up and looks at me, his eyes big and shining. "Every time I move you jump like a mouse."

I shrug and look away. I don't know what to tell him, I feel so sick inside. "Maybe it's Juan," I lie. "Ever since he went away I can't trust nobody, not even Clara."

"But you went out with Orlando. The whole street know you went with him, Bianca. How come him and not me?"

A big lump comes up in my throat when he says that. "I don't even wanna hear that name!" I yell, and I put my hands over my ears.

Roberto touches me lightly on the knee, like a bird pecking. "Hey, Bianca, take it easy," he says, quiet and serious like he can be. "Don't worry 'bout it. You don't have to say nothing 'less you want."

I stare at the ground for a while. The asphalt under us is all tore up, grass growing in clumps and chewing gum wrappers glinting in the sun like jewels. When the lump is all the way back down my throat, I say, "What's he been saying about me anyhow?"

"Nothing much. Just that you went out with him one time."

"Oh yeah, is that all? Well, whatever he's saying, it's a lie. He's evil. He's a devil in human skin. He's dangerous."

"I know, Bianca. He's into scary shit. He hurt you?" Roberto puts his head to one side and looks at me real gentle, no pressure, and all of a sudden I feel like this plug is pulled outta me and a giant gush of feeling comes rushing up, all the stuff that Mami said, and the baby going, and that coño Orlando, and my fucked-up life, and suddenly I'm crying and Roberto has his arms round me and he's saying, "Go on, baby, let it all out. I'm gonna look after you, don't you worry. Let it all out."

Teresa

La Virgen de la Altagracia, I hope You are in a forgiving mood, even for a sinning woman like me. I feel ashamed in my heart with all my lying and scheming, but also I am feeling a tiny bit good inside. I can't help thinking that maybe things are going better for Teresa Rodríguez and her poor little nieta for a change. I got that Miss Goldin back over here finally, though I know she didn't wanna come. Forgive me, but You understand it was for mi Rosita, and not for myself.

The lady never came back after she left that last time, even though she promised, so that is why I called Miss Mandel and asked her to come over here instead. I wanted to find out about adoption, how it is done and how it can work if both the natural mother and the adoption mother wanna do it. I know she didn't like what I was saying 'cause her face it went pink and she pulled her long back up straight as a mop handle, but she did give me answers and those answers gave me ideas. So I let a few days more pass, then I called Miss Goldin at home. "Miss Goldin?" I said when I heard her voice, "can you talk?"

"I wish you wouldn't call me at home, Teresa," she said. She sounded real upset. "What do you want?"

"I got some more information about my landlord. Something for the tenant's lawyer you told me about?"

"You can't tell me on the phone?"

"No, I am at a phone booth. Those thugs, they took my phone, remember? Anyhow, it is something I gotta give you, not tell you."

"Can't you just mail it?" She sighed, her voice real tired.

"I am afraid it'll get lost—I don't trust that post office in my neighborhood. The people who work there, they got the brains of a sheep. Come on over here, it won't take long." She tried some more to get outta coming but I wouldn't let her, so she came the next day after work. She looked even more worn out than before, her face thin and kinda transparent, like dirty glass. I sat her down on the couch. "You okay?" I said. "You look like you don't feel too good."

She waved a hand. "I'm okay. I've been covering some tough stories lately." She smiled, but her smile was shadowy and sad and for the first time I wondered if this lady, she is too old to be a mother to my Rosalba. My eyes ran over her. She looked strong enough. Just overworked, I guess, like us all.

"Well, what have you got for me, Teresa?" she said.

I handed her a piece of paper, some raggedy thing I found in my drawer, scribbled with writing I couldn't make out. She tried to read it, wrinkling up her eyes. "What's this?"

"I don't know. I thought maybe it was important. Maybe it could help get my landlord off my back, yes?"

The lady flings down the paper and crosses her arms over her breasts. "Honestly, Teresa, what nonsense. What did you drag me up here for, really? I'm busy enough."

I raised my eyebrows when she said this. I didn't think this lady, she would talk so rude to me. Maybe it is 'cause I told her about Bianca and the pinching. Maybe she has lost respect for us. I didn't say nothing for a while 'cause I was too hurt and angry to trust my words. I wanna keep Miss Goldin on my side, but I don't take to rudeness from nobody.

"Oh dear." I hear her sigh. "Look, I'm sorry. I shouldn't have said that. I'm in a terrible mood, some difficulties at home, some . . . health things . . . You're right, I'm not feeling so well. Sorry, Teresa, I really am."

I look over at her from my chair. "You having husband trouble, is that it?"

She blushes and smiles like it hurts. "That's part of it. How can you tell?"

"I can read these things. They are written on a woman's face like a book. But don't you worry. These men, they always give a wife a hard time in the warm weather, you ever notice that? I think it is seeing all the girls out there with almost nothing on, y'know? The men get restless like a bull locked away from the cows. It will be better now it is the fall."

Miss Goldin shrugs. "Maybe."

"Anyhow," I say quickly, "you are right. I know this piece of paper, it is no good. I wanted you to come here 'cause I got something to ask you." I stop and pull at my fingers a while. "Miss Goldin? I can't keep Rosalba here no more. I can't stay outta work this long. The landlord, he is back again with his bills and his threats. I don't wanna lose my home, lady, you gotta understand that. And Bianca, she is doing real good in school now—you would be proud of her. But I can't leave the two of them alone, Miss Goldin, I just can't do it. Rosalba don't even smile at Bianca no more, she just looks scared around her. My babies never looked like that, I didn't even know a baby could look so scared. I gotta find mi nieta another home."

Rosalba is playing at my feet the whole time I am talking. She is six and a half months now and sitting up straight and

steady, her little legs folded in front of her like a queen. She
says "Guggle, giggle, gurgle," she lies on her back sucking
her toes, and she smiles at me when I cuddle her in my lap.
I pick her up, kiss her soft head, and rub her back. I do
these things almost without thinking, but there is a proud
voice inside of me saying, See, lady, see how much love
she gets?

Miss Goldin watches me, her gray eyes watery and troubled, but she don't say a thing, so I keep talking. "Rosalba,
she is used to having love, Miss Goldin. Look, I understand
you don't wanna take her, but how am I gonna find her a
good foster home? I don't want no mean woman taking her
in just to get the money. I hear enough about those people,
abusing the babies and carrying on with perversions and
cruelty. How can I find somebody I trust? I was hoping you
maybe would know about this."

Just then Bianca sticks her head in the door, looking like
she wants to ask me some favor, as usual, and as soon as
Rosalba sees her she clings to me with her little hands. She
does that all the time now—she is so afraid of Bianca it hurts
my soul. I hope Miss Goldin notices so she sees the truth I
am telling her. "Bianca, what you want now?" I say, but
Bianca doesn't answer me. She just looks at Miss Goldin like
the woman's una culebra.

"How come we didn't make it into your paper?" she asks
her suddenly. "I looked and looked after the last time you
came here, and I never saw us in any of the stories under
your name. How come you reporters are always breaking
your promises, huh?"

Miss Goldin blinks and goes red. She blushes real easy,
I've noticed—Mamá used to say that was a sign of a guilty
conscience. "Bianca, don't you be so rude to our visitors," I
say quickly. "Now what you want, hunh?" But before the
words are all the way outta my mouth, Bianca slams the
door shut again, and she's gone. "I am sorry, Miss Goldin,"

I say with shame. "I try to teach her manners, but she is so . . ."

"No, never mind," Miss Goldin says quietly. "She's right, really." She smiles at me, and I notice she looks real sad. "Now, what were you saying?"

"Well, I was gonna ask you, do you know a good place to help me find my Rosalba a home?"

Miss Goldin gives herself a little shake. Her face has gone tense, like she is in pain, and I wonder what is going on with her. "Uh, yes, one of the other reporters did a story about adoption once," she says after a minute. "I'll find out from her, if you want. Are you really sure about this, Teresa? Can't you send Bianca to a relative or something? Why does it have to be the baby you send away?"

I reach down to smooth Rosalba's hair. "I got no relatives left in this country but my sister, Miss Goldin, and she I could never trust with Bianca. My daughter, she would only end up running wild. I wanna keep an eye on her, keep her in school so she can amount to something. Did you find out anything more from those lawyer people, y'know, who help tenants?" I ask this quick, to change the subject. I don't want her questions making me tell her about Hernán and Luis and my fears for my daughter. I am too ashamed of all the mistakes in my life.

"No, sorry. I haven't been able to make it back down there yet. I've been so busy. . . ." She waves her smooth hand in the air, like it is too much even to speak of her suffering. What does she know about suffering? A few little squabbles with her husband and she thinks she got the world's trouble on her back? "I'll go soon, I promise."

Yeah, sure, I am thinking. Haven't I been telling myself all along not to trust nobody else to do my business for me? "Maybe I better go after all," I say. "Just tell me what to do."

"No, I promised. I'll do it," she says.

"You sure, lady? 'Cause things are getting pretty tight round here."

"Yes, I'm sure."

"Okay," I say, hoping I pricked her conscience enough to make her get up off her lazy butt and do something, and then I go on and talk and talk and talk about Rosalba and my landlord and my life until Miss Goldin is just sitting there, slumped in her chair, looking like she been hypnotized.

Finally, when the sky is getting dark and Rosalba has fallen asleep against my chest, Miss Goldin rubs her face and stands up slowly to go, like it hurts her even to move. That woman needs more sleep. "Don't leave yet," I say quickly. "I got something to show you. Hold the baby a minute, hunh?" I put Rosalba in her arms, which makes the baby wake up suddenly and start crying. "Bounce her a little, up and down," I tell Miss Goldin, who looks frozen with panic. It makes me wanna laugh, a grown woman so scared of a baby's cry. "Like this, yes. Then she will like you, no problem."

"Like this?" she says, jiggling Rosalba.

"Yeah, you got it," and sure enough mi ángelita stops whimpering and twists her little face up to look at Miss Goldin. My Rosalba, she's got these big black eyes and thick eyelashes, and her cheeks are so smooth and perfect— she could charm the horns right off the devil. She pokes a finger in Miss Goldin's mouth, exploring, and that lady, she begins kissing her plump fingertips like she is under a spell. Rosalba giggles, showing Miss Goldin a glimpse of her pretty white teeth.

"She's growing up," Miss Goldin says while I am rifling through some envelopes stuffed with photographs. Now I got her trapped with the baby in her arms—and Rosalba, she is no lightweight—I can take advantage.

"Ah, here they are," I say. "Yes, look here how much Rosalba, she has grown." I hold one of the photos up so

Miss Goldin can see. There is Rosalba, a newborn, scrawny and raw, her black eyes squinting scared into the light as if she is saying, Mi Dios, what is gonna happen to me now?

"She was always beautiful," Miss Goldin says, and she smiles again, that same sad, sweet smile I saw the first day we met. She gives mi Rosita a kiss, hands her back to me, and picks up her bag and leaves. I pray to You, Virgencita, make her think over all I planted in her head.

"You like la doña?" I say to Rosalba after Miss Goldin is gone. "You think she is gonna want to be your mamá?" Rosalba, she smiles and pulls a strand of my falling-down hair to her mouth so she can suck it. I keep my eyes looking at her face for a long, long time, hoping to see her future.

Roberto

I'm gonna kill that mothafucka. When Bianca told me what he did to her I could hardly see nothing outta my eyes it made me so burning mad. How could he do that to such a sweet girl? He mighta made her pregnant or given her AIDS or anything! Every time I think of her, that little face with those big eyes under her bangs, those sweet lips, it burns me up. Why everybody beating up on her? First that Juan abandoning her with the baby, then her moms whacking her in the mouth over every little thing, and now that mothafucka Orlando who thinks he be so cool with his stupid-ass car and his dope-fiend friends. I'm gonna fix him for you, Bianca, he ain't getting away with this.

Orlando ain't from our street but I remember him when he was a kid 'cause we was in the same school together. He was always the businessman, cheating other kids outta their good comics which he traded for duds, getting the better of everybody with his slick words and his mean jokes. The other boys collected round him like flies round shit; they thought he be the Man. I guess that's 'cause he was smart, but smart don't necessarily make right. I used to hang with him, too, back when we was thirteen or so, 'cause I thought that'd make me big, but soon as he got into dealing and selling guns I got outta there quick. Maybe that fucka don't care about the little kids in the hood, giving ten-year-olds guns so they can shoot them off like firecrackers never realizing they can end a life that way, but it ain't right, it ain't Christian— it ain't even human. Bianca said the truth when she called that asshole a devil. He always been a devil, using his brains for evil insteada good.

I feel so bad for Bianca, though. That fucka put her through all that hell, treating her like she was no better'n some junkie whore, and she can't even tell her moms about it. She said her moms told her not to go with Orlando so she'd just say it was Bianca's own fault. I don't know if Bianca is right about that 'cause I think Mrs. Rodríguez is a good woman, even if she do got a hot temper—maybe she'd make Bianca go to a doctor at least. Sometimes I think Bianca don't know how lucky she is still having a moms. But I guess I don't know. I seen the bruise on Bianca's mouth where her moms hit her, and I heard the woman screaming at that girl outta their apartment window enough times, so maybe Bianca be right not to trust her. I just don't know.

Still, I'm happy Bianca told me what's in her heart. It's just like I thought, Bianca and me, we got the same kinda troubles and the same kinda mind, and that means we can help each other out. Ever since that day in the park, me and her got a new relationship. We be best friends now, telling each other our lives. She told me her troubles and I told her mine. I told her about what my dad did, and about my dreams—how I'm gonna make that man pay with sorrow for all he done to us for the rest of his miserable life. The only thing I don't tell her yet is my dreams for her. She wouldn't like it, I know, 'cause she gets mad if I talk love. She ain't ready yet, I understand. I know I gotta give her time after what that motha did to her, but it's hard to keep my patience. I look at that girl sometimes, with her pretty nose turned up just a little, and her dark eyes full of soul, and my heart feels like it's swelling with love so fast it's gonna pop right outta my chest. I gotta use all my willpower to stop my hands reaching out for her. I want so bad to hold her close up to me, to feel her little back under my palms and her softness against my chest, her hair tickling my lips. I want so bad to tell her how I feel, to hug her tight, wrap myself round her and never let her go. I got so much love in me it could fill up the street, smother the cars and seal over the windows and stretch right up to the top of the roofs. I need her so bad sometimes my whole body seems to be singing right out, Bianca, I love you.

Bianca girl, you gonna be all right. I know it, deep in my heart I know it. I'm gonna beat that mothafucka Orlando till he begs for mercy for what he did to you, then I'm gonna take you outta this place, girl, far away from all your troubles. I'm gonna help you forget your sadness and give you the peace of mind to love the baby you got, and the ones you gonna get from me when we be married. Just you hold on, sweet love, and you'll see. Roberto be like your knight in shining armor. I'm gonna ride into your life and set it right. Just you wait.

Bianca

Some weird shit is going down round here. Things are happening so fast I feel like I got up and left my head on the pillow. Like today. I'm just walking outta school, talking with some girls like we always do about how cute Mr. Jonas is and other stupid stuff, and suddenly I hear my name being called and there is Mami! I mean, Mami's never come to meet me at school since I was a little kid! She is standing in the street looking skinny and clean in a white shirt and her white stretch jeans, her hair in a fancy braid on top of her head, and she got the baby all dressed up in the stroller. I'm so surprised and embarrassed I stare at her like she's a ghost. "Mami, what you doing here?"

"Bianca, come with me," she says, looking round like she thinks she's being followed. "Listen Biancita, we got trouble. Our landlord? He locked us out. He changed the locks on us and now we got no place to stay 'cept Miss Goldin's house."

"Shh." I look over at the girls, hoping they don't hear, but they've all gone. "Miss Goldin?"

"Y'know, that reporter lady? I called her on the phone

and told her what happened. She said we could stay with her till we get this stuff worked out."

"Why don't you just break the lock, Mami? I can get Roberto to do it. I got all my stuff in there!"

"I know, mi amor, but I don't wanna make no trouble. If we break the door, the landlord, he will make me pay even more. I just gotta see him tomorrow with some money I owe, and maybe he'll let us get our things." Mami squeezes her hands together, pulling at the knuckles. "All along I been scared he would do this to us, bastardo!"

I'm so shocked by what she's telling me I sit down on the sidewalk. "Mami, I'm scared. It's like we're homeless or something."

"Get up, Bianca, it is dirty down there. Listen, we go to Miss Goldin's house now, okay? Then tomorrow, we will see. Maybe we can go stay with Yolanda, like I said. Come on now, get up. You got no reason to act so surprised, I told you we might have to move."

I stand up, but I'm real upset. "But why we going to this strange woman's house and not to Tía Yolanda's place, Mami? I don't understand."

But Mami tells me to stop making problems, and we take the bus down to Eighty-sixth Street, where she says Miss Goldin lives on Riverside Drive. All the way on the bus she won't explain anything to me, she just rocks the baby to sleep. "The two of you, you give me so much trouble," she says. "Whining and complaining all the time, whining and complaining. It is like I got two babies."

When we get to the reporter's front door, I can't help it but I'm pretty impressed. She lives in one of those fancy buildings looks like a wedding cake, with a big glass awning over the front door and iron gates all twisted and black like the opening to a haunted castle. A doorman's standing there, a little fat guy with a pink face and no eyebrows, and when I push the stroller in he steps right in fronta me so I almost run it over his feet. "May I heelp you?" he says in some kinda horror-movie accent. This makes me mad right away 'cause I know he thinks we don't belong in a building like this, but Mami acts real dignified.

"We are here to see Miss Sarah Goldin," she says in her best English. "Miss Goldin, she is expecting us."

"Vat ees your name?" the man says, and he looks at us with these suspicious little eyes, like he thinks we no better than thieves.

"Mrs. Rodríguez and Mrs. Díaz," Mami tells him, her head up high, and the man blinks when he looks at me. I lift my hand up and scratch my nose, just so he can see my wedding ring. He shuffles over to a phone in the corner—he's got some kinda limp, I notice—and pushes a button. "Mees Goldin?" he says, still staring at us. "There's two ladies heer say they vant to see you. Mrs. Rodigaz and . . . who?" He looks at me.

"Mrs. Díaz," I say. All Juan left me other than the baby was a ring and his name, so I might as well get the most outta them.

The man hangs up the phone. "Go up to zee eighth floor. Eees number eighty-eight." He points to a corner of the big marble lobby behind him. While I'm pushing the stroller round it I see myself in this huge mirror in a gold frame that's hanging on the wall. My hair's all wild from the wind and my lipstick's eaten off, but I think, Bianca girl, you could break that man's heart in a minute.

In the elevator Mami's real quiet. She stares up at the numbers while I look around. The elevator in my building is lined with this puke green metal that's all bent and scratched, and it's got graffiti all over it, even on the buttons, but this one looks clean enough to eat off of. The walls are real wood, polished and glowing, and the buttons and the gadgets are this shiny gold brass. It's so big you could put a bed in here. "Hey, Mami," I say, "we can move in here if we can't find no place else to live."

"Bianca, don't gimme that smart-ass talk," she says, sounding real tired. "This is shame enough for me without you making trouble, hunh?"

"Yes, Mami."

We go down this long hall till we get to a door with 88 painted on it in gold, and Mami rings the bell. The noise wakes up the baby, who opens her eyes and right away starts making her little pig noises. "Shh, cuquita, shh," Mami whispers, and sticks the bobo in her mouth. The door opens.

"Hi, Teresa, come in," says Miss Goldin, smiling and nodding like she's having us over for a party. She looks pale, I notice. She should get more sun. "Hi, Bianca." She opens the door wide so I can push the stroller in, then she leans over and gives the baby a kiss on the head. "Hello, sweet thing," she says in this gooey voice makes my skin crawl, and kisses her again before she stands up. "You can leave the stroller here in the hall. Would you like some coffee or a cold drink? I've got some Coke if you want, Bianca."

I shrug. "Okay." I feel so embarrassed I can't look this lady in the eye. I feel like I'm some junkie from a shelter she's found begging in the street. Mami picks the baby up outta the stroller, and we follow Miss Goldin into the kitchen. I watch the lady walking in front of me, her fat ass jiggling in these silk pants she's wearing, and she looks so rich and white in her blue silk and this palace that's her home that I just wanna die. I look at Mami to see how she feels and I can tell she's as embarrassed as me 'cause her face is strained with no smile on it. Why'd she bring us here like this if she was gonna feel so bad?

"Have a seat, if you'd like," the reporter lady says, waving to these tall white stools she's got around a counter in her kitchen. I climb up onto one, but Mami has a hard time balancing on hers with the baby. Miss Goldin don't seem to notice though. She just gets out a long, thin glass with bamboo branches carved on it and puts a bunch of ice and Coke into it for me, then she takes down these two mugs covered with blue flowers from a cupboard and fills them with coffee. I look around. I've never seen a kitchen this big outside of TV. The floors look like red brick, and the cupboards are shiny brown wood with brass handles, and it's all lit up with these glass lights like flying saucers hanging from the ceiling. There's a big round table in the corner with enough chairs for six people—hell, ten grown men could walk around in here without banging into a soul. I think about our kitchen, where me and Mami bump elbows every time we chop an onion, and I wonder what Roberto would say about this place. He likes to preach about how the whites got everything good in this world. This place would make him real mad.

"Bianca," Miss Goldin says. "There's a TV in the living room. We've got cable if you want to watch."

"Sure." I shrug and look down at my ice cubes, so stuffed in the glass they can't move.

"Are you hungry? Can I get you anything?"

"Uh, you got any potato chips?" I still can't look her in the face. I just see how the ice, it begins to turn around real slow in the glass, like the room's spinning.

Miss Goldin opens a few more cupboards. "Nope, sorry, but I've got some peanuts. Here." She pours them into a blue bowl that matches her coffee mugs and hands it to me. The nuts still got the shells on but I'm too embarrassed to tell her. "The TV's through there." She points out the door and I go, since she's shooing me out so fast.

In her living room I stand still for a while, the bowl of nuts in one hand and the Coke in the other, just looking. I never been in a place like this before. For one thing, this room? It's like two rooms joined together but with no doors in the middle. I mean, it is huge! You could play basketball in here. There's these big, clear windows stretching all round it, and even from where I'm standing I can see the treetops turning yellow and the Hudson River shining this silver-gray, and the light's pouring in like we're in the middle of a park having a picnic. Then there's these wood fans in the ceiling, with shiny brass bits on them like in the elevator, and they're spinning slowly so the breeze makes you feel like you're on that river you can see. And the floor? It's shiny wood with patterns of darker wood all round it, like a puzzle, and in the middle is this big old rug, all red and dark and soft. There's books everywhere, too, in shelves round the walls that look like they're sunk into the plaster. This room is so damn big and fancy it takes me five minutes just to find the TV.

I turn it on to MTV and sit on the floor to watch but I can't see a thing, the room's so bright. The windows all got these silky white shades, so I let them down to make the room dark, lie back down on my belly, and start shelling the nuts. What a lotta work for a few nibbles. I'm halfway through the nuts, listening to some sappy love song, when a man's voice right behind me says, "Hello," and makes me jump outta my skin.

I turn round and squint up in the dark, and there's this real tall, thin white man with gray curls all over his head like a mop, a long nose, and thick lips. "Who are you?" he says in this snooty accent like he's reading the news, and I see his lips move some more.

"Huh?" I say, 'cause the music's up so high I can't hear him. He walks over and turns the TV off, just like that. I sit up, annoyed.

"It's a little loud, don't you think?" he says. "You aren't Bianca Rodríguez by any chance?"

"Díaz," I mutter.

"Well I'm Sarah's husband, Graham Levy. How do you do?"

I begin picking up the shells I dropped all over his rug. "Hi," I say, real quiet.

"Do you happen to know where my wife is?" He sounds polite, but I can hear he's angry underneath. I would be, too, if I came home and found this strange girl in my living room, spilling Coke and nuts all over some priceless rug.

"She's in the kitchen with my mother."

"Thank you." He walks out and I watch him go. His legs, they go on forever, way up high like flagpoles, and he's got this linen suit on like I seen in the magazine ads, a pearly cream color for summer, and it hangs off him like sheets in the wind. His voice is kinda weird, like he's got cotton stuffed up his nose, but otherwise this man is cool.

I get up with my hands full of nutshells and follow him into the kitchen to see what'll happen. "Graham!" I hear the reporter lady say, sounding like she's more surprised to see her own husband than she was to see us. She's holding Rosalba, I notice, and her silk shirt's all messed up in front. "Let me introduce you to Teresa Rodríguez. Teresa and the children have come to stay the night."

Mami gets up off the stool, almost falling 'cause she's so short she's gotta jump. "Oh, Mr. Goldin, thank you, thank you so much," she says, nodding her head up and down like she did with Miss Mandel. I hate it when she does that. She looks like a stupid little rabbit in her tight white clothes, bobbing around at the feet of this man so tall she's only up to his chest. "You and your wife, you so kind," she says. "It is terrible what they done to us."

"They've locked her out," Miss Goldin explains, putting the baby down to play on the floor. "Teresa came home from shopping and she found her lock changed. The landlord didn't even warn her. She can't even get at her own belongings. Isn't it outrageous?"

"Pleased to meet you," the man says, reaching down to shake Mami's hand, but I see him give his wife this angry look.

"Oh, Mr. Goldin, thank you," Mami begins again, but he cuts her off.

"It's perfectly all right," he says. I can tell Mami is embarrassing him, and that makes me feel even worse. "Sarah," he says then, "I have a meeting tonight so I'll leave you to it, all right?"

"You might ask if there's anything I need," she says with this sour edge in her voice.

"Well I don't have much time. What can I do?"

"Drive over to Lucy's for me, will you, and get the porta-crib? I've already okayed it by phone."

He looks at his watch. "I only have half an hour." Miss Goldin gives him a frown, which nobody seems to notice but me. They don't notice the baby, neither, who's drooling all over the floor and playing with her spit. "All right," the husband says with a sigh, and he turns to Mami. "I'm Mr. Levy, by the way, not Mr. Goldin."

"Yes, sorry," Miss Goldin says real quick. "I forgot to tell you. I don't use my husband's name."

"You don't?" I say, stepping in the kitchen, the nutshells still filling my hands. "Why not? I mean, you and him, you are married right?"

"No, we're living in sin, actually," the man says. "We don't believe in marriage."

My mouth drops open, but just then Miss Golden speaks. "He's just kidding, Bianca. Of course we're married. We've been married for fourteen years. Graham, just go get that crib." She squints her eyes at him and he leaves like he can't wait to scrape filth like us right off his shoes. She smiles at us nervously. "Don't mind him. It's his oddball sense of humor. I know he's glad to have met you—I've told him so much about you both."

I bet you did, I think. I can just imagine what she been saying about me and Mami. What's she want outta us anyhow? I stare at her across the kitchen, crumbling the nutshells in my fingers, wondering why Mami likes her so much. I don't see anything in her to like 'cept she lives like a queen. She's crabby with her husband, she treats me like I'm a moron, she acts so phony with Mami it makes me sick, and she slobbers all over the baby like she's in love. Maybe that's it. I give her the evil eye. Yeah, of course that's it: This lady's after my baby.

"Bianca?" Her voice comes stomping in on my thoughts. "Would you like to throw those nutshells away?"

"Oh, no thanks," I say, and I dump the shells on the counter and walk back to the living room. I'm not letting no baby thief boss me around.

I been watching the TV a little while longer when I hear the husband come back in, panting while he hauls this folded-up crib he's carrying down their hallway. I hear a scraping sound and him cursing, so I go over to watch the show. There's a big gray scrape now along their nice white wall and he's mad as hell. He heaves the crib into the kitchen and props it against the counter. Rosalba's on the floor banging some pot lids together, Mami and Miss Goldin are talking hard at the counter, and my nutshells are still messing up the place like a squirrel's been making a nest. "Here's the crib," Mr. Levy says, shouting above the baby's noise. "Sarah, may I have a word with you in private?"

"What?" his wife says, and I can see that makes him even madder. I lean up against the kitchen door and fold my arms. This is better than TV. She looks at me a second, then gets back to her husband. "Oh, sure. Could you put the crib in the spare room, darling? I'll be out in a minute." She flashes him a smile even I can see is fake. I follow Mr. Levy to a little bedroom and watch him fighting with the crib, trying to open it up for about five minutes.

"Do you know how to open this cursed thing?" he says to me, panting, but I tell him I don't. By the time his wife comes in he's all red and sweaty.

"Let me do it," she says, and presses a couple of invisible buttons. The crib springs open. "Thanks, sweetie. I've put aside the yellow sheets for the sofa bed, and we can use the flowered ones for Teresa. Do you have time to run out and get some more pasta and juice? Then we'll have enough for everyone." She looks over at me. "Bianca dear, would you leave us alone for a minute?"

I shrug and leave the room, but insteada going back to the kitchen I hide in this little nook in the hallway so I can listen. I wanna know what they're plotting.

"Sarah," I hear Mr. Levy say.

"Oh, and some milk and baby formula," she goes on. "I'll write down what kind. Those poor people have nothing but what they had on them when they got locked out today. Can you imagine?"

"Sarah!"

"What?"

"What in the hell are you doing?"

I hear her sigh. "Look, don't start," she says, sounding tired, like they been through this a whole lot already. "For just this once try not to stand in my way, okay? These are my friends, and what I do about them is my decision. These people need help. It's no different from what you'd do for your buddies."

"But I thought you were trying to get that woman to leave you alone!"

"Yes, but what could I do, turn her out on the street? Look, G, the fact is if I'd nailed her landlord she might never have been kicked out. She was counting on me. I only dropped the story because my asshole editor didn't think it was sexy enough. Anyway, I like Teresa. It's not her fault she's landed with a crooked landlord and a messed-up daughter."

I put my hand over my mouth to stop up my voice. Who the fuck says I'm messed up? What do they think I am, some kinda public property? I hear them fiddling round with the crib some more and try to quiet my breathing, which is real hard and angry, so I can keep listening.

"Are you sure this crib is safe?" the husband says then. "It won't fold up and make a baby sandwich in the middle of the night? I wouldn't want them to sue us on top of everything else."

"What the hell's that supposed to mean?"

"Look, darling," he says, "let's be practical. How long are these people going to stay here? And what are you going to do with them while we're at work? I wish you'd told me before you let them all in here."

"I didn't have time. Oh, don't worry so much," says Sarah. "Bianca goes off to school early in the morning, so she'll be out of the way, and Teresa's going to see about getting her things back from the apartment. She said they'll move to her sister's tomorrow. It's no big deal."

Out of the way! Is that all I am, just some nuisance in everybody's way? I hear Sarah flapping sheets around and making the bed. "This'll be good for you," she says finally. "See how the other half lives. Eviction is only a problem that affects thousands of Americans every year."

"Don't you dare preach to me!" He shouts this so loud even Mami must be able to hear it a block away in that kitchen. "You better make sure they do move out. I can just see them settling in here, living off that liberal guilt of yours. You've got a heart like butter, Sarah!"

"You used to like that about me."

"Listen, darling." He's trying on the gentle act now. Jesus, he's no better than Juan, but I gotta see his point. I wouldn't want no strangers moving into my house, neither, specially not with a slobbery baby. "I know you feel guilty about not doing that landlord story but this is a mistake, Sarah, can't you see? That woman is exploiting you just when you're at your most vulnerable, and I don't like it."

"Who's preaching now?"

The two of them go quiet for a while and I'm just beginning to slide myself along the wall back to the kitchen, when Mr. Levy starts up again.

"Sarah? There's something behind this, isn't there? What is it? Tell me."

She sighs. "Okay. Well, you're not going to like this, G, but I've promised. You won't have to do a thing. I'll take on all the responsibility. I can take the rest of my vacation time from work, and I'll get Lucy to help."

"What are you talking about?"

"I promised Teresa I'd take Rosalba for a few days while they get back on their feet. Now don't panic. It's just that she doesn't want to leave her with Bianca or her sister while she deals with this landlord—she says neither of them is reliable. I told you about the sister being a crack addict, right? And you remember when the baby ended up in the hospital? Well, that was Bianca's fault. Don't look like that. At least Teresa's being responsible."

"Who's Rosalba?"

So that's what Mami says about me. I'm a no-good nobody who can't even look after her own baby! I don't like this Sarah. I don't like the way she talks about me and Mami like we're both no better'n children.

"Oh, God, you mean the baby?" the husband says. "You're going to keep the baby here?" He sounds so astonished, his voice squeaking like a rubber duck, I almost laugh out loud.

"Look, I want to do it, okay? I need to do it. It'll help heal me." Sarah sounds like she's begging all of a sudden, her voice shaky and weak.

"For God's sake, Sarah, you are so wrongheaded sometimes!" I hear the bed creak like he's dropped himself down on it. "This isn't going to heal you, it's just going to make you feel worse." There's a pause, the two of them silent for a second. "Does that woman know you were pregnant?" he says quietly. "Did you tell her about the miscarriage? Is that what this is all about?"

Miscarriage? So that's why she been looking so sick and tired lately. I guess I feel sorry for her, but that don't mean it's okay to go round talking about me and Mami like we be nothing but crooks. I hold my breath 'cause Sarah's saying something again, real quiet.

"No, Teresa does not know about it, as a matter of fact. You know I don't even like talking about it. Why do you always have to see the worst in everyone?"

"I'm not seeing the worst, I'm being practical. You're so gullible, Sarah. You're letting this woman walk all over you! First she moves her whole damn family in here, then she tries to foist her baby on you—she'll be getting you to pay her rent next!"

"You have no sympathy at all, do you?" Sarah's voice sounds hard and angry, and I gotta say I'm glad. I don't like the way this husband of hers is pushing her around, and I sure don't like the way he be talking about us. "You can't think about anyone but yourself, you know that?" she goes on. "You don't give a damn about what happens to these people, and you don't give a damn about me, either. All along I knew you didn't really care about us having a child— you just pretended. I think you're actually relieved I had that miscarriage! Now you can go on and lead your Graham-centered life with nobody getting in your way!"

"Sarah, please. Don't say those things. You're being irrational."

"Irrational! Who was it who went through years of pain for the chance to have our child, huh? Who was it who mourned its loss like a death? Not you, was it? You hardly gave it a thought!"

"Stop it. You sound hysterical."

I wait, staying as still as I can to hear what this woman's

gonna say back to him now. She's always seems kinda mousy when she comes over to our house, speaking to me in her bad Spanish like I'm gonna eat her if she doesn't make a good impression, so I'm curious to see how she handles her man.

"Screw you, Graham Levy," she says, and her voice sounds calm but kinda dangerous. "You aren't willing to do even one thing to help me cope with all this, are you? You're just a self-centered bigot, and I'm sick of it!"

That's better, I think. You tell him, lady. I'm glad you got some guts. But I better get outta here before somebody commits a murder right in fronta my feet.

Roberto

Okay, I got my plan figured out about Orlando. Bianca put her trust in me when she told me what that fucka did to her, and I been holding that trust next to my heart like a jewel. She wants me to do something about it, I swear. Why else did she tell me?

My plan is this. I'm gonna find Orlando at his house, when he be away from his homies, and beat the shit outta that mothafucka till he ready to kiss his ass good-bye. I know where he lives, so I'm gonna catch him in his stairwell where nobody can see and crack him in the nuts. I got a baseball bat ready just in case he pulls something. The only thing I gotta do is find him when he don't got his gun.

The whole thing is set out in my mind. "What you want with me?" the fucka is gonna say when I back him up in the corner.

"I'm gonna teach you a lesson, faggot," I'll say to him. "Going round raping girls like some kinda pervert."

"You be so lucky," he gonna say back. "No girl ever gonna look at you, your face like a mutt."

"Oh yeah? I don't need to rape nobody, mothafucka. You so desperate it's the only way you can get a girl."

"That bitch is a ho anyhow. What's the difference?" He gonna say that, I know, 'cause they all do. But I'm gonna have my answer:

"You wouldn't know a ho if she sat on your face. You a criminal and a pervert, and I'm gonna fix you good." Then I'm gonna do it, beat on him till he begs for me to stop and never, never hurts nobody again. In a way, it's something I been wanting to do all my life.

I thought about maybe getting some friends to help me but I didn't know who to ask. Truth is, I ain't gotta lotta friends. I been so busy trying to keep my dad from busting heads open in my house, hiding Diego and my sisters away from him when he was in one of his evil moods, and so busy trying to make some money for them now he's in jail, I ain't had time to hang with nobody but Bianca and Clara and my family. It's a waste of time anyhow, hanging with homies talking bitches and blunt. I don't like it, it just seems dumb to me. That's how my dad ended up the way he did, thinking no further than his dick and his bitterness, and whatever happens to me, so help me God, I ain't never gonna end up like that mothafucka. I hate my dad so bad it eats inside of me like acid. That's why I need Bianca worse and worse. When I'm with her, she be like medicine for my heart, the only thing ever makes me feel better, the only thing brings relief to my mind. I ain't felt a need like this since I was a little kid waiting on my mother, waiting for her to wake up outta her nod and gimme a smile. That's why I gotta win Bianca's love if it kills me to do it—win her and get her to marry me.

I can marry her nice and legal now 'cause I turned eighteen last week. My birthday was cool. Diego woke me up bouncing on my head, and the girls were yanking my feet, trying to pull me up outta bed. Aunt Maria cooked me eggs for breakfast, and they sang me "Happy Birthday" before school. Then my aunt and Uncle Carlos, they gave me a five-dollar bill in a red envelope—maybe enough to buy the toe of one sneaker—but to tell the truth I was surprised they remembered at all. Diego drew me a little scribble on a paper in crayon, which I got on the wall above my bed, and Juanita gave me this box she made at school outta popsicle sticks, which she stuck all over with paper flowers. Carmen didn't have nothing for me, 'cause she wanted to gimme this lollipop somebody bought her but she couldn't wait and ate it instead. Well, she be only five. She was so sorry she cried all morning no matter how much I kissed her. But I was real touched 'cause my aunt, she told me the birthday presents was the kids' own idea they come up with without even a nudge from her.

So now I'm eighteen I'm a man, and I can do what I want with my life, like teach that Orlando mothafucka a lesson. I ain't gonna tell Bianca my plan for him, though, 'cause I don't want her worrying about me or feeling the pain all over again of remembering what he done to her. I'm just gonna creep in there and do the deed. I'm gonna teach him that nobody can mess with my Bianca, nobody, never. Then, next time that sweet girl sees that fucka on the street, crawling round so ashamed of hisself he won't know where to look, she'll see him with two black eyes and a busted nose, and that's not all. Then I'll tell her somebody who loves her gave him what he deserved. Maybe then, maybe she'll look up at me and she'll think, Y'know, that Roberto, he may be kinda short and funny looking, but he's brave and he's straight. He's the kinda guy a girl like me could love. And then I'll get her to marry me.

Teresa

Four days in Miss Goldin's house and my Rosalba she has won that woman over like some witch poured love potion in the lady's coffee. I gotta thank You, la Virgen de la Altagracia, for making this work, but please forgive this sinner if I don't feel too happy about what I done. Now Miss Goldin has found out she wants Rosalba, it is like mi nieta, she is gone already. I will miss her so bad, her tiny smile and those soft dimples. I don't like to say this after all You have done for me, specially not after all that lying I been doing, but how will I wake up in the morning without mi muñeca beside me, no gurgling, no babbling, no baby skin to touch in my sleepiness? When I see her shining face and that look she has like everything is new and bright to her, all the ugliness of the world washes away like dirt. Even those days I left her at Miss Goldin's house made me miss her so much the ache got into my bones. You know that pain too, Virgencita, so help me bear it, please.

I told Al about it, it has been weighing so heavy on my mind. He came round to see me after we got back from Yolanda's place and I took off the plastic for him so he could sit on my clean red couch like a king. "I can't go to no movie with you," I told him, "I gotta stay here with my granddaughter."

He poked his big finger in Rosalba's stomach and wiggled it till she laughed. "That's okay, I like babies. Maybe one day I'll have some grandchildren to call my own." He smiled over at me, his thick glasses going white in the sun.

"Al, don't be in too big a hurry," I said. "Make sure your daughter's got a husband before you get yourself grandchildren." And I told him about Juan. "I am thinking of letting this relation take Rosalba for a while," I said, looking away from him 'cause I was afraid of what I might see on his face. "Just till I can get Bianca straightened out."

"Yeah, that's what my sister did." Al picked up Rosalba and bounced round the room with her. She looked like a cabbage so tiny in his arms. "She gave her baby to my mother to look after while she finished school. Seemed to work okay. How's Bianca feel about it?"

I pulled at my fingers. "She don't know yet. But I told her we gonna have to do it sometime. I hate to say this Al, but I think that girl was relieved. She is having a hard time, la tremenda." I stopped and took a swallow 'cause my throat was choking up with words I was afraid to say. "Did your sister . . . did she take the baby back?"

"Nope. Guess she liked her freedom better. She visits sometimes, but to him his grandma is his mom. My sister's more like his aunt."

Rosalba begins to cry then 'cause he's scaring her whirling round the room like she is on a roller coaster, so he stops. "Here, you better take her. She don't like me."

"Sure she do. You just being too rough." I take mi nieta and give her soft body a squeeze. "It is her nap time anyhow. Let me fix her bottle and put her down."

Then Al does this thing makes me feel good inside, I can't help it. He comes up to me from behind, slips his big arms round my middle, and says, "Hey, little thing, then maybe you and me can have some private moments, huh?" And he nuzzles my neck, his broom mustache tickling me.

"Al, calm down. Let me put this baby to sleep like a civilized woman." I carry Rosalba to the playpen and lay her down, slowly, like I am afraid of what will happen when I don't got her to protect me. No man has looked at me for years, never mind touched me. I feel rusty and stiff like an old hinge on a gate. Al follows me into the bedroom and I hear him close the door.

"Bianca's at school, right?" he says. "We got the place to ourselves?"

"Yeah, but Al?" I turn round and find my face up against his chest, which is as big and flat as a mattress. He puts his arms round me and runs his hands up and down my back.

"What is it, gorgeous thing?"

"I don't know. I don't know if I feel ready for this. I got too much on my mind."

Al rubs his face in my hair, his hands slipping down over my hips. "You just relax, honey. I'll make you ready." Then he takes off his glasses and lays them on the dresser and for some reason that makes me want him, as sudden and strong as a flame licking through me. Every part of my body he touches is tingling like the dead awakening on Judgment Day, but my mind is still resisting. I see flashes of Rosalba crying while she is being torn away from my arms mixing in with the touch of Al's hands, his chest, his sex. Wish I could just shake my head and drive all the worry out like scattering raindrops.

Al kisses me then, his lips springy and soft, his big hands running over my body like a blind man feeling a sculpture. Pretty soon he is unbuttoning my shirt, and my skirt is down round my feet. He lays me down on the bed and undresses me slowly, kissing and looking at me like he is discovering something beautiful, and I am lying there, my hands on his round, hard arms, feeling twenty years old again and as sexy as a movie star. "You got the body of a teenager," he tells me, and I laugh and slap his head for saying such nonsense. But when I get his shirt off, I find this big chest, skin as smooth and soft as my velveteen couch, the muscles hard from all those years of swinging mops and buckets, pushing brooms, chasing pickpockets, with barely a belly on him for his age, and, Lord forgive me, but I do forget all my troubles, just like Al said. I let myself sink into the sweet thrill of being wanted again. I let myself go, and it felt like a healing rain. I needed that so bad.

So, la Virgen de la Altagracia, my heart it is aching at the idea of giving up Rosalba, but my mouth, it is smiling, too—not so much 'cause of what Big Al gave to me, though I thank You for that nice surprise in my life, but 'cause he made me feel like I am not a terrible abuela, throwing away a baby like she is no more than a used-up box of soap. I am only doing what a lotta women do, giving the baby up so she don't have to live in fear. That is not so evil, right?

Bianca

It sure was a relief to leave Tía Yolanda's house. The noise was so bad up there I hardly got a wink of sleep. I swear I heard gunshots mosta the night. Mami couldn't sleep neither, so we sat up late together in the living room for three nights watching the front door, expecting some gangbangers to come tearing in any minute shooting machine guns. Tía Yolanda told us we was full of shit to act so scared but I noticed she jumped, too, whenever we heard a bang outside, even if it was just a garbage can lid, and she kept running to see if her tugboat baby Jonny was okay. I was glad we didn't bring Rosalba with us. That place was too scary.

So to make ourselves feel better, Mami and me cuddled up on Tía Yolanda's ratty couch, and Mami told me these great ghost stories she remembers from the DR. My favorite was this one about Don Juan, who's really a devil, and he follows people on his horse with his head turning round and round on his neck till he scares them to hell. I guess he's Death, not the devil—I was too sleepy to get it—but I love those ghost stories, they make my skin prickle all over. That storytelling woulda been real fun 'cept my tía, she was drinking too much, and that really bothered me. I watched her get through four or six beers every night, just between supper and bedtime, and I could tell Mami didn't like it either 'cause she kept whispering to Yolanda and making her look mad. My tía would start out each night kinda tired out and sad, then she'd drink till she got happy and funny, then she'd drink more till she was sad again, and get all bitter and sorry for herself. Mami was sitting there on the couch, her arms crossed and a frown on her face, while Yolanda bumped around the room like a blind driver and I stared at the floor, real embarrassed that I ever listened to her advice. She mighta been right about Juan but she sure was wrong about Orlando. And I don't understand why she ain't fat from all that beer.

Still, if I thought coming home was gonna let me relax after those scary nights uptown, I was wrong. Soon as we walk in the door, Mami springs this thing on me makes my head spin.

It started when we got back from picking up Rosalba at Sarah Goldin's house and Mami found her key fitted the lock again. "They musta put the old locks back so we don't have to buy new keys," she said, surprised, and we went inside. It looked just the same, 'cept to me it seemed real small and poky after Miss Goldin's fairy-tale palace, and it smelled funny, like cooking beans, old steam and bodies, a smell I realized I don't notice normally but that I kinda like. Seems that landlord never touched a thing, thank God—I was afraid he'd trash the place or steal our stuff like Mami said he did before. "How come that bastard's being so nice all of a sudden?" I asked her.

"Bianca, I paid the rent, okay?" she said, putting Rosalba down in her playpen. "Now stop bothering me with these questions."

"But Mami? We gonna be safe here now? I mean are they gonna lock us out every month we don't make the rent?"

"No, no, it is okay now. Miss Goldin, she got these lawyers to fix it so the landlord can't go threatening us no more. And we will make the rent, niña. I am going back to work."

"Who's gonna look after the baby then? I'll be in school, you know that. You going back on the night shift?"

Mami looks real uncomfortable for a minute, and she starts pulling on her long fingers like she does when she's praying. "Biancita, I got something to tell you. I wanted to say it at Yolanda's house, but she is a chismosa and this is private business. Sit down, mi muñeca."

I sit on the bed and look up at her, wondering what surprise she's gonna spring on me this time.

"You know I told you about putting Rosalba in foster care?"

"Yeah. You really gonna do it, Mami?"

"Listen, lechuza. Miss Goldin and me, we been talking and she tells me she wants to help us out."

"Like hell she does. She just wants to push us around."

"No, Biancita, she es una buena mujer. She wants to adopt the baby. She wants to take Rosalba in and bring her up like her own child. Is that good news or what?"

"I knew it!" I shout, making Mami jump. "I knew she wanted that baby. She been sniffing round her like a dog after a bitch."

Mami puts a hand on me. "Bianca, calmate. Why not let her have Rosalba? It is better than some stranger taking her in, some person we don't know who might do child abuse or anything. Miss Goldin, she is a good woman, and she wants a child so bad. Look how good she did with Rosalba while we were up at Yolanda's, hunh?"

I fold my arms and stare down at our rug, which is more string than carpet it's so worn. "How long she gonna take the baby for?"

"She is gonna adopt her, Biancita. That means she will be the mother, not some foster woman filling in time."

I look at Mami all confused, but then I start to feel mad. "How long you and her been plotting like this?"

"What you mean?"

"When you were talking in the kitchen in her place all those hours? Is that what you were planning together—to take my baby away?"

"What put a crazy idea like that in your head?"

"Puh, never mind. I ain't such a fool as you think."

"What you got against Miss Goldin, Biancita? She been good to us, helping us with the landlord and stuff."

"I don't like her, that's all." I look away from Mami's eyes and stare at her arms instead. They're getting all stringy and wrinkled, and I notice how her skin is dry and crinkly round the elbows.

"Explain to me what you mean."

"I don't like the way she acts with us. She treats us like we're not human. And that husband of hers, you can't tell me he wants the baby. Didn't you hear them fighting when we were there?"

Mami takes my arms in her bony hands and she holds me tight so I gotta look right in her tired eyes. "Bianca, mi hijita, listen to me. That lady, she is gonna be a good mamá to Rosalba, trust me. I been watching her a long time, I prayed to la Virgen de la Altagracia, and I know it is gonna be okay. And don't you worry none about her husband. Men, they always act like that about babies at first. Give him some time." Mami pats me on the head like I'm a pet dog, and then she switches her voice so it's all tough and businesslike. "Now, Bianca, I am gonna go change clothes. The caseworker, she is coming to see us today, so you clean yourself up good, okay?"

"What caseworker? You mean the one from my school?"

"No, no. This is the one who is gonna help us with the adoption, cuquita. She got some papers for us to sign."

"Today? But Mami I ain't had no time to—"

"Go, don't give me no arguments." And Mami shuts herself up in the bathroom.

An hour later, we all look like we just came from church. Rosalba's in pink frills like a birthday cake; Mami's made me put on my yellow shift with the ruffles round the hem and a ribbon in my hair, with no makeup or nothing so I look about nine years old; and she's in her dark pink suit and heels. She straightens up the plastic in our living room and tells me to keep my mouth shut and to act real young. I'm so confused, one minute at Tía Yolanda's house, cuddling up for a story, the next sitting here in my good clothes like it's my confirmation—my brain feels like mush. I do what Mami says but I wish she'd give me more time to think this out.

The caseworker is a tall, skinny, black lady with her hair sprayed so heavy it looks like a hat. She stares at us like she thinks we're evil—what we ever do to her?—and she makes us sit for a long time while she talks to us in Spanish like we're these campesinos right off the farm. She makes me explain all about Juan and how he left the country before the baby was born and we ain't never heard from him since, no letter or nothing, which is why he don't have to sign the papers, and then she asks us at least twenty times if we're sure about getting Rosalba adopted. Mami keeps saying, "Sí, sí," and I say it too, 'cause I wanna get this woman outta here so I can think.

Suddenly, the woman turns to me. "I don't think you're in touch with your feelings, Bianca," she says in English. "Have you thought about what this means?"

"Yeah, 'course I have," I say, wriggling on my plastic. "I wanna get on with my studies and finish school." I got that from Mr. Jonas. "Get on with your studies and finish school," he says every day. He tells us to chant it in the shower to keep our minds on what's important.

"But Bianca, do you understand you are giving your child up completely? This is not like foster care, you know. You can't go back in a few months and reclaim her. You can't take her home if you miss her. She'll be part of somebody else's family and out of your life forever. Do you understand that?"

"Well, that Miss Goldin, she's rich, right?" I say, sticking my chin out.

"Bianca!" Mami hisses; then she slumps back in her chair, Rosalba kicking on her lap.

"Mrs. Rodríguez, you have something to say?" The woman speaks with this sharp edge in her voice, like my mother's a kid in trouble at school.

"Yeah, I do." Mami sits up a little. She looks exhausted. "Miss Goldin, I think she will make a good mother, but lady, do you think I am right?"

"Well, we'll do a home study to ascertain that as much as we can, of course. That's part of the procedure. We won't let her have the baby if we find something inappropriate. For one thing there's the matter of religion. How do you feel about the fact that she's American and, uh, Jewish, Bianca?"

"So long as she's rich I don't care. I ain't prejudiced. She's got a big husband and a big house She can give the baby all kindsa things she never gets round here."

"Yes, her husband's a renowned history professor." The woman looks impressed just saying the words.

"¡Carajo!" I say sarcastically, but I gotta admit I'm impressed, too. I like the idea of my baby having a man like that for a daddy, somebody who's smart and important and cool, even if he is kinda snooty like his wife said. Least he's not some loser from the street like Roberto, who's full of those bullshit dreams, or Juan, who's probably starving to death in the DR just 'cause he's afraid to come back to me. Not like that coño Orlando either, who's gonna get busted any day now, I swear it, he deals so wide open on the street. "My baby's gonna have a daddy then," I say out loud. "That's more'n I got. She'll be lucky. Maybe go to college like him . . ." Suddenly I can't speak no more. This thing goes click in my throat and I remember how I used to say to myself that the baby'd grow up proud and smart, not like me, not trash, and how she'd learn to mind her mami. Maybe that dream'll come true now, but no thanks to me. I look away quick, swallowing those thoughts back down where I can't feel them no more. I don't want that snot-nosed woman seeing my face. I don't want none of her social work pity.

"That Miss Goldin, she is gonna be all right," Mami says then. "You know she been trying to have a baby for five years and no luck? She is gonna be a natural mother, I can tell by watching her with my Rosalba. She is so sweet with that child! That's more important than what kinda religion she got, even the Lord knows that. Just give my daughter those papers to sign, lady, and let's get outta here. I got things to do." She don't mention dropping Rosalba off at Miss Goldin's house and leaving her there for four whole days, I notice, and I guess she don't know about the miscarriage, but I decide I better keep quiet about that.

The caseworker sighs and opens her briefcase. "Family Preservation won't like this," she mutters, but she takes out some papers and hands them to Mami. "This one is the English version. Do you need a Spanish one?" Mami shakes her head impatiently. "All right. Read the papers carefully. You, too, Bianca, because this is your out-of-court consent. That means it's the surrender of the child, okay? You do understand that you have forty-five days to change your mind, but after that it's irrevocable? Then there'll be another six months before the adoption is finalized in court, but that part is usually a formality and I doubt you'll have to attend. Do you understand what I'm saying, Mrs. Rodríguez?" Mami nods.

"Good. Once you sign you must get it notarized, then I'll get it checked by the lawyer."

"How much that cost?" Mami says, sounding real tired again. Her face has gone kinda pale under the skin, I notice, like it does when she's sick.

"The lawyer has told me that Sarah Goldin has offered to pay any such expenses."

Mami looks worried but all she does is put the baby down on the floor. She starts to read the fine print, pretending she can understand it, and I stare at Rosalba, who's playing with the rattle I bought her for her half birthday. "Will I get to see the baby after that lady takes her?" I say.

The caseworker looks upset. "That's what I've been trying to explain, dear. You are giving up *all* rights to the child."

"But she's my baby! She came outta my body!" I'm sitting up now, hot in the face.

The woman glares at me. "Haven't you been listening at all?"

I look at Mami. "Is that true? Why can't we get her back if we want? I thought you said this was only till we want to take her home!"

"I never said no such thing, Bianca. Don't make trouble now." Mami frowns at me to shut up, so I do, watching her while she reads the papers. Finally she hands them over to me. "Take them, Bianca," she says.

I look at the papers and sit still for a while, trying to clear up my thoughts. My mind feels like it's whirring around in a bunch of colored clouds. "Is this forever?" I ask.

"You have forty-five days in which to change your mind," the woman says again, slowly. "And in a few months we do a second visit to the woman's home to make sure everything is okay before the adoption is finalized. Of course we discourage passing children back and forth, it's too disruptive for them."

"Miss Goldin wants to be Rosalba's mother, not some baby-sitter, Bianca. Now stop making trouble and sign it!" Mami looks like she's in pain, and she's staring at me so hard I feel like I'm a puppet and her face is the strings.

"Mrs. Rodríguez, no pressure please," the woman says.

I ignore her and pick up the pen. "Okay, okay. Shit." I sign and hand it back to Mami. I can't even think about what I done.

The caseworker closes up her briefcase with a snap and walks out the door so fast it's like she can't wait to get us outta her sight. "Mami?" I say soon as the woman's gone, "Mami, I don't know if I feel good about this. It's so sudden and everything. Why didn't you give me more time to think?"

"Leave me alone, Bianca. Now go on, get outta here," and suddenly she's mad and crying and splotchy in the face. "I'm doing this thing for you, isn't that enough!" And she grabs the baby up and runs into the bedroom, slamming the door behind her. I stand and stare at it for a while, wondering what to do. Should I go in and try to make her feel better? I know she feels bad, much badder than I do. I know she'll miss the baby something terrible. But then I think, I'm sick and tired of all this worry. I don't wanna deal with Mami or crying or the baby or bad feelings or any of it anymore. And I got nowhere to go but out.

When I get downstairs I decide to go find Roberto at work so I can talk this out with somebody who's not gonna scream at me or lead my mind round like a puppy on a leash, so I walk down to the liquor store on Broadway. Mr. Aquino's behind the counter, doing some adding up on a piece of paper.

"¡Hola, linda, estás muy hermosa hoy!" he says, winking and looking me up and down like I'm in an underwear ad. "You looking for your boyfriend?"

Mr. Aquino's short and fat, with a droopy mustache like a Mexican's, and he's real nice to Roberto and the other boys.

He's just a pain in the ass to the girls. "Maybe," I say, and I crouch down to play with the black-and-white cat he keeps in the store.

"Don't be too sweet with him, now. I wanna keep him fierce for the mice. Lover boy's out on a delivery. He'll be back in a few minutes Then maybe you can keep him outta trouble."

"What trouble? Roberto never gets in no trouble." The cat's lying on its side, purring while I stroke it, but I notice its white patches are looking real dirty. "I thought cats are s'posed to keep themselves clean," I say. "This one looks like it's been mopping the floor."

Mr. Aquino comes round from the counter. "Yeah, I think he is sick. They say cats stop washing themselves if they get sick, y'know?" I feel his hand touch my head and creep down to my neck, but I push it away.

"It's got fleas, too," I say, standing up and looking that dirty old man right in the eyes. "Big ones."

"Bianca!" Roberto comes in, pushing his delivery cart.

"Your girlfriend's gotta mouth," Mr. Aquino says, but he looks like he thinks it's funny.

"You got any more deliveries for me?" Roberto asks him.

"Nah, go ahead. Give her a kiss for me."

Roberto glances at me, embarrassed, and that's when I see what Mr. Aquino was talking about. Roberto looks like somebody pushed him down and jumped on his face for ten minutes Every piece of it's bruised or cut.

"Jesus! What happened to you?"

Roberto don't answer. All he does is grab his baseball cap from behind the counter—Mr. Aquino won't let him wear it when he's working 'cause he says it looks disrespectful—and follow me out.

"Well?" I say. "You gonna tell me who beat up on you?"

Roberto stares down at the cap, turning it round and

round in his hands like he's searching for the label. "Nah, just some creep."

I cross my arms. "That kinda answer ain't part of our deal, Roberto. What're friends for, right? You wanna talk about it in the park?"

He turns around and walks with me down to Riverside. "How come you came to see me?" he says. "Your moms been giving you a hard time again?"

"I want my answer first before I tell you."

"It was just some fight I got into at school. Some dumb thing, y'know."

"That's all you're gonna say?" He shrugs but he stays silent. "I'll find out from Clara then. She'd know if a roach got married."

Roberto don't even smile. It makes me feel bad to see him sad and beat up like that. "You in trouble, Roberto? You're not getting into that dumb-ass dealing are you?"

"You know better'n that." He sounds so offended I know he isn't lying. Roberto would never touch drugs.

"So you ain't gonna tell me nothing more?" I say. He shakes his head. I guess he's ashamed since it looks like he got the worst of the fight. He reaches out and takes my hand, which normally I wouldn't let him do, but I feel so sorry for him I let him hold on. I even give it a squeeze.

"How 'bout you, Bianca? You gonna tell me what's up?" He glances over at me with his mashed-up-face.

"Yeah, I guess." And I tell him about the caseworker coming round, getting me to sign the surrender papers. Just talking about it makes me feel sick inside. Giving away my own baby like that—it don't seem right. It don't even seem human.

"Listen, girl," Roberto says when I'm finished. "The whole trouble is you ain't white and powerful, you ain't got the law and the land on your side. You and me, we come from one of those little places down there underneath America—that's all them white folks know 'bout our home."

"How d'you know?"

"I know 'cause I asked. At school I asked my teacher, 'What's nearer to the U.S., Puerto Rico or the Dominican Republic?' She went red in the face, Bianca, 'cause she couldn't give an answer. These people, they don't even know where our home is, I swear it. And you know why they don't know? 'Cause they don't care."

I rub my eyes. Roberto's making me tired with all his talk. "What this gotta do with me?"

"I'm saying that's why they think they can take your baby away. 'Cause you ain't white and powerful, and 'cause you only fourteen, see? They think they can do what they want to you. But don't let them get to you, Bianca. Treat yourself right, don't let them make you treat yourself like they treat you. Maybe the white folk in this city think we're nothing, maybe a lotta people do, but it ain't true and don't let them make you think it is. We gotta stick together and give ourselves respect. 'Cause if we don't, nobody will."

"Will you shut up? Jesus, it's like listening to some preacher on TV."

But Roberto ignores me. He's got this burning look in his puffed-up eyes, and he's hopping up and down when he talks, his thick body bouncing boing boing boing like a basketball. "Listen Bianca," he says, his voice so excited it squeaks. "If you marry me, then we can take the baby nice and legal and they can't do nothing 'bout it. I'm eighteen now and I got my rights."

"I can't marry you. I'm already married." Don't wanna marry you, neither, I add to myself.

"Yes, you can. I talked with Father O'Hearney and he say the church can annul your marriage 'cause you so young and Juan went away almost the day of the wedding."

"I thought you have to be a virgin to get annulled," I say, laughing. "I don't care. I'll get a divorce."

Roberto looks shocked. "But you a Catholic! You can't do that!"

"That's old people's stuff. My mother's stuff. I don't care. This is the modern day, Roberto, I can be a free woman if I want. Mr. Jonas says so at school."

Roberto stops bouncing and squints at me through his bruises. "Mr. Jonas, Mr. Jonas. Don't you got nobody else to talk about?"

"What's it to you? I'm getting outta here anyway. I'm getting my diploma and going to college and the next time anybody on this damn street hears about me I'll be a scientist, like I told you. I'll be a professor like that Sarah Goldin's husband!" Well, why not? Better than being married to Roberto, who I feel sorry for but I don't love, and having a lotta children crying at my feet. I know I'm hard, I know I sound like I don't have a heart, but I'm trying to be realistic. I seen too many women sink down to the bottom 'cause of this romance and marriage and babies shit. Like my tía. It's a big lie.

"What about that baby, Bianca? You can't just forget her like that."

I shake my head. "You want her? Then you adopt her."

Roberto grabs my arm, right there next to this playground where the kids are throwing sand in each other's faces. "Listen, Bianca, stop that talk! You don't mean a thing you say, I can tell. You just acting cool and covering up the truth from yourself. How will you live the rest of your life knowing you gave your own child away to some stranger? Nobody else can love her the way you do, nobody!"

I pull my arm out of his hand. "My mother's the one loves that baby, estúpido, not me!" I shout at him. "Can't you get it through your thick head? She loves that baby so bad she be giving it up to save it. I can't give that baby a love that deep, never ever!"

Roberto stares at me, "Your mother?" he says. "What you saying?"

"Never mind, never mind. Forget it." I fold my arms and look down at the ground, kicking the sidewalk with my toe. "Listen Bianca," he says. "Just think about it, okay? Just think about marrying me. You know you got no more chance of being a big-shot professor than I got of being president. But it won't be like you're alone. I know how to look after kids, you seen that. And you know how I feel 'bout you. Will you think it over at least, please? You don't wanna be doing the wrong thing and feeling bad about it, do you?"

I shrug and kinda grunt at the same time, half no, half yes. I've never met anyone so straight as Roberto. I don't know what to make of him 'cept I know he means what he says. "Okay, okay," I say finally, "I'll think it over if you stop bugging me about it. Okay?"

"It's a deal," Roberto says, and he grins this big grin, cut mouth and all, like he thinks he's already won.

Teresa

Miss Goldin took Rosalba and me shopping Saturday. She came round in the morning 'cause I still got no phone for her to call me on, and she asked me to come with her to get things for the baby. "Teresa," she said, screwing up her eyes like she do when she is worried, "I don't know what kinds of things Rosalba is going to need. Would you like to come with me and help me choose?"

I was real surprised, but my heart was touched. It is like she still wants me to be a grandma, even now. I told her she could have the high chair, though I promised the playpen to Yolanda to keep her youngest out of trouble in, but she said no, she wanted new stuff. "I don't mean to offend you, Teresa, it's just that I've dreamed about furnishing a nursery for years now and this is my only chance to do it. I'd like to get a matching set, white or maybe wood. I've seen some beautiful things in this store on Amsterdam. Will you come?"

I tried to tell her she could get it cheaper downtown but she wouldn't listen, so I dressed Rosalba and out we went. The first thing she does when we get to Broadway is stick her hand out for a cab.

"It is not so far, we can walk," I tell her.

"No, let's save our energy." She smiles at me and I see she is all excited, her little face pink and shiny, her hair blowing in her eyes. I hope she knows there is more to being a mother than shopping. She asks to hold Rosalba while I fold the stroller and I look at the two of them cuddled up there in the wind, my heart bleeding. Still, I can see this woman, she loves mi nieta already, 'cause she rests her lips on her soft head and rubs her mouth in her hair. "She's so warm and sweet," she says, her light eyes sparkling. I look away and nod.

In the store we put Rosalba back in her stroller and look at the cribs. The store is not so fancy as I expected, all crowded and messy, with boxes piled up and mothers trying to get their strollers past each other like it's a traffic jam, but the prices are so high I gotta rub my eyes and look at them twice. "This place, it is too expensive," I try to tell Miss Goldin, but she is so busy getting excited about this mobile with balloons and clouds floating around to music that she don't hear me.

"Look, Teresa," she says, "isn't that cute?" She picks up Rosalba, who laughs and reaches out her fat little hand to the clowns. "See? She loves it." I just stand there, feeling like a shadow somebody forgot. I watch Miss Goldin order the mobile and this white crib with colored balls along the edges, and a matching high chair that folds into a table, and sheets with little clowns all over them to go with the mobile . . . and more and more like money is for nothing but play. I never seen anybody spend like that, so I just stand there, my mouth open, thinking about how many weeks of welfare checks it would take to save up for even one of those tiny sheet sets. Mi Rosita, I think, looking at her kicking all excited in Miss Goldin's arms, you gonna be spoiled rotten, you lucky niña.

After Miss Goldin is finished buying most everything in the store, toys and baby dishes and bottles and all kinds of safety gadgets my children did just fine without, as well as the bedding stuff, she tells them to deliver it all and takes me out to a diner. "Shopping makes me starving. Isn't it time for Rosalba to eat, too?" she says, and she tells me to order whatever I want. I sit across the table from her, mirrors and lights wherever I look making me feel all dazed and confused, wondering why she is spending so much money before the adoption is even cleared. I guess if you are rich, and you been childless all the way into your forties, I guess the temptation is too much. For her, buying all that stuff must be like a reward after a long time of suffering. So I smile at her and look down at the menu. We might as well all have fun.

We get Rosalba some soft eggs and rice, which I show Miss Goldin how to mash up so the baby can eat it, since she only got four teeth, and I order myself some chili. Miss Goldin, she has nothing but salad and crackers. "You not on a diet, I hope," I say. "You gonna waste away to nothing if you are."

She laughs. "No, no. I thought I was hungry but I'm just too excited to eat. Let's go to Macy's after this and get her some clothes."

"But I got clothes. I will give them to you when you come."

"I know, but I'd like to get her some new things, too. Maybe for her to grow into. Okay?"

I shrug and laugh at this crazy woman. There she is, a big smile on her mouth like a child at Christmas, the happiness vibes spreading out over the table so strong I can feel them like heat. Rosalba squeals and whacks her high chair tray with a spoon, making us both jump and laugh. When this lady, she takes my baby away, she is gonna take a piece of my heart with her—but least I'll know that piece will be happy.

Now I am back at home, though, spending my last few days with Rosalba, it is harder. Big Al, he came round last night and took one look at my sad face and said, "Teresa, let's get outta here." And he made me go with him for a walk up and down Broadway, pushing Rosalba in her stroller like a coupla old people proud to be grandparents for the first time. He put his arm round me trying to shield me from the pain. "Don't make yourself sad now," he said. "This is only for a while till Bianca's ready to help out more, right?" I nodded 'cause I am too ashamed to tell him the truth. He thinks I am giving up mi nieta to a relation, and only for a short time. He don't know I am throwing her away to a stranger.

It is getting dark earlier now, the winter creeping up on us, but the air last night, it was fine and fresh from the fall rains. The streetlights on Broadway were all turned on and the stores were shining warm and happy inside, begging us to get in there and buy. When I was young and making good money for the first time in the subways, and I only had one baby to feed, I always was so tempted by those stores. José, he had to stop me from spending all the time. "You don't need that, mi lechuza," he would say, tickling me under the chin—he always called me his little owl 'cause my eyes, he said, they got so big when I saw things I wanted to buy. "You just getting suckered in by all that glitter." It was true, the greed was strong in me then. I'd grown up with so little in my life, toys I had to share with all my sisters and brothers, clothes handed down from bigger girls. I wanted to fill up my home with new things, shiny and bright with no holes, no shredding hems, no cracks or missing legs. My kids, they had better than me, but not like little Rosalba is gonna get. Miss Goldin said mi nieta, she is even gonna have her own room, with pretty curtains and a red rug and the sun shining in to wake her up each morning. That girl is gonna live like a princess. I never could have given her that.

So there I was, walking down Broadway with Rosalba, Al trying to make me happy with his arm round my shoulders,

and all I could think about was my past and all its mistakes
while the store lights glittered on the wet street like nothing
but money matters in this world. Back when I had a handsome young husband I never woulda believed that one day
I'd be handing over my own nieta to a stranger like this. If
some devil had whispered in my ear what was gonna happen to me in the future, I woulda promised anything to
change it. José, he was full of ambition for himself in those
days and I thought my little babies would grow up to make
me so proud—I was foolish enough back then to think the
Rodríguez curse wouldn't stop me dead. Why didn't Dios
spare me at least one son? Why did both of them have to fall
to the devil's ways? No sons, and soon no granddaughter.
How can He make it so that outta all the children in my life
I only got one left, and even she I am fighting every day
to save? I still don't get it, what I done to deserve such
treatment.

Sometimes I think about leaving all this mess and going
back home to la República to join my no-good brother Alfredo who was deported there, the one who sends me the
perfume. I don't know what he is doing with himself, he
don't tell me in his letters, so I guess it is nothing good.
Maybe Bianca, she could find herself some work in Santo
Domingo where I got some family still, and learn some of the
old ways to keep a woman straight and narrow. But I know
in my heart I will never do this thing. I think of the sweet
air I remember from my childhood, and the guayaba trees
steaming in the rain, but those memories, they are too far
away to feel like anything but somebody else's dream. If I
went back what would I do 'cept sit around being poor and
feeling like I failed? Here I got neighbors seeing my troubles
and that is bad enough, but there it would be family looking
down at me and laughing. I got too much pride for that.

So I guess we are stuck here, Bianca and me and the
mess we made of our lives. I will get through these days

with Rosalba somehow, giving her the last precious moments of abuelita love she will ever get. Big Al, he will try to help but he can't do much not knowing the truth. La Virgen de la Altagracia, help me bear what I gotta bear. I lost children before but I never gave up one on purpose. You done it, Virgencita, you gave up a child. How does a woman stand such pain?

Roberto

I can't believe this shit Bianca be telling me. She gonna give up her child, her own baby came outta her own body! I think about my moms, who woulda killed anybody who ever tried to take us away no matter how bad she was suffering, and I can't believe Bianca will do this thing. The only reason my moms left us was 'cause my dad made her life such a living hell she couldn't help us no more even if she tried. She didn't know what she was doing when she jumped in fronta that train, I'm sure of it, 'cause the moms I remember from before the smack, she was as loving and strong as a mother could be. So I know somebody musta been brainwashing Bianca, maybe Mrs. Rodríguez, or some powerful white folk who don't see her as human 'cause she be young and Dominican . . . but I still can't understand it.

Maybe it's 'cause of that fucka Orlando. Maybe he messed up her mind by what he did even worse than she knows. When I went to teach him a lesson, he said things about Bianca made me wanna drag his guts outta his stomach and squeeze them till he screamed out in pain. He don't see Bianca as human, he just thinks she be some kinda joke, or game, like poker. He thinks he made himself big by forcing her like that. If he said any of that shit to her, he probably messed up her mind real bad.

I didn't do all the things to Orlando I wanted. I'm short but I'm strong, and I mighta got him real good 'cept he be a dirty fighter, a cheat like he is in everything else in life. He even bit me, like a girl, then one of his homies showed up and the two of them . . . well, I gave him a few good cuts, anyhow. He ain't gonna look so good as he used to under them shades, not with half his cheek sliced off.

Still, I don't feel satisfied. It wasn't good enough hurting his body—I guess what I wanted was to hurt his soul. I wanted to make him pay deep inside for what he did to my Bianca, but I didn't know how. How you make someone feel sorry for hurting a piece of dirt? That's how he sees that poor girl. He don't see the light shining outta her eyes like I do, he don't see the soul in her heart. He too blinded by greed and self-love. I guess that's what it means to be evil. I wanna combat evil, but I ain't a god. I ain't even a superhero. I ain't nothing but a short, ugly guy with a whole lotta love and a whole lotta bad luck.

Still, I got one mission I can do. I can stop this terrible thing happening to my Bianca. I ain't gonna let nobody take her baby away. I ain't gonna let nobody hurt her that bad. That's what they used to do to slaves, take their babies away. Those days are over, and I'm gonna prove it if I have to lay down my life to do it.

Bianca

Every day now when I get home from school some kinda sadness is going on. Mami's either crying, or she's got her face set up tight and grim and she's looking at the baby like she's afraid it's gonna die and float up to heaven any second. I can hardly stand it she makes me feel so bad, so I just creep around trying to help out without bothering her none. I wish she could lighten up a little and relax. I mean it was her decision to give the baby away, so why can't she be happy about it? I thought the whole idea here was to make things easier for her and me, but so far it's just worse.

"Biancita," she says to me today when I come in the door, her voice sounding kinda croaky, "pack up Rosalba's things, mi linda. Put the ones that fit her in a bag for Miss Goldin. The ones she has grown out of you can do with what you want. I don't even wanna see them. Miss Goldin, she is coming in a few minutes."

"What's she coming now for, Mami? I thought she couldn't take the baby till next week."

"She just wants to visit." Mami screws up her mouth like she's trying not to cry. "I want Rosalba to have some of the clothes and toys she is used to in her new home, so she don't feel too lonely." Then her voice cracks and she whisks the baby off into the kitchen to give her some dinner. I hate to see Mami hurting so much.

When I start going through the drawer at the bottom of our dresser, though, pretty soon I'm feeling bad, too. Here's that little dress we put the baby in when we took her home from the hospital, with skinny arms and a long skirt that ties at the bottom like a sack. And here's the white one with frills under the skirt she wore for her christening, and the matching shoes with lace on the side and a button. I pretend it's just doll clothes so I can fold them up without it seeming like my baby's died. I don't know if I'm even gonna want to look at them again, it might make me feel too bad, so I shove them way back outta sight at the top of our closet. Then I put the clothes that still fit her in a plastic garbage bag with a label on it so Sarah Goldin will know not to throw it away.

While I fold the clothes, some of the things Roberto said about it being wrong to give up my own flesh and blood keep echoing in my ears. Mosta the time I don't take him too serious, but this time, deep down, I worry that he's right, so I try to look at it this way: I'm giving the baby the best home she can have. I won't ever be able to give her what she needs, what any human being needs: money, a good education, a nice home, and, most of all, a daddy. And I gotta admit I ain't exactly been the world's best mother. But Sarah Goldin can give her those things and that makes my baby a pretty lucky girl. Roberto thinks he can be her papi, but he don't know yet I'm not marrying him. Not for nothing. I'm done with men. No, I'm giving the baby a good home this way and that's a mother's first duty, right? I don't think I'm gonna go to hell for that.

Sarah rings the doorbell just as I'm folding the last pair of lacy socks and Mami says to let her in. At the door I notice she's looking more nervous than ever, her brow pinched and her fingers picking at each other, which makes me wanna ask her how many more fights she been having with that big-wig husband of hers. I flash my eyes over her. Something about her embarrasses me, maybe 'cause she looks like ghosts visit her in the night. Maybe it's her conscience does the visiting, like part of her knows she's a thief. "I got some of the baby's things for you," I say, leading her to the bedroom. "Here, in the bag."

She peeks inside. "Are you sure you want to give all this to me? It must have cost a fortune."

"It did." I look at her hard and it works, 'cause she reaches for her purse.

"How much do I owe you? I know your mother can't afford to just give all this away."

"A hundred bucks at least," I say quickly, hoping Mami don't hear.

"Well, I don't have that much cash. I can give you sixty."

She's just about to hand it over when Mami walks in, holding Rosalba. "What's this?" she snaps.

"I want to pay you for all these lovely clothes," Sarah says. "Please, Teresa, I know how much they must have cost."

Mami pulls the air in through her nostrils and sticks her chin in the air. "I ain't selling my baby's clothes and I ain't selling my baby." Her back's up straight like a tree. "Keep your money for the lawyers."

"Sorry, I didn't mean to offend you." Sarah stuffs the money back in her wallet and I'm mad. It feels like I should get something outta giving up my very own baby. I mean I was the one who had the labor and everything—nobody seems to remember that. Sarah closes her purse, looking all pink and blotchy. "You're right about the lawyers—they charge a fortune!" She tries to smile but nobody else does, so she turns red and we stand there in silence, none of us knowing what to say. At last she looks at Mami. "Can I hold Rosalba again?" she says, all meek and humble in that way that makes me squirm. "I've missed her terribly these past two days."

Mami nods and hands the baby over. Rosalba seems to know Sarah 'cause she kicks her fat legs and smiles, reaching for the woman's nose with a giggle like this is some game they played before. The baby don't act that nice with me, that's for sure—she still cries whenever I try to hold her. The whole thing makes me sick.

Mami looks at me and it's like she notices the evil eye I'm giving Sarah 'cause she hisses, "Bianca, get yourself outta here. All you do is make trouble." I don't wanna watch that woman stealing my baby away anyhow, so I give her the finger behind her back and go downstairs. Jesus, they treat me like I got nothing to do with that baby at all. Who do they think its mother is anyhow?

Downstairs, I decide to visit with Clara to help me get my mind off of Sarah Goldin. Clara lives in the projects east of Columbus and usually I hate walking there 'cause it's gangbanger territory and it's scary, but today even that's better'n staying at home. There are these guys who hang on Clara's block looking like they came right outta jail—I saw one with a big knife in his hand once, which he flashed at me just to see the look on my face. Clara told me she was chased down the street one day by a man who said he was gonna kill her. Anyhow, I try not to think about all that, and when I get there I go up to her apartment quick as I can, where she lives with her grandma. On the way up I remember the day Clara's little cousin was shot in the crossfire between some gangbangers. Just a little kid playing outside on her bike and a bullet she had nothing to do with went straight in her head. That's one thing Roberto's right about: we all gotta get out of this sick city before every one of us ends up dead.

Clara's up there fighting with her grandma as usual, so she's glad to see me. She lives way up high in this building and you can see the roofs of Harlem out her window, but the place is falling apart. There's no doors on the closets, the rail for the shower curtain's come outta the wall, and the tile in the ceiling keeps falling off and whacking somebody on the head. It smells bad, too, like an old woman who hasn't washed—maybe it's her grandma, or maybe it's rot under the rug, I don't know, but I can't stand it. I hop from foot to foot while Clara looks for some money to put in her pocket and tries to run a comb through her sticky hair—she keeps on using too much hair spray no matter how much I tell her to stop. "Come on Clara, move your ass," I say. Her grandma stares at me, saying nothing and playing with her false teeth. Sometimes I think that woman's putting a spell on me 'cause she's jealous that I'm pretty and her granddaughter ain't— she sure gives me the creeps. "Clara," I say, "if you don't move it right now I'm leaving."

"Okay. Jesus, what's eating you?" She sticks her comb in the back of her jeans and at last we get down to the street.

Clara's hooked on some new boy now, like Roberto said, some guy in his twenties who sounds no good to me but she says he's real fresh and she tells me about him all the way down the stairs. I don't mind—at least she's forgotten about Juan. We never talk about him no more: he's like a dream now, something that zips by my mind once in a while and makes me feel sad. I just push it away. I got no time to moon over that bastard no more. I got my studies to think about, and how to get free of the things in my life weighing me down And at least me and Clara, we can be friends again.

When we get outside I ask Clara if she knows anything about what happened to Roberto. "He looks like somebody used his face for a trampoline," I said, "but he won't tell me nothing."

She looks at me sideways. "I don't know," she says, which ain't like her at all. "I heard something but I don't know if it's right."

I pinch her in the ribs till she squeals. "Then tell me, estúpida!"

"Okay! Get your hands off of me, bitch! I heard he got into a fight with that sleazy guy on your street with the red Z-car. Y'know, the one you went out with once? He probably jealous. Roberto's always jealous. Anyhow, the other guy looks pretty bad, too, but not so bad as Roberto. He ain't much of a fighter, I guess."

I let her keep on talking while we walk over to Broadway so I don't have to show how I feel. I'm shocked, but something worse is going on inside of me, too. I feel like some big hand reached down from the sky and took my willpower away. The baby, Mami and that caseworker, and now Roberto—everybody making decisions about Bianca's life 'cept Bianca herself. What made him think he had the right? I feel like Rosalba would feel if she had the brains—people pushing me around like I'm nothing, nobody listening to me, nobody thinking about what I might want, nobody asking me if I got an opinion. Nobody even thinking about me as a human being.

When we get to Broadway we walk downtown, looking at the stores, Clara blabbing away about boys and stuff. She tells me about all the ways to shoplift she's learned from friends, and we take a few hair clips and a lipstick. But then we get the giggles and laugh at every stupid little thing till the salespeople kick us out. It's fun to have a friend again—I been feeling lonely so long—and it gets my mind off Mami and Roberto and the baby. But even through the giggles it don't feel quite right. All the time I be laughing and looking at the clothes with Clara and daring her to take some panty hose while the saleslady is helping somebody else, I feel a little hole inside of me, a sad little hole that makes everything I do seem phony. I feel like I'm not really me, like I'm putting on an act for somebody who's watching me, but I don't know who it is.

Teresa

We gotta go to court. The caseworker, she told me this wouldn't happen, but something has changed and I don't know what it is. I hope they are not gonna accuse my Bianca of some evil thing, pobrecita. All I know is, we gotta go down to court today and see some judge about this adoption. And we gotta bring Rosalba with us, 'cause if things go the way they s'posed to, today is the day Miss Goldin is gonna take her away.

La Virgen de la Altagracia, will I ever see mi nieta again once that lady takes her? Will I ever know what she is like when she begins to walk and her hair grows long, and her first words come, and she turns into a girl and then a woman? Will I ever feel her little arms around my neck and her voice whisper to me, "Te quiero abuelita"? Forgive me for even thinking all this, Virgencita, 'cause I know I started this whole thing and You been merciful and answered my prayers. I just pray mi Rosita won't ever remember this day, that she won't remember the things Bianca done to her, even that she won't remember me. It is a hard thing to pray that your own nieta will forget you, but for her sake I hope she wipes these eight months of her life outta her little brain, and grows up happy with Miss Goldin.

I get her into her little white dress with the ribbons threaded through the neck and hem, and her white sweater with the yellow patterns on it, and her lace hair band, all of it breaking my heart. Then I pack the rest of Rosalba's things Miss Goldin didn't take yet in a bag and make Bianca put on something decent, though her idea of decent is to dress in clothes so tight she looks like she been shrink-wrapped in the supermarket. I put Rosalba in the stroller and we catch the subway downtown to the courthouse. Bianca, she keeps looking over at me like she wants me to show her how to act, but I don't have the strength to help her right now. I gotta hold myself together just to make it through this day. When Rosalba is safe in her new home, then I can give Bianca all the attention that silly niña needs.

The caseworker said to go to family court, but when we get there I can't believe this is the place we s'posed to be. It looks like a giant tombstone, huge and black and shiny and hard, like it was custom-made for all the killers and rapists who hell is waiting to give a home. What idiot built a place like that for kids and their troubles? It is so big and creepy it makes you feel like an ant about to be stepped on. I grab Bianca's hand, as much to keep me in one piece as her, and we push the stroller between these gigantic black pillars and through the front door, only to find we gotta wait in line so some cops can check us out at the security gate. It is a long wait, and all the time my heart is beating like a gong and I am thinking, Don't change your mind, Biancita, don't.

After the cop is done looking down my tampons and messing with my personal business, they let us through these electric gates like they have at airports, the ones that go beep over every metal button, and we get to the elevators. The caseworker said to meet the judge on floor nine so up we go, squashed in against all these people looking miserable with their troubles, every one of them dark like me, and the lawyers in their greasy suits, every one of them white like Miss Goldin, and all of them breathing germs over my Rosalba's little face. And the first thing I see when I get out on the ninth floor is this sign saying, PREPARE TO SPEND ALL DAY IN COURT.

"Jesus," Bianca says when she sees that. "What they expect us to do here, huh? They coulda put in a snack bar at least. Shit."

"Bianca, keep your patience." I look around, noticing these teenage kids sulking on the orange and blue chairs, and their mamas and grandmas looking as tired and worried as me. In one corner there is a boy about ten, with a round face and a new suit so tight he can hardly breathe. I wonder what mamá or papi is throwing him away, and I remember that little naked boy me and Al found on the subway car. "Everybody gotta wait, and that means you, too," I tell Bianca, and settle back into my sadness.

The walls around us are this gray concrete, depressing as hell, and the floor is pale orange under the fluorescent lights—the whole place looks like some kinda nursery school for crazy adults. Everywhere I see big silver doors, each one of them locked to keep us campesinos out, with only the lawyers in their smart suits allowed in, clicking past in their leather shoes. I get this vision of me sitting here forever, growing old, while these skinny white people march over my bones.

"Mami?" Bianca says, touching my knee. "What's gonna happen now? I mean why we gotta wait with all these ho's?" She looks around at the other girls, raising her eyebrows.

"What makes you think you any better? The caseworker said to wait here till our name is called."

"But why we gotta go to court, Mami? I thought we could do it all with paper."

"I don't know why. They said we got some trouble with

Miss Goldin." I look over Bianca's shoulder so I don't have to see any expression on her face. I don't wanna make her feel like a criminal, even if that is how they gonna treat her here. She don't know it, but they got every one of those pinches she did to Rosalba on record somewhere, down forever like a stamp.

When we get the call, after they make us wait so long I know it is a punishment, I am surprised to see how small the courtroom is inside. There's these light wooden tables in a circle, with the judge's desk up on an elevated platform, only it is empty now, and a few chairs around the back of the room. I guess it is s'posed to make us feel like this is all friendly and equal, not some criminal court where we get judged, but it don't fool me. I know who is Us and who is Them here, and I never felt so Them in my life.

The caseworker tells me and Bianca to sit on one side of the circle, and she says the judge will be there in a minute. I try to ask her what is going on but a man comes in and she scoots off to talk to him in the middle of my question, so I gotta wait. We pull up our chairs and I put Rosalba on my lap, where she plays with her teether and drools down her front. Bianca slumps down beside me, her chin almost touching her stomach.

"Bianca, sit up," I say. "You behave like a lady in this place." But she ignores me, and, like I said, I don't have the strength to bother with her now.

I look around for our caseworker, who I see whispering in a corner with some other woman, then I see Miss Goldin come in with her lawyer. He looks tense and ready to spring like a tigre. Miss Goldin has dressed herself up real smart in this cream-colored suit like a nurse's uniform, I notice, but she seems worried. I don't put it down to nothing, though— she always seems worried. I hope Rosalba will drive that worried look off of her face. I hope they both can be happy.

She nods at me, but I can't look no more. I am too afraid I will cry.

At last the court officer shouts, "Order," and we all gotta stand while the judge comes in and sits down at her desk. She is plump, maybe in her fifties, with stiff gray hair and a straight back, and she seems tired out but dignified. She looks at the files on her desk while we stand, me with Rosalba in my arms, then she nods to the officer. "State your name and relation to the respondent," the court officer barks at me, and I don't even know what he is talking about.

"My name is Teresa Rodríguez," I say, clear and proud, "but I don't understand your question."

The judge turns to him. "This is an adoption surrender," she says, and he seems to understand some code 'cause he begins to act nicer.

"Your relation to the baby," he says.

"Abuela. Grandmother."

Bianca gives her answer, too, then they tell us to sit down. The judge calls for Miss Goldin's lawyer to hand her the papers and looks them over, then she asks him to summarize the case. He tells her that the surrender papers have been signed and notarized, that the home study went well, that the baby and Miss Goldin know each other and the adoption has been privately arranged, and that Miss Goldin has the certification. "There should be no obstacles to my client's petition," he says, and the judge looks at him over her glasses.

"What are we doing here then, Mr. Fielding?" I see her eyes dart about a little, then she adds, "And where is Ms. Goldin's husband?"

The lawyer stands up again. "Ms. Goldin is formally separated from her husband, Your Honor. We have the separation agreement here."

So that is why we got dragged down to this tomb building like a coupla thieves. It is nothing to do with the pinching Bianca done. I look at the judge, surprised as she is, and see her frowning and taking a paper from the lawyer's hands. "Why didn't you tell the court this right away, Mr. Fielding? Ms. Goldin, have you anything to add?"

Miss Goldin stands up, blushing. "I'm petitioning to adopt as a single mother, Your Honor," she says. "My husband has agreed to stay out of it."

The judge frowns again. "Is there nobody here to speak for this child?" she asks, looking at us. Our caseworker is about to stand up when Bianca shoots to her feet.

"Hey!" she shouts. "Hey, what's that you say?"

"Mrs. Díaz, please don't shout," the judge says. "You have a question?"

"Yeah!"

"Sit down!" I hiss at her, tugging at her sleeve, but she pulls her arm away. "What's that the lawyer said about separation?"

"Keep your voice down, young lady," the judge says, but she is looking at Bianca with kindness. "Ms. Goldin is apparently soon to be divorced. She is adopting your child as a single mother."

"Oh no she is not," Bianca says loudly, shaking her head. "That wasn't part of the deal. I want my baby to have a father. That's why I agreed to this."

"But you've signed the papers, Mrs. Díaz," says Miss Goldin's lawyer.

"Mr. Fielding!" snaps the judge, glaring at him. "Will you kindly refrain from speaking out of turn?" The lawyer apologizes, which I gotta admit makes me grin inside, and the judge turns back to Bianca. "Go on, dear."

"That caseworker lady told me I had forty-five days to change my mind!" Bianca says loudly. "Am I right or what?"

"Quietly, please, we can hear you fine. Yes, that is since you signed the consent form. Did no one tell you about this separation before?"

Bianca's eyes are flashing now, and she is waving her

arms like she is trying to stop a train. I sit there holding Rosalba close to my chest, the dread so thick in my throat I can't even swallow. What is my daughter doing to me now?

"No! Nobody told me about no separation. She's a liar!" Bianca points at poor Miss Goldin, who looks like she is gonna faint. "There's no way in hell I'm letting my baby move in with a liar!" she says again, her voice echoing round the room.

The judge turns to the lawyer. "Why wasn't the girl told about this before she signed, Mr. Fielding?"

"The client's situation has only recently changed, Your Honor." The lawyer's gone droopy in the face, like a puppy caught eating somebody's dinner. "The separation agreement has only just been formalized."

"When is 'just', Mr. Fielding?"

The lawyer shifts his feet. Miss Goldin should fire him. "Well, in point of fact, Friday morning."

"I see." The judge looks at Miss Goldin for a moment, who stares back, squeezing her hands together. Then the judge turns to the papers on her desk and leafs through them for a long time. "The husband apparently was not present for the home interview, but the client said he was away on business. Ms. Goldin, please stand."

Miss Goldin stands up, and I notice all over again how short she is. She looks like a little white pear with a scared face.

"Was your husband away on business when the caseworker came for the home visit, Ms. Goldin?"

She clears her throat. "No," she squeaks, and the judge leans forward like she can't hear.

"Take your time," she says, her voice kind again. "We can wait."

Miss Goldin nods. "Thank you," she says in this little voice, and clears her throat again. I hold Rosalba tight on my lap, my heart beating so hard it aches. I don't even know what I want. La Virgen de la Altagracia, is this a way out?

"He wasn't away on business," Miss Goldin says finally. "I lied about my husband. He had left, you see, and I didn't know where he was, and I was afraid it would wreck my chances of getting the baby if I told the caseworker that, so . . ."

"You should have told the truth, Ms. Goldin. Do you often lie?"

"No!" I see Miss Goldin look over at me like she thinks I am gonna help, but this is outta my hands now. All I can do is pray that whatever happens it is the Lord's choice for what is best for Rosalba.

"Nothing like this has ever happened before," Miss Goldin goes on. "I didn't use the best judgment, I realize that. I'm sorry." Then she turns and looks at Bianca, who stares at the ground, kicking the table in front of us. "I'm sorry I'm not all you want, Bianca," Miss Goldin says. "I know you must have had dreams about the perfect home you could give your baby. I know this must be hard for you and your mother. But I promise I will give Rosalba everything she ever needs. I tried to have a child for years, Bianca, and I know I will love Rosalba more than anything in the world. I already love her. She will have a good life with me, I promise you. Please give me a chance."

I am nodding at Miss Goldin while she talks. Keep going, lady, keep going, I wanna say, tell them how it is, but I am too choked up to speak. Miss Goldin, she has got tears running down her face, too, and now I know I have chosen the right woman.

The judge nods, gripping her mouth tight. "Is your husband likely to cause trouble, Ms. Goldin? We don't want the baby put in a home of fights and turbulence."

Miss Goldin shakes her head, unable to speak, so her lawyer steps in. I guess he has decided he is gonna be some use at last. "Your Honor," he says, "my client's husband is in Boston. He has agreed not to interfere. This is a consensual adoption between my client and the birth mother, if I may remind you, Your Honor."

I look over at Bianca, who is still kicking the table. Mi Dios, she looks like such a baby.

"I am aware of that, Mr. Fielding. Must I ask you again to refrain from speaking out of turn?" The judge looks at Bianca. "It is up to you, Mrs. Díaz. You are the child's mother and no one can force you to do anything you don't want. Would you like to think it over?"

Bianca shrugs, then glances at me. "Let her do it," I whisper in her ear, but she pushes me away. My eyes are crying with Miss Goldin's by now, but all this emotion, all this to-ing and fro-ing, it is making my heart grow hard. Finally, Bianca stands up.

"Okay, this is what I want," she says clearly, her head high, and I look at her real surprised to hear this tough, sure voice coming outta my troubled niña. Maybe, I think for a second, maybe this smart hijita of mine is gonna get far in life after all, just like I always wanted.

"I want my baby to have a good life and to go to college," Bianca says then, "but most of all I want her to have a daddy." She pauses, frowning and staring at the big windows on one side of the room, and at these words of hers I feel my hopes crashing down again. If she sends Ms. Goldin away, I see our last chance going away with her, and the years of welfare and no money and Bianca and Rosalba turning evil with fear and anger like my sons, all of it stretches out in front of me like a prison sentence. At last Bianca speaks again.

"Okay. This lady can take my baby home, but only if she promises me something. If she don't make it up with her husband, or if she can't find a good man by the time my forty-five days are up, I wanna take the baby back."

¡Tu estás loca! I wanna say, that is an impossible de-
mand, and I wait to hear the judge tell Bianca so, but all the
woman says is, "Are you absolutely sure, Mrs. Díaz? Remember, once the baby enters an adoptive home it is best for
everyone if she remains there for good."

"Yeah, I'm sure. I wouldn't say so if I wasn't!"

The judge turns to Miss Goldin and nods. "Well," she
says, "it seems you have the birth mother's permission to
take the baby. I am not happy with the circumstances under
which the consent was signed, however, or with how your
profile as an adoptive home has changed, so I must remind
you that this is not the final surrender. If circumstances
change substantially in the birth mother's home, the court
may see fit to review the situation. Mrs. Díaz?" The judge
turns again to my Bianca. "You have thirty days left before
your consent becomes irrevocable, do you understand? But I
remind you again that it is in the baby's best interest not to
be tossed back and forth between families. A baby is not a
beach ball. Do you understand me, Mrs. Díaz?"

Bianca blinks and shrugs. "Yeah."

"You will address me as Your Honor, Mrs. Díaz."

"Sorry. Your Honor."

"Ms. Goldin, is this satisfactory to you?"

No, my heart cries out, no more torture, no more not
knowing. But Miss Goldin nods. "I'll try my best, Your
Honor," she manages to croak. "Thank you." I guess she
knows that is the best she can get.

After it is all over, and we file outta the courtroom, me
feeling like I just been to a funeral, we drive home in Miss
Goldin's car, me in the front with her and Bianca in the back
next to Rosalba in a brand-new baby seat. I never could afford one of those for my babies, but I was always nervous in
those crazy gypsy cabs, driving around without so much as a
seat belt to protect their little heads. When we get to my
door, Miss Goldin looking all happy and pink in the face,

she asks me if there is any advice I wanna give her before she takes mi nieta away.

"Yes," I say, the hurt so bad I can hardly get the words out, "there is. Cover her face when she is sleeping so the evil spirits, they don't disturb her, and put shoes on those little feet to keep the dirt off." It has always bothered me the way some American mothers, they let their babies play outside in the park in bare feet like savages. Miss Goldin, she just smiles when I say this, and I can see she don't agree with a word I am saying. Well, I gotta let her have her American ways, I guess, but she better know how to rock that baby and sing her to sleep when la pobrecita is scared and tired. I pray to You, Virgen, don't let little Rosalba miss her abuelita too bad. I don't want her to feel pain, her heart as little and fresh as a dewdrop. Let her love Miss Goldin quick, so she can be safe and happy in her new home

"Miss Goldin?" I say before I get outta the car. "I got a question I hope you don't mind me asking. Now you and your husband are apart, how you gonna look after the baby on your own?"

"That's a fair question." She smiles at me gently. "I get three months leave from work, just like after giving birth. Then I can go back part-time until Rosalba's three years old. If it gets too hard I'll go freelance."

"You won't be hiring some baby-sitter to look after her all day? It is you I want for her mother, not some stranger."

Miss Goldin shakes her head and leans over me to open my door. "I didn't go through all this just to dump her on a baby-sitter, Teresa. I'm not giving up my chance to be a mother for anyone, especially not after what Rosalba has been through."

I nod and study her face from the side a while. I was a mother so young I never had time to long for it and dream about it—it just happened. First Hernán came along, then two years later Luis, then a pile of troubles till Bianca popped out. It must be different when you been wanting a child for five years and everybody's got one but you. I think it's gotta make that baby extra precious—I mean, Miss Goldin's even given up her husband for the chance to have my Rosalba! Yes, I am sure Miss Goldin is right for mi nieta.

I climb outta the car and lean in the window to say my last good-bye, but when Rosalba sees me out there she starts crying. Miss Goldin, she is biting her lip and looking from me to the baby, her brow scrunched up with worry, so I come back and lean in the car window again. I stroke Rosalba's little head and talk in her ear till she calms down enough for me to stick the bobo in her mouth. Once Rosalba is sucking and Miss Goldin is watching her, her eyes soft and tender, I say to her, "Talk to Rosalba. Let her know you are here for her. Let her hear your voice so she don't feel alone."

And Miss Goldin, she says, "Hey little Rosalba, it's okay, it's okay, I'll look after you." She sounds so shy saying it that I think, You'll do better on your own, lady, I gotta leave you to it.

I turn to Bianca, who is standing next to me with her face screwed up like she got a stomachache. "Biancita, you say good-bye now. We gotta go in." Bianca throws her eyes at the baby then away again, quick, like she is looking at something ugly. Then she glares at Miss Goldin.

"Remember what I said," she says with a hiss.

"I remember, Bianca." Miss Goldin is being real patient, 'cause I know she was not happy about what Bianca did in that courtroom.

"Miss Goldin?" I say when Bianca is gone into the house. "Don't you pay no attention to her. Y'know all these threats she makes, they will come to nothing. The judge knows it, too. Bianca, she understands inside this is for the best."

Miss Goldin sighs. "I hope you're right, Teresa. You know I'll love Rosalba, don't you? Will you help Bianca believe me?"

"I will try, with God's help. I gotta go in now." Then this

sadness, it comes up in my heart so strong it makes it so I can't speak. "I better go in and be with Bianca," I say when my voice comes back. "She is probably not feeling too good."

"Thank you for everything, Teresa," Miss Goldin says, squeezing my hand. "You've been so good to me. And here, please take this." She hands me an envelope. It is the rent money, I know. It shames me, but I take it. Forgive me, Virgencita, but I am too poor to refuse.

"Give your thanks to la Virgen María," I say, then I remember Miss Goldin is Jewish. "Or whoever it is you thank."

"God." She looks embarrassed.

"Okay, God. You got friends to help you out?"

"Oh, yes. I know lots of women who've had babies. Teresa?"

"What?"

"You can . . . you can come over and see her sometimes if you want. We don't live so far away."

I was wondering if she was gonna say this, but now she has I know what I gotta do. It is hard, but it is right. "Miss Goldin," I say, "thank you, but no. It is better she gets used to her new family, you know? And for me, I think it would be too painful. It is better she is just yours now."

"Are you sure?" she says, but I can hear the relief in her kind voice.

"I am sure. Good-bye miss, and good luck." I shake Miss Goldin's hand, give my Rosalba one last look, her little face so helpless inside that car, and walk up to my apartment alone.

PART FOUR

Bianca

Things are real quiet these days. November's come, I'm going to school, Mami droops round looking like somebody died. I hang with Roberto and Clara, going to the movies when we got the money, or just listening to the radio. I even let Roberto kiss me once now his face is all healed, just to liven things up, but I didn't like it much. I feel strange, kinda fidgety and restless and bored. I feel like I'm waiting for something to happen, but I don't know what it is.

I asked Mr. Jonas if he's married last week, just for something to do. The other girls dared me to ask, so I did it. It seemed like no big deal at the time. Me and him are friends anyhow, I thought, and he knows all about my private life 'cept the adoption, so why shouldn't I know about his? So I went up to him at the end of class, put my hands on my hips and said to him real sassy, "The other girls want me to ask you something."

He looked up from his work, tossing his dreadlocks off his face like he do, then he leaned back in his chair and smiled. He wears these like African shirts with a V neck down the front, so you can see his chest hairs and his beads all tangled up in them. "What do you want to ask me, Bianca?" he said in his deep voice.

I shrugged and looked away from him, so he wouldn't see how nervous I was. "It's just the other girls, that's all. I don't care."

"Well, what is it? I don't have all day."

Then suddenly I felt real stupid. "Oh, it don't matter. I'll see you," I said, and turned to leave.

"Don't go. If you promised them to ask me something, you should keep your promise. I won't mind."

I stopped and turned back, looking at the window over his shoulder like I didn't care. "Well, it's Yasemin. She wants to know if you're married. I told her it ain't none of her business, so you don't have to answer if you don't want."

Mr. Jonas chuckled. "Tell Yasemin and whoever else wants to know that I'm not, okay?"

I felt like my face was so hot by then it'd burn him, so I ran outta the room. I am never, never, never gonna do such a dumb thing again. Mr. Jonas and me, we respect each other, and I feel like I almost ruined that just 'cause those other girls be trying to invent a romance for us. Just 'cause he makes me feel giggly and proud when he talks to me don't mean I'm falling in love. Those ho's, they're just bored, that's all. They're just using me for entertainment. And even if I do like him sometimes, that's a secret I'm gonna keep deep down in my heart where nobody, 'specially not him, is ever gonna know about it.

Anyhow, now the baby's gone and it's real quiet at home, Mami says she wants me to get a job. She says she wants me to learn how to be more responsible and to earn my own money insteada spending all of hers. There's this flower store on Amsterdam that's looking for a girl, she told me, and maybe I could apply there to work after school and on weekends. I told her I don't have the time. When would I do my homework and see my friends? "If you can have a baby you don't want, you can take a job you don't want," she said. Every time she says something like that, I feel like I been shot. Mami just wants to keep me outta trouble, I know. So I let a week go by and I told her I applied and they said they didn't want me. I mighta taken the job if she hadn't been so pushy, but if she's gonna say something mean to me every time she opens her damn mouth, then I'm gonna lie right back to her till she don't know which way is up.

Still, mosta the time, Mami and me don't fight so much anymore. She's gone back to work, the six-to-two shift, getting up before it's light and stomping outta here in her work boots and that orange vest makes her look like a road sign. The new shift means she's home now when I get back from school, but it's not like she wants to talk and play around like the old days. There's a kinda silence in the house now, Mami acting like her fire's gone out, never having anything to say to me. Sometimes in the night, I wake up sudden 'cause I think I hear the baby crying and I look over past Mami's bed to where the playpen used to be, and there's nothing there. Then I get this hot panic shooting through me like I think somebody's kidnapped the baby, before I remember. I think about her warm little belly and how she used to laugh when I rubbed my nose on her ribs, and I crawl into Mami's bed and cuddle up against her back so I don't feel so lonely. I hope the baby's happy where she is now. I mean there she is, not even old enough to get a spoon in her mouth the right way up, and she's living in this stranger's home. I hope Sarah isn't messing up with her, 'specially now she don't even have a husband to make the money. I hope I did the right thing.

Roberto don't help none. He's still mad at me. "You better get that child of yours back before it's too late," he keeps saying. "You gonna feel bad the rest of your life if you don't, believe me. You can't give your family away like that, Bianca. It's wrong and it's evil. It's hurting too many peo-

ple. Your moms looks old and bitter with grief, the baby's
gotta be missing you so bad, and you, Bianca, you don't
look happy, neither. I can tell you care inside, you do, no
matter what you say."

"Shut up, Roberto," I say. "Who the fuck you think you
are?" But he always makes me wonder inside. Like, right now
I know I'm not ready to look after a child. I don't feel too
proud about the things I did to her, and I'm sorry to say it,
but I like my freedom. But how will I feel when I'm seventeen or eighteen, like him? S'pose I try to have another baby
with some man I love and I can't, like happened to Sarah,
and Rosalba's gone forever? If I took her back, though, who'd
look after her? I don't even know if they'd let us have her
back, or if they'd stick her in another stranger's home.

I asked Mami about that last night. We were cleaning the
kitchen after dinner, and I said, "Mami, if I wanted the baby
back before my thirty days are up, would they let us take
her home?" She looked at me like I'd turned into a demon.

"Bianca, forget that baby," she said, her voice sharp and
hard. "Rosalba, she is out of our lives now, and that is forever. Don't you go trying to change that, niña. She got another mamá and another family now."

"But, Mami, how come we can't just see her? I mean,
she's my baby!"

Mami sat down, pulling off her rubber gloves and
smoothing that lotion into her hands like always. "Biancita,
don't you understand? We gotta give Miss Goldin time to
love that baby now. She needs to spend time with her alone,
she needs to show her to her new family, grandmothers and
aunts and uncles. We can't go butting in there and messing
up her mind. She and Rosalba, they gotta learn to love each
other."

"But . . ."

"No, mi hijita. I know, I suffer, too. But it is for Rosalba's
sake. She is gonna get a good life from this, I checked it all

out, the whole family, everybody, that caseworker told me all about them. Trust me, mi linda. You gotta let it go."

I shook my head, but I couldn't find the words to make Mami understand. It's not for me I'm thinking about this, it's for her. I can see she's dying from missing that baby, I can see her soul shriveling up like a raisin. Mami, I wanna say to her sometimes, don't do this for me. It's killing you, I know. I wish you loved me that bad, but I don't wanna hurt you this much. Take her back, Mami, and let me be the one to move out if it's gotta be that way. But I don't say it 'cause the trouble is, I don't know where to go. I can't move in with Clara 'cause her grandma hates me and they don't even have enough money to fix their own ceiling so it won't keep smacking them on the head. I can't move in with Tía Yolanda 'cause she got enough kids and, anyhow, I think maybe Mami's right when she says my Tía's on crack. And I sure as hell can't move in with Roberto, not with him trying to get into my pants, which I know he is no matter how goody-two-shoes he acts. So that's that. There's nobody else in my life, 'cept maybe Mr. Jonas, and I can just see me going up to him and inviting myself to move in. Just imagine the headlines! Teacher Busted for Living with Teen Student. A nice dream, Bianca, but dumb. So I guess I'm stuck here, watching the sadness grow over Mami like mold on cheese, and feeling helpless to do anything about it 'cept hug her and wonder how one little baby can cause so much grief.

Teresa

Big Al, he is like part of the family now. He comes round every week to eat with us or to take me to his place when Bianca is busy with her homework, and he tries to make me feel better when the missing of Rosalba gets too rough. "Don't you fret yourself," he tells me, rubbing my back. "The pain'll get less. Every day passes, it'll get less. Anyhow, you can always go see her if you can't stand it no more. Don't you be shy about that, Teresa, you ain't no child." So even Al don't know why it still hurts, and it hurts bad.

But he does help mend my soul a little with his big body and that warm skin that is like a shelter to huddle up in. He is no God's gift to look at but he is a kind man, and I feel so lucky to have him, like I found a gold button in the gutter. He makes me feel like my body is still there for love, not just for slaving, and he helps me remember how it is to be heated up with desire, hot and strong like life hasn't left you behind.

Bianca she don't seem to mind him too much. He knows how to talk to her 'cause of his own daughters her age. He knows the music she listens to, which I never bothered with, and the movies those kids like, with the gore and the blood and the axes chopping. I don't get it myself, I don't get why anybody who lives in this evil world would wanna go to a movie just to feel worse, but Bianca and her friends, they love this stuff. Those kids spend hours giggling over these movies that make my hair stand on end, movies about people with ugly masks on their faces tearing up young girls with nails and saws and the Lord knows what. It is sick, that's what I say. But anyhow, Big Al, he can always get a smile outta Bianca by acting the fool.

The other day, for instance, he was round here for supper when Bianca, she was in one of her moods. Her face was all pouty, she wouldn't look him in the eyes, and I had to say every little thing twice to get her to move her butt. "Bianca," I said, "get on up outta that chair and pour us some water."

Bianca kicks the chair, but she don't move.

"Bianca, did you hear me demonia!" I am just about to let my yelling loose when Al, he starts making these faces so ugly even I can't stop staring. He's got this big square head, and with his thick mustache he ain't exactly Mr. Perfect, but when he began sticking out his lips in this tube like a sucker, and rolling his eyes behind his glasses, and wiggling his ears, his face got so ugly my mouth was stuck open with surprise.

"Oogle boogle," he says, staring at Bianca. First she just pretended she couldn't see him, but I saw her eyes fighting not to watch. Then this little twitch comes over her mouth. And finally she says, "Stop that. It's disgusting," and she bursts out laughing. I never woulda thought of that. To me, Bianca, she seems too old for silly faces. But Al, he showed me wrong.

Al tells me not to worry so much, my Bianca is okay. "I know these girls can tear your heart out," he says, "but Teresa, that child loves you."

"What do you know about it?" I say to him. "You don't see that devil look she sends me, the things she done."

"I can tell by the way she follows you with her eyes. She might be sitting there sucking her teeth like a lemon's in her mouth, but those big eyes of hers are following every move you make. She is just dying to have you say something good to her."

He tells me she is beautiful, too, and I can't help it but that makes my heart melt with pride. "That girl looks like a movie star," he said to me once. "You better protect her, Teresa, 'cause every guy on the block is gonna be after her, if they ain't too afraid to try."

"You call that a blessing?" I told him. "I say it is a curse." But the truth is, who wants an ugly daughter?

So things with Al they are going good, and then I got work to occupy me, too, and to help take my mind off of Rosalba and the empty hole she has left in my life. The MTA, they gave me trouble at first 'cause I quit, but I said it was medical problems and 'cause I got seniority, they let me back. Well, it brings in the money and keeps me busy. More than that, there is a pride I feel in keeping the trains clean for the people of this city. We don't let a single car go till we have cleaned every last scrap of graffiti off it: better to make the train late than let it drive around with those angry black scrawls all over, making every soul who looks on it feel bad. Those kids who do the graffiti, they just shoving their anger in our faces like it is gonna make some change, but all it does is make things worse. We got a kinda war on, the kids with their spray cans messing up the cars when they on the move, us with our snowy white rags and our paint remover, ready to run in and wipe it off the minute the cars get to the terminal. I kinda like standing there like a soldier with my cleaning cart next to me, and my rags and my fluid and my mop and my broom, ready to attack the dirt and the litter and the graffiti to make this one dark corner of the world a little bit brighter.

La Virgen de la Altagracia, keep my mind on these parts of my life going good for a change so I can hold up under the pain of my Rosalba being gone. I feel like mi nieta, she has died, I can't help it, mi cuquita belonging to another. True, I don't have to worry about Bianca hurting her no more, or where the money for the rent is coming from, and my landlord, he been lying low since Miss Goldin got those lawyers on his case. But I never realized how much a baby fills up a home, her noise, her clothes, her toys and bedding and stroller and high chair and bottles . . . it is like the guts of my house have been ripped out and I am walking round in a shell. Even when Bianca is here with her trouble and her loud voice and her mess, my life still feels empty, and my arms still ache for Rosalba's little body and her soft, sweet smell.

La Virgen de la Altagracia, mend my heart fast so I can fill up my love need with my daughter. I know she needs me bad, and Virgencita, I need her, too.

Roberto

I think I'm getting through to Bianca at last. She was so mad at me after she found out what I done to Orlando I was afraid she'd dump me like she always be threatening. "It's none of your business, Roberto," she said to me. "You don't own me."

"But Bianca, what kinda man you think I'd be if I just sat on my ass doing nothing and knowing what that mothafucka did to you? You think I could live with myself like that?"

"Yeah, but it don't help almost getting yourself killed. Anyhow," she says, pouting up her pretty red lips, "you coulda asked me first. I don't want you messing in my life like I can't look after myself. It's my private stuff." But I think I got her to see my side of it in the end 'cause she let me give her a kiss. It's kinda scary for me to say, but I think she trusts me now. She knows I be looking out for her the best I can, she knows I be the only one in her life who counts. Ain't I the only person ever treated her nice? Ain't I the only one she could lay her little head on and cry? Ain't I had the patience of Job waiting for her to come round to loving me?

Believe me, I know what's what with Bianca. That's how come, when I was with her yesterday, I could tell something was bothering her the minute I saw the look on her beautiful face.

We was in Riverside Park, fooling round on the tire swing in that playground at Ninety-seventh Street like we do after school—I was pushing her round and round and she was squealing like a little kid. It was one of those sparkly fall days, when the sky's blue like ice and it makes you cold, but the leaves are all yellow and orange like fire, so it makes you warm. She was swinging, her bangs flapping up and down on her smooth forehead, her round mouth open and happy and we was laughing at all the little kids waddling in their snowsuits like penguins, when her mouth kinda freezes half-open and her eyes suddenly get wide and sad. I grab the swing and stop it. "What's wrong, babe?" I put my arm round her. "You look like you seen a ghost."

"It's her." She ducks her head down behind me like she be trying to hide. I look over and that's when I see Rosalba. I don't recognize her at first 'cause she's dressed in this weird outfit with baggy legs makes her look like a red clown, but then I see her cute little face. She looks just like Bianca, the same big eyes and curly mouth. She be sitting in a new stroller, looking up at this stumpy white woman who I can tell right away must be her new moms 'cause she be smiling and talking to the baby, unstrapping her round the waist and babbling some nonsense or other. The woman lifts Rosalba outta the stroller and stands up. "Let's get outta here before she sees us," Bianca says, and she grabs my hand and tries to run away.

"Wait up a sec," I say. "You go on home, Bianca. There's something I gotta do. See you later."

"Why?" she asks, still ducking and hiding behind me.

"I'll tell you later. You go on back home."

"Since when d'you get to boss me around?" Bianca folds her arms and flashes those pretty, big eyes at me.

"I ain't bossing you, I'm asking you. Just do me a favor. You'll be happy when I tell you."

We argue for a while, Bianca saying she don't want no more of my secrets after seeing my face from Orlando, but finally she goes home, looking mad, and I hang out by the tire swing and watch Rosalba and that lady till they make a move. They play a long time, feels like forever, while I get more'n more freezing, jumping up and down on both my feet and blowing on my bare hands, wishing I had gloves. This is a hell of a cold November. Even the playground, painted all these bright colors, red and yellow and blue, and those yellowy green dinosaurs they put up that look slimy like they're made outta snot—even this place ain't much fun in this weather. The lady don't seem to think so, though. First she pushes Rosalba in the baby swing a long time, then she slides her down the slide—my heart's in my mouth watching them 'cause I think the stupid woman's gonna kill her, but she don't let go of the baby, so it's okay. Then Rosalba wants the swing again, so they do that more. Jesus, I'm thinking, don't that woman got nothing better to do than spend two whole hours at the park in the middle of the afternoon? She gonna spoil that baby rotten if she don't freeze her ass off first.

Finally, the lady sits down on a bench, takes Rosalba on her lap and gives her a bottle, so I gotta wait more while the baby sucks it down. They look warm enough—the lady's got a pointy wool hat on makes her look like Santa Claus, and the baby's so bundled up she can't move her arms—but it's a different story for me. I swear my nose is gonna chip off like a piece of ice. At last I see the woman stand up, put Rosalba in the stroller, and start to push her up the hill outta the park. I hide behind a tree till they're ahead of me, then I follow them. Bianca told me the lady moved apartments after her husband dumped her but she don't know where to, so I'm gonna find out for her. I know Bianca won't be too happy about what I'm doing, but I be doing it for her, and one day, I believe deep in my heart, one day she gonna thank me for it. She can't let them take her baby away like this, it's wrong, and I ain't gonna let them do it. I keep telling her that and I know she don't listen to me, but one day she will.

So I follow that lady up the hill to Broadway and I hang behind a car while she goes into a fruit store decorated with pumpkins and these bright orange paper turkeys for Thanksgiving. Then I hide again while she stops to buy bread in this fancy bakery for rich people, where even the muffins got silver skirts; then again while she looks at some baby clothes in a window, where one tiny coat costs as much as the stuff Juanita wears in a year, and again when she goes into a supermarket and comes out with milk and diapers. By now the stroller's hanging with so many bags I'm sure it's gonna tip right over backward and spill Rosalba out on her head, but the lady keeps on walking and keeps on shopping till I be thinking, Jesus Christ, don't this lady got a bottom to her purse?

But I stick to it and I follow her all the way to Ninetieth Street, right between Amsterdam and Columbus, past the back of that old building they turned into stables, with horses peeking out the second-floor windows like they bought their own apartments, and those big gardens people be growing vegetables in among the weeds, and the projects on the left like giant blocks of concrete, and those fancy new red brick town houses on the right, and all the rest of that city crowdedness. I watch that lady struggle to carry the stroller and the baby and all those shopping bags up the steps of her own damn house, and she never even notices me.

Bianca

I got no place to feel at home. My house is filled up with
Mami's new boyfriend, this big fat man with a bushy mustache that gives me the creeps and glasses so thick his eyes
look like paddling pools. He and Mami moon round the
apartment holding hands like those valentine bears whose
paws are stuck together with Velcro, ignoring me like I don't
exist. She's even taken the plastic off the furniture so he can
sit his big ass down on the velvet like he's the president!
They make me feel like I'm nothing but in the way, but if I
go over to Roberto's house for some relief it's no better. His
aunt stares at me like I'm trying to steal away her precious
nephew, his little brother and sisters fight all over me like
I'm a piece of furniture, and he just starts preaching at me
about the baby till I feel worse than ever.

He says I only got one week left before the thirty days is
over, and after that the baby's gone forever. He keeps pushing and pushing me, acting sneaky and full of plans like my
opinion don't count for nothing. Ever since he beat up on
Orlando he thinks he's got the right to boss my life around.
Okay, so it was weird seeing Rosalba in the park with Sarah

Goldin pretending like she's her moms, but that don't mean I was ready to go do what Roberto did.

Three days ago he comes round after school and tells me he has a surprise. "What surprise?" I say. "I told you, I don't need no more surprises in my life. Cut it out."

"No," and his brown eyes are twinkling and sparkling like he's found the greatest present, "trust me. Get your jacket on, let's go."

I can't help it, he's got my curiosity up, so I follow him. He heads toward Amsterdam, stepping over the garbage, torn open and spilling its stinking guts all over my street, but I tell him I want Broadway 'cause I like the stores better. "But it's longer that way," he says.

"You don't have no right to lead me around like a kid, Roberto."

He throws up his hands and says, "Jesus Christ, Bianca," but he agrees, and we turn around. The truth is I don't like going anywhere near Amsterdam 'cause that's where Orlando hangs out with his dopehead gangbangers.

We go on down Broadway, which is getting all dressed up for Christmas even though we ain't had Thanksgiving yet, the windows glittering with little nodding Santas and tinsel and gold ribbon. We pass that place which sells kinky underwear, red panties with no crotch and those bras you're s'posed to stick on without straps like they'll hold your titties up with just glue—I never did understand how they work. Then we go past Mr. Aquino's liquor store. He's done his windows up in stockings and reindeers with plastic snow on their heads, which could look cute 'cept they're covered in dust 'cause he never cleans them. Next to his place a line of people is waiting in fronta the Korean news store to buy their lottery tickets—that always gets me down for some reason, seeing those sad people trying to change their tired old lives with nothing but a dollar. Then we get to those pawn shops that sit all in a row like dusty devils waiting to buy your soul, and I stop to look at some gold earrings, hoping maybe I'll find the ones the landlord's thugs took from me 'cause I heard these stores are where a lotta stolen goods end up, but Roberto tugs at my arm. "We wasting time, Bianca," he says. "Come on."

"Jesus, what's the hurry? And where we going, anyhow? You gonna make me walk all the way to Times Square?"

"Ten more blocks and that's it," he says, grabbing my hand.

"Don't push me around." But I follow him anyway, down blocks and blocks of stores, wondering what this loco is up to.

Finally, we turn left at Ninetieth Street and walk back over to Amsterdam, cross it, and go down a block with lots of trees turning yellow with the fall and that stinky ginkgo stuff making it smell like a hundred people vomited all over the sidewalk. I hold my nose, stepping over the dog shit, wondering what asshole planted those trees in a city. You ever notice how those stinky trees are only in the poor neighborhoods? Like along the top of Central Park at 110th? I bet there isn't a single one of those things on Fifth Avenue or in the Village or where those houses that look like palaces are on the East Side.

"Hey, Bianca," Roberto says, yanking at my sleeve. "This is it."

I look up and see this shabby old brownstone, with the paint crumbling on the stoop and cracks in the plaster. The front door has glass in it, that frosted kind, and I guess it's s'posed to look cool, though to me it just looks dirty. "Where's this at?" I ask, but Roberto's run up the stoop already and he's ringing one of the bells. I hear the buzzer and in we get.

"Don't that person use the intercom?" I ask him. "What a fool." But Roberto's still ignoring me. He's got this scary look on his face, with his teeth clenched and his eyes narrow and hard. I stop in my tracks and grab his arm. "Hey, Roberto, wake up. Are you listening to me? You tell me what this is about, else I ain't going another step."

But he shakes me off like I'm a flea and begins leaping up the stairs. I hope he's not taking me into some weird crack house. I always thought he was clean, but ever since he got beat up by that coño Orlando I decided you can never tell with guys, not even with him.

After we get up three flights of stairs, he stops in front of a green door and rings the bell. I'm behind him, my hands in my coat pocket trying to get warm, feeling like I don't belong here, when the door opens and insteada some tooth-rotting crackhead like I expected, there's Sarah Goldin, her cheeks all red and bright and her smile freezing into shock when she sees him.

"What do you want?" she says, quickly trying to push the door closed again. Then she glances past Roberto and sees me. "Bianca! What are you . . . ?" But before her sentence is out Roberto's pushed by her into the room, me right behind him.

Wow, what a change. Has this lady come down in the world or what? I look around the little living room and I can't help feeling kinda embarrassed for her. Okay, so it's sunny and the walls are painted a new white so it looks bright and happy, but it is *tiny* compared to her old place— I mean, Jesus, this whole apartment could fit into the bathroom she had before. And what a mess! Toys are all over the floor, there's a sofa bed in the middle with the sheets and pillows tangled up, a crib is stuck in one corner, and unpacked boxes are stacked against the corners. All this 'cause that husband of hers up and quit on her. I look at Rosalba, who's sitting in the middle of the floor, real cute in a little red dress and white tights, playing with a block and a rubber duck. The minute she sees me she hits herself in the face with the duck and begins to cry. I take a step over to help her out but Sarah gets there before me, grabs her up, and gives me a look like I'm a child murderer. Wait a minute, wait a minute, my brain is saying, but I'm too surprised at even being here to speak a word.

"There, there, little Rose," Sarah croons, rocking her and kissing away her tears till the baby stops crying. Rose? Since when's her name Rose? The baby looks at me, her big black eyes wet and scared, her nose running. I'd forgotten how long her hair was getting, black and wavy round her face, her thick bangs right down to her eyebrows like a Chinese doll's. Her lips are so red. I wonder if she remembers who I am.

"What are you doing here?" Sarah says then. "You're not allowed to do this."

"Don't be scared," I find myself saying. I don't want this to turn into some kinda ugly scene, but just when I'm looking for the words Roberto butts in.

"We wanna know what you're doing with Bianca's daughter," he says real loud, and he stares at Sarah with so much hate I can feel it heating up my skin.

"Get out of here!" Sarah says. "You have no right to force your way in here and talk to me like that. And you're frightening the baby."

I pull at Roberto's arm. He's acting like some movie Rambo, like he thinks that's gonna impress me. "Roberto!" I hiss at him.

"How did you find me?" Sarah says more quietly now. "Bianca, was this your idea?"

"Yeah, it was," Roberto says. "She misses her baby. She wants her baby back."

Sarah sighs. "Try not to shout, please, you're scaring her. You might as well sit down. If you'd just fold up the sofa bed there, you can sit on that. What's your name?" she asks Roberto.

"Roberto Valdes," he grunts while he's pushing the sofa bed back. Roberto Moron, I could add. We sit down and he puts his arm around my shoulders. "We come to tell you we want our baby back."

Sarah ignores him and looks at me. "Does your mother know you're here?"

"It's none of her business," I say, getting angry myself now. Why's she have to bring Mami into this? Who's she think the mother of that baby is, anyhow? "You and her been planning together from the beginning to take my baby away from me, and you can't deny it!"

"That's right!" Roberto says, and his arm tightens round my shoulders. "We're tired of being pushed around!"

"Calm down, both of you." Sarah shifts Rosalba up on her hip. Sarah's wearing this old navy blue sweat suit, I notice, and her hair looks like it hasn't been washed for a week. She looks a real slob. I guess she's learning what it's like to be a mother. "Let's talk about this like adults," she says then. "Shouting only makes Rose cry."

"What's this 'Rose' shit!" I yell. "That's not my baby's name!"

Rosalba begins to cry again, so Sarah walks back and forth across her messy room, soothing her, while me and Roberto sit on the couch. "See?" Sarah says, "I told you. We'll never be able to talk unless you are quiet and stop scaring her. Especially you, Bianca," and she gives me that baby-murderer look again. Suddenly I get this horrible thought creeping into my mind. Does she know about the pinching as well as the high chair? Did Mami betray me so much she even told her about that? "How did you find me?" Sarah says when Rosalba's quieted down.

"That ain't your business," Roberto says. "She has a right to know where her own baby is."

"I wasn't asking you. Will you let Bianca speak for herself, please?"

"She don't mind. I know what she wants." Roberto puts his hand on my knee.

"And what's that, I'd like to know?" Sarah pulls Rosalba's little head down onto her shoulder and strokes it. The baby's whimpering and holding on to that woman like a monkey hanging off a cliff. It makes me feel real weird to see Rosalba clinging to Sarah like that. Sarah's got her arms around her in this comfortable, protective way, the two of them fitting together like pieces in a puzzle, and I see Rosalba sucking on Sarah's shoulder, making this little round wet spot on her sweatshirt like a kiss. The whole thing makes this pain start up in my chest so all I can do is look down on my lap and swallow. "What has all this got to do with you, anyway?" Sarah says to Roberto.

"We gonna get married and take that baby back, that's what," Roberto answers. "I'm gonna be her daddy."

"Oh, you are, are you?" Sarah smiles in this nasty superior way that makes my blood hot. "Bianca's too young to marry you, Roberto. They could arrest you for statutory rape."

"I am not too young to get married!" I shout. "I already done it once. And what about your promise in court, lady? I don't see any man round here. Where's your husband at?"

The baby starts crying again, so Sarah has to raise her voice. "That's none of your business, Bianca, don't be absurd." She holds the baby's head against her and gives me a look like she wants to burn me up, but just then the buzzer goes again. She walks over to the door and presses the intercom. The doorbell rings and, this time, she squints through the peephole before opening it.

"Come in," she says, "I have company." In waltzes this tall white lady with blond hair and a wool coat on I can tell right away musta cost more than Mami makes in a month. The woman is pushing a stroller with a baby in it. She stops dead inside the room and stares at us like we're a couple of giant purple mushrooms. Rosalba catches sight of the new baby and stops crying again.

"Lucy, this is Bianca Díaz and Roberto . . . sorry, I've forgotten your last name."

"She's Rosalba's mother," Roberto says. "The rest don't matter."

"Oh dear," this Lucy woman says, pushing her stroller into a corner. The baby in it is asleep. He looks round and big and blond, like his mother. The woman walks over to us, puts her hands on her hips, and stares down at the two of us sitting on the couch. "You know as well as I do, kids, that it's against the agreement that you are here at all," she says in a voice like we're no older than the fat baby in that stroller. "I don't know why you came, but I can guess. You're not getting a penny out of Sarah and unless you get out right now we're calling the police."

"Lucy . . . ," Sarah says, but Roberto suddenly jumps up.

"We don't want your fucking money! We just want our rights!" he yells.

The blond woman doesn't even blink. "If you care at all about this child and her welfare, you will remove yourselves from the premises this moment. What you are doing is harassment, kids, and you can't get away with it."

"Roberto," I say, "let's go. This is getting to be a pain in the ass."

Roberto seems about to slug this Lucy woman he looks so mad, and I notice she backs away and kinda hides behind Sarah. I gotta say I don't blame her. "Listen," Sarah says to me, and now her voice sounds all friendly. "I understand what you're trying to do. You just want to make sure the baby is safe and happy, right? That's understandable. But don't worry"—she peers round the baby's head to look at me—"she's fine. She's healthy and comfortable here, she knows me now. We are happy, can you see that? You made the right decision, Bianca, you did. It is very hard and brave to give a baby up, but you did the right thing."

I stare at the floor the whole time she's speaking, noticing how clean the pink patterns on the new carpet are now and wondering how long they'll stay that way, but even though I'm trying not to listen, her words sink into me like little arrows of poison. "We gonna think about it," is all I can get out. "Let's go, Roberto, this whole thing stinks."

Roberto looks at me like he finally remembers that this is my scene, not his. He takes my hand and follows me to the door. "We'll be back!" he shouts, and slams the door hard behind him. We walk down the stairs, our footsteps echoing against the hard brown walls and the green iron steps, and we don't say a word till we get outside.

Finally, I turn on him. "What a fucking nerve telling that lady you're gonna marry me! You're not and you never will if you carry on like that!"

"But Bianca, I just don't want her pushing you round, that's all. She's a tricky bitch. I got more experience than you dealing with those people."

"What experience, asshole? You made me look so dumb in fronta her, interrupting me and acting so mean and scary. If you hadn't acted like that maybe she woulda let me hold the baby one more time, just to see how it feels. I didn't even get to kiss her or nothing. I didn't even get to touch her, Roberto, and it's your fault!"

"Oh Bianca, don't be saying things like that! It ain't my fault, it's that bitch's fault. She never woulda let you touch that baby. Didn't you see how she was holding her away from you like you got some disease?"

"Get your ugly face outta my sight!" I told him, and I went home alone, feeling like somebody big and heavy was jumping all over my heart.

For three days now, since that visit, it's been like I got somebody else's head on by mistake. I wish I could tell Mami what happened. I mean, I thought Rosalba was gonna get a rich mother and daddy, living in that palace with MTV and extra rooms and the park outside like her very own backyard. But instead she's living in two rooms with one moms and mess all over: that's no better than when she was with us! I mean maybe Sarah does kinda love that baby, but so does Mami. I feel like I been cheated, like Rosalba's been cheated, Mami, too. It's true what Sarah said, I did give that baby up so she could have a better life. But I don't see no better life with Sarah Goldin. All I see is a fuckup.

Teresa

La Virgen de la Altagracia, I need Your help with something personal only another woman can understand. Today at work me and Al had our first fight, and it hurts so much it is bruising my soul. I know he is a good man—please help him feel right by me so we can stay together. Big Al, he is the only good thing that has happened in my life for so long, and I need him bad.

This fight started 'cause I had a crisis at work about Rosalba, pobrecita, and her new life. I was cleaning up my spills, shoving my big string mop 'tween the feet of those boys who ride the trains all day long by their own little selves, and I think suddenly, Have I done Rosalba wrong? I worked on Miss Goldin for months to get her to take mi nieta, which not even Bianca knows, thinking it was the only way, and all of a sudden there I was filled with doubt as strong as a thunderstorm. Was there another way I didn't think of? Some other way that would not just end up with Bianca hating the baby even worse? This doubt, it made me feel so bad that when I saw Big Al at the end of my shift, I held on to him like I was drowning.

"What's the matter, little thing?" he said, grabbing my elbow. "You shaking like a leaf."

"Take me home, Al, I feel like I am gonna drop."

We sat on the train on the way home, not talking but holding hands, and my legs, which are always tired after eight hours on my feet, they were shivering in my boots. I thought I was doing right, making a sacrifice to save Bianca and to give Rosalba a chance to escape the Rodríguez curse and her jealous mamá, but suddenly I didn't feel right no more. I felt evil.

When we got home, Al sat me down and made me some coffee. He wouldn't let me do a thing. "You look sick, Teresa," he says. "You look like you getting some flu."

"No, I don't have no flu, Al. I just miss that baby so, and I worry 'bout her new mother. I hope she knows what she is doing. S'pose I made a mistake? I feel so bad."

"Teresa, stop that talk." He sat down at the table with me and put his big, hard hand over mine. "What you did was just fine. It's a sensible thing to get relations to help out when things get tough. You just feel bad 'cause you miss her, that's all."

That is true enough. Over three weeks have passed by since I gave her up, and I miss Rosalba more now than I did when she was first gone, her soft little hands on my cheeks and her giggle when I kiss her toes. "But Al, it isn't just that," I said. "It is making me sick inside that I won't ever see her again."

"What you mean? I don't understand." He took his hand off mine and he stared at me. "Can't you go visit her whenever you want?" And even though I shoulda known better, I told him the truth. He never knew before. Even in all the weeks we been rolling round together in bed I never told him about how I got this stranger to take Rosalba away 'cause Bianca was hurting her. He thought it was a cousin took her, not some white lady I picked outta the blue. "I feel like I sold my own grandchild," I told him. "I feel like I made some deal with the devil." I said all that 'cause I hoped he would tell me I did right.

"I don't understand," he said again, staring at me from behind his thick glasses. "Who'd you give her to?"

"This reporter called Sarah Goldin I met when she was doing a story on my landlord." I looked over his shoulder 'cause the expression on his face, it was giving me pain. He looked shocked, and worse, he looked disgusted.

"You gave her to some white lady who ain't even a relation?"

"Yes," I said, pulling at my knuckles. "She wasn't no stranger, Al. I got to know her over the months. Miss Goldin, she is a sweet woman. And she wanted her own baby so bad."

Big Al, he stood up then and stepped back, putting a distance between us he'd never done before, a distance that felt cold and wide. "I don't know 'bout that, Teresa," he said. "I don't hold with giving away our babies to no white people. They got enough of the world already."

That's when I got mad, Virgencita, forgive me. "White got nothing to do with it!" I said, standing up sudden and glaring at him. "It is love that counts, Al, not color."

"It's family that counts, Teresa. You gotta stick with family."

"Why? What is so great about families? My family didn't do no good. Nobody in my family stayed round to help. And don't you read the papers? What about all those fathers doing incest on their little girls, hunh? And those mothers beating their children with electric cords? Family is bullshit. Love and money, that is all that counts. What is the matter, Al, you don't trust my judgment?"

"You said yourself you getting doubts, Teresa. Sounds like you think yourself you mighta done wrong."

Now I was too upset to think straight, and I began saying the opposite of everything I was trying to say before. I only wanted Al to comfort me. "I don't think I done wrong!" I yelled. "Maybe it is you who thinks I done wrong!"

Big Al, he folds his strong arms cross his chest when I say that and looks at me a long time, like he is studying me. "Maybe I do, Teresa," he says, real quiet and serious. "Maybe I do." Then he picks up his jacket off the chair and walks out.

Oh Virgencita, why this punishment? I need so bad to have Al's good heart behind me. If he thinks I done wrong, then maybe I have. I am in so much pain not knowing. I gotta get him back, la Virgen de la Altagracia, please. If you do this thing for me, I will thank You forever, from the bottom of my heart.

Bianca

Mr. Jonas told me this morning he wants to see me after school today for a talk. I wonder what it's about. I told Yasemin and some of those other girls about it at lunch, like the dumb ass I am, and they woudn't stop teasing me. They said he be trying to get me alone so he can start up our romance. Thing is, I like him and everything, and I'd really like it if he likes me, but I don't know if I can handle this whole thing 'cause I got so much on my mind with the baby and Roberto pressuring me, and 'cause I been thinking about being alone with Mr. Jonas for so long that the idea of really doing it is making me sick with nervousness. Part of me wants to be alone with him, but part of me is real scared. He's a lot older'n me, and after what happened with that stinking coño I don't trust nobody 'cept Roberto, and I only trust him 'cause he's too stupid to do anything wrong.

It's funny that Mr. Jonas asked me that today 'cause just last night I had this real embarrassing dream about him. We was on Juan's bed in his home, like in the old days, and Mr. Jonas was explaining this math proof to me while his hands were going up my skirt. I been having a lotta these dreams about him to tell the truth. He's always kissing me and shit, and it makes it difficult to look him in the eye at school the next day. In the dreams he's real gentle, and younger—I think he's kinda mixed up with Juan. He's got his dreadlocks and deep voice, but he's smaller and skinnier, with Juan's hazel eyes. Then when I see the real him in the classroom the next day, he just seems old and annoyed and more like a daddy than a boyfriend. Dreams are spooky.

Still, now he's got me alone in the classroom, I feel so nervous I don't know what to say. "What's the matter, Bianca?" he asks me in this bass guitar voice of his, "is your mother expecting you home?"

"Yeah, I mean no, I don't think she'll mind if I'm late." I look down at his desk and rub a deep old scratch on it with my finger.

"You look worried," he says. "Anything you want to talk about?"

I look up at him, and all of a sudden it seems like it'd be great to talk to him about the baby and everything else on my mind. I mean, he seems to know so much, but he isn't all hard and snappy like Mami, or snooty like Miss Mandel. He isn't full of bullshit preachy stuff like Roberto, either. And it'd be a dream come true if somebody like that was in love with me, like when I was thinking about moving in with him. He gets up and walks round his desk, looking so fresh in his African shirt and his beads and these braided bracelets he wears all over his strong arms.

"Let's sit down," he says, and pulls up a chair for himself and me. We sit next to each other. His dreadlocks are almost brushing my arm and I can smell his aftershave, this musty scent that's like a bedroom in the morning. My stomach starts to flutter and my hands are trembling, so I stick them under my legs. I feel sick inside. I wait for him to try to kiss me or something but all he says is, "Okay, I'm listening. Now, what's the problem?"

I stare at the floor, trying to find the words to start with. How do you tell somebody outta the blue that you've given your baby away? Maybe he'll think I'm some kinda monster if I tell him, just some coldhearted bitch out only for myself. Maybe he'll decide I'm no different than the other ho's in this school, thinking 'bout nothing but men and babies and sharpening their nails for a fight. How do I tell him I gotta make up my mind in the next two days whether to get that baby back or not? I shift in my chair, wondering if he's gonna make his move and kiss me.

But he don't make the move. Instead all he does is sigh and look at his watch, like I'm nothing but a nuisance to be pushed outta the way. "Bianca? Are you going to tell me what's on your mind or not?" he finally says, his voice sending a tremble through me like a drum. But he sounds so cold and teacherish that I'm too embarrassed to look at anything but that floor. This lump comes up in my throat as big as an orange, so I couldn't talk even if I knew what to say. I feel like he's kicked me. How could I be dumb enough to think he wanted to kiss a stupid brat like me?

Mr. Jonas waits awhile longer, neither of us moving in our chairs. Anybody watching would laugh, the two of us sitting there like frozen mummies, but I don't know what to do or how to act. I mean all the men I know in my life are either old and ugly like Big Al, who you just make faces at behind their backs, or guys to flirt with. I don't know what to do round a man who doesn't want me.

Finally, he yawns and stands up. "Okay, you don't have to say anything if you don't want. Anyhow, I asked you here 'cause I want to set up some extra tutoring with you for the next few weeks. You're one of the smartest kids in math I've had for years, Bianca, and I want you to do extra well in the next tests so we can get you into a good high school. What do you think?"

All I can do is nod, sick with myself 'cause I thought he asked me here for love, when all it was is math.

"I'll give you a letter for your mother so you can get her permission. She'll have to sign it." He pauses, looking down at me, but I'm still paralyzed in my chair, feeling so dumb and ugly and embarrassed all I can do is sit there on my hands like a little kid on a potty, staring at this squashed gum next to my foot.

"See you tomorrow," Mr. Jonas says, and he walks out.

When I get home I go into the bedroom and shut the door, hoping Mami don't come in and mess with me. I lie down 'cause I need to think of some way to get this hurt outta my chest. It feels like this hand is squeezing my heart real hard, and it's kinda difficult to breathe. It's not just Mr. Jonas, it's Mami and the baby and everything. I feel like nobody but Roberto even likes me anymore, and even he's mad at me since I gave up Rosalba. I'm having such a hard time deciding what to do with my life and her life and all the people like Mr. Jonas who don't want me around it's giving me a headache day and night.

I lie there with these two sides making arguments in my brain, just like when my bad angel fights with my good angel. On the one side is Roberto, saying I been robbed of my rights and treated like dirt 'cause I'm poor and Dominican and nobody even thinks I got human feelings, and when he says that I get so mad at the world I wanna shoot somebody. Then on the other side is Mr. Jonas, who says he wants me to try out for a math prize so I can show the world teenage mothers aren't all stupid like the newspapers seem to think, and so I can make something of myself. . . . How am I s'posed to know who to believe? I don't think God created people to make decisions like this. There's something about civilization that is real fucked up, and now we gotta pay for it by thinking about things only angels and God should ever have to decide—things like whether to keep a human baby or give it away.

The thing is, I know Mami'd be so happy if I brought Rosalba home, never mind what she says. She's been looking so gray since that baby's been gone it's like all the light's gone out of her. I know she don't want me to even talk about the baby, but if I brought her home, like a surprise, and it was all legal and everything, I can just imagine the light coming back into her face. She'd be so happy she'd cry! And then she'd forgive me everything and love me 'cause I did the right thing, and we could be a happy family again. That's what my good angel says to me, anyhow. Or, maybe it's my bad. How am I s'posed to know?

I look at the clock on the dresser. In two minutes I gotta get up 'cause I promised Roberto I'd go for a walk with him in the park, but right now I just wanna lie here and never move again. I can see Mami's Virgen María staring at me from the altar, her beady eyes shining in the gloom like she got a spell on me. I guess whoever carved her tried to give her a motherly expression, but she just looks scary to me with that white paint in her eyes that glows in the dark. I wish Mami'd bought one of those plastic Madonnas that light up inside—at least they look friendly. This one comes from the DR, she said, and some cousin she once had a crush on made it for her, so she won't never throw it out. It haunts me, like some kinda spooked-out zombie trying to put a curse on my head. I stare right back at it to let it know I ain't scared. "Virgen María," I say out loud, "why don't *you* help me decide what to do 'bout this baby?"

I hear Roberto ring the doorbell, so I drag myself off the bed, run a brush over my hair, put on Mami's lipstick, and go down to meet him. I didn't speak to him for three days after we visited Sarah I was so mad at the way he acted with her, but he kept on coming round, looking at me with those sheep eyes of his like a little kid just begging for love. He's such a funny guy. I mean, to look at him you'd think, whoa, what is that, a fire hydrant? He's short and pudgy, and he's too small for his baggy pants; he's still got baby fat, for Christ's sake. But then those big eyes, and the way he does what he believes in, even like risking his life to teach that coño a thing or two. I don't know. He's got his own kinda power, I guess. Anyhow, I meet him on the stoop like we agreed and we go down to Riverside Drive to walk along the top of the park. It feels good to be with him today, somebody I know and trust, not somebody sexy and scary like Mr. Jonas, who makes me feel like I'm just a kid and not a woman. The trees along the path are mostly bare now, their leaves lying all over the sidewalk like presents, but it's real pretty with the river showing through the tree trunks, the old stone wall on one side of us and the little squares of grass on the other. It's kinda like walking around a castle if you look away from the ratty squirrels messing in the garbage and those homeless pissing on the stairwells. That's what I always liked about coming here—it feels old and grand and heavy, with big trees bending over us in an archway, and fancy paving stones like a hundred gray throat lozenges squeezed together in a puzzle. It seems real far away from my street, like I'm in an old movie from the days of horses and carriages and people in long cloaks and furs. It seems like a different world.

So me and Roberto walk along, not saying much, me thinking about Mr. Jonas and all the decisions I gotta make, when I see this young couple coming by just like us, pushing a baby stroller and holding hands. The girl isn't any older than me and the boy looks about Roberto's age and they are smiling and talking love words to each other in Spanish. How come she can do it? How come she can have her baby and keep her man and be happy—why can't that be me? She ain't so pretty—she's fat, and she's got this pasty skin—how come she gets happiness and I don't? It makes me miss Rosalba, seeing her, and it makes me think of Juan and my dreams again. If he'd stayed around like he promised I wouldn't be in this mess. I really loved him. We coulda been happy. I'm never gonna love anybody like I loved him.

Suddenly, in the middle of me feeling like I missed out on all the good things in life, Roberto tells me he wants to go see Sarah again by himself. He says she's smart and tricky, that she'll just talk me outta wanting the baby back before I even know where my feet are. He says he wants to handle it alone 'cause he's tough and he knows how to deal with these slimy white people. "Listen up, Bianca," he says to me, getting his preachy voice on again. "All that counts in life is love, the rest is nothing. Without love, it don't matter how much money you got, what kinda job you can strut out, or what kinda clothes you wear. Here you are letting this white woman take the one thing you got away, the baby's love for you. You just a little girl, a smart girl but a little girl, and you been hurt so bad it's like your life's got broke. So trust me, sweet thing, I'm gonna fix it."

"You don't know nothing about my feelings, Roberto, and I wish you'd quit acting like you do. Anyhow, it ain't your baby so what makes you think she'll listen to you?"

"She'll listen to me 'cause she has to. I'll make her listen, 'cause she knows what she done is wrong."

"She only wanted Rosalba 'cause she couldn't have her own baby. Is that so wrong?"

"Yeah, course it is. She stole your baby away from you, Bianca, 'cause she's white and rich and she's used to getting whatever she wants. It's got nothing to do with her own pain."

I think about this for a while, remembering what Sarah said in court that day. She sounded like she'd really love Rosalba to me, but maybe it was a trick, or maybe she just wants her 'cause of her miscarriage. S'pose she starts hating Rosalba 'cause she isn't her real baby, the one she lost? And what about a daddy for my baby? Where's he at? And why'd she have to go changing Rosalba's name, anyhow? What's wrong with her name?

"What about if she calls the cops?" I say. "That other lady said she would."

Roberto sticks his head up proud when I say that. "I don't care what she do, Bianca. I'm on the side of right, and God knows it and you know it, and that's all that matters. I'm gonna save that baby for you, Bianca, you wait and see."

Suddenly, I don't know why, I feel so angry I can't stand it. "Roberto?" I say. "¡Mama huevos!" I'm tired of other people making me do things. Mami making me give up the baby, Mr. Jonas making me take all these tests, the girls at school making me think he got a crush on me when I didn't even want that to begin with, and now Roberto saying he's gonna get the baby back like he thinks he knows what I want better'n I do. I am sick and tired of everybody pushing me round like this. So I turn to Roberto, who's standing stiff and strong like he's a soldier marching off to war, and I say to him, "Listen. I don't want you messing in my life no more, okay? I told you before! That thing with Orlando was bad enough, but this is my baby, it's my life, and I'm gonna make up my own mind. Leave me alone!" And I walk off outta the park leaving Roberto behind me, his mouth gaping open like a stunned fish.

When I get to a phone booth outside Woolworth's, which got its windows full of weird things like diapers for grown-ups, I pull out the card that social worker gave me after I signed the papers. I been keeping it in my pocket and looking at it almost every day, trying to decide what to do. I'm tired of waiting round with this sick feeling building up inside of me, getting worse and worse, like somebody stuck their hand in the guts of my life and pulled out the heart. I gotta fix this feeling for myself, and for Mami. So I push 0 on the phone, and I tell the operator that I wanna make a collect call to the caseworker whose name is on my card, 'cause I'm gonna tell her to get my baby back.

Roberto

I been lying awake in my room all night, afraid to fall asleep in case I fuck up my plans. I listened to Diego having some bad dream, his little fists punching out in fronta him in his sleep, and Juanita and Carmen whimpering next to him in the bed, disturbed I guess by his noise. I hope they ain't all dreaming about our dad. I heard my uncle grunting while he put on his clothes and went outta the door for his night-time security guard job. I even heard my aunt get herself to bed, praying and moaning in Spanish, her raspy breath rattling like a rusty old fan. Then I just laid there, listening to shouts and screams and sirens all night long, to bangs of cars or guns, who knows which, to that city rumbling noise like a song in your ear never stops, and I made my plans. No matter what Bianca say, I know she hurts inside and I know she needs me to help her out. I'm gonna make it so the sun comes back in her face and she won't be mad at me no more. I know she can't handle all this trouble she got now. She needs a man to do it for her, somebody whose soul ain't all confused by giving up love. I showed that Orlando he can't mess with her and get away with it, now I gotta show Bianca what she needs, too, and I gotta do it now.

Finally, when the light at the window's just getting a little bit gray I get up, put on my darkest sweats so I can hide in the shadows, and pull my hood up over my face. I slide my knife down in my pocket and tiptoe over to the bed where Diego and Carmen and Juanita are all curled up together like kittens, sleeping in peace now their nightmares be leaving them alone. I kiss them good-bye and sneak out before my aunt wakes up to make us breakfast. If everything goes right for me today, I'll be in school by eight and nobody'll know the difference.

Outside the street is real quiet this early, with those homeless sleeping next to the church in their cardboard boxes, and only one or two people going off to some job they be lucky enough to have. None of the daytime racket's started up yet, not the garbage trucks nor the street cleaner, so yesterday's mess—paper bags and cups, greasy food wrappings, broken bottles, crack vials—is still laying all over the ground, wet and muddy, and the whole street looks asleep in the gray-pink light. I wanna sneak into church for a quick pray to get some luck, but I look at my watch and see I don't got the time so I just cross myself in fronta that Jesus, shining up there on his pedestal so white. He got a new pair of hands, I see, the fourth pair I remember this year. They the wrong color for the rest of him, kinda greenish—they make him look like one of those amputees out of a war, with plastic hands that never work right. That Jesus ain't doing a very good job in this hood, I gotta say. Maybe if they painted him brown like all of us people who live here, maybe then he'd do better looking after our souls insteada watching funerals and losing his hands every month. I walk on over to Amsterdam, glad not even the dealers be around this early, and look up at the sky. It's this light, pearly blue, with pink streaks, real soft and pretty. By the time I get all the way down to Ninetieth Street, the first birds are just starting to sing.

It's cold out. My breath is puffing clouds in fronta me like a cigar. I can hear the horses snorting in those apartment house stables, but nobody else is around so I know this is gonna be easy. I walk up to the lady's stoop and ring one of the bells. "Yeah?" I hear this sleepy old man's voice say.

"Gas man" I call, and he buzzes me in, simple as that. I go upstairs and wait by the door. I'll wait all day if I got to. I know what I want.

Inside, I can hear the reporter woman talking to Bianca's baby. I figured she might be up this early, with a baby to wake her. Diego, he still gets us all up at six. "Come on, sweetie, time to get your sweater on," I hear her say, then she laughs. "No, no, little one, not Mommy's nose."

Huh, calling herself mommy. What a liar.

Then the lady begins to sing this really dumb song, in a voice so bad it squeaks like an old door.

Hello little baby, hello little thing,
This is my love song, to you I will sing.
Hello little mouth, hello little nose,
Hello little feet, hello tiny toes.
You are my baby, so little and light,
You are my baby, so sunny and bright,
I love you Rosy, with all of my might,
You are my baby, so sweet and so bright.

Okay, so the lady likes being mommy to this baby. I feel bad for her, I do, but Rosalba is not her baby and she is full of shit. It ain't right to make yourself happy by stealing happiness from other people. Just then the door unlocks and the lady comes backing out, pulling the stroller behind her. Rosalba's so bundled up inside of it she looks like a stuffed pillow. I sneak up behind and grab the woman by the arm, but before I get a chance to clamp my other hand over her mouth she lets out a scream so loud I jump right up in the air. She whirls around to look at me, the baby starts crying, and my heart's beating so hard all I can do is stare back at her.

"Roberto! How dare you?" she says. Her cheeks are flaming red and her light eyes look like they'll jump out at me. "You almost gave me a heart attack, sneaking up on me like that. I thought you were a mugger. What the hell do you think you're doing, you maniac?"

That makes me mad, calling me names like I'm just some nutcase, doing wrong 'stead of saving a baby. I push her against the door and reach for my knife in my pocket. She struggles against me, but I ain't been pumping all these years for nothing and I don't want this woman thinking for one moment I ain't the one got control here. "Go inside or else you'll be sorry."

"Oh, for God's sake," she mumbles, like she don't even take me serious, but she opens the door again. "All right. Just don't touch me or the baby or I'll kill you on the spot."

"I'm not here to hurt no baby." She got me all wrong, but she's gonna know soon enough. I see her rolling her eyes, though, and that makes me even madder. "Move it!" I yell.

"Okay, okay, calm down. I'll let you in, but I warn you I have friends coming around in five minutes and if you try anything you're going to end up in a prison cell."

"If you got friends coming round, how come you be going out? Get in there." What's she take me for?

She's just pushing the stroller back in the apartment when Rosalba drops her pacifier on the floor and cries even louder than before. I pick it up to give it to her, but the lady snatches it outta my hand. "Don't let her have it, it's dirty," she says. "Now I'll have to wash it." She sighs, like she's real annoyed. "I just spent hours getting Rose in all these clothes, and because of you I'll have to take them off again. This is such a nuisance, Roberto. What do you want, anyway?"

I follow her in and shut the door behind us. "I'm here to

take Rosalba home to her rightful mother." I watch her wash the pacifier and plug it back in the baby's mouth, then I cross my arms and spread my legs so she won't be able to push me around.

"There is no way in hell you are ever going to touch this child," the woman says, pulling off Rosalba's jacket and sweater. "What are you doing this for, Roberto? It's crazy, can't you see that? It's not going to help anybody."

"I know you think what you doing is right, lady, but it ain't. That's Bianca's baby. You know how much it hurts me to see you treating that child like it's your own? You can't take a child from its natural mother, it ain't right."

"Not by force you can't, that's true," she says, taking off her own jacket, then picking Rosalba up outta the stroller. "But Bianca agreed, Roberto, she agreed legally, in front of a judge. Rose is my child by law now. I am her mother. Bianca has given up all claim to her. You have no right to be here and no right to take Rose anywhere. Why are you meddling in this, anyway? I know you aren't the father."

"Yeah, but it was force! Not like snatching the baby outta her arms maybe, but by using your white power to force Bianca to give her up! That's a worse kinda force. You think she truly wants to give up that baby, lady? You think she knows what she's doing? Her and her moms, they both so sad they can hardly stand up straight. You stealing that baby from their love, and I don't know how you can look yourself in the mirror knowing how evil that be."

I can see my words sinking in 'cause the lady stares at me with her big gray eyes like I've shocked her. She shifts Rosalba up on her hip. "You don't know anything about it, Roberto," she says then.

"Oh yeah I do. I can see the whole fucking thing clearly. I know exactly how you white people work. You got the judges and the cops and the courts and everybody else on your side—what fucking chance we got to be treated fair?"

"Roberto, do you know what was going on with this baby when I got her?"

What's she talking about, this tricky bitch? "Yeah, course I do."

"You think she was in a safe, loving home, do you?"

"Well, maybe Bianca's kinda young, but I know sure as anything she loves that baby."

"Why do you think Rose kept ending up in the hospital, then?"

I shrug. What's the witch getting at? I look her up and down, trying to figure her out. She's dressed in this purple sweat suit, I notice, which makes her look even shorter and wider than she is. Her face is kinda pretty but she looks old, and, right now, she looks fierce.

"Do you have any brothers or sisters?" she says suddenly.

"Yeah, three."

"Well, you seem to care about kids. Are they younger than you?"

"What's that gotta do with anything?"

"You wouldn't like to know someone was hurting them, would you? If you did, wouldn't you want them to be somewhere safe?"

"What are you talking about?"

"You ask your girlfriend, Roberto. Or, better still, ask her mother. This whole thing was Teresa's idea in the first place, if you must know, so you are quite wrong in supposing I used any kind of force."

I watch her a moment while the baby plays with her hair, then I give my head a shake. This lady's like a snake charmer. She be trying every dirty trick in the book. She's dangerous! I pull out my knife and point it right at her. "Enough of that bullshit. Gimme Rosalba."

She stares at the blade like she turned to stone, and for what feels like years we just stand there together, my knife pointing at her gut, my mind willing her to do what I say.

Without taking her eyes off the knife, she starts slowly moving over to the phone hanging on the wall by her desk. I follow her, the knife still pointing, but I don't seem able to
move my arm. It's like paralyzed or something. She switches
Rosalba onto her other side, picks up the receiver, tucks it
under her chin, and dials 911.

"There's a man in my apartment with a weapon," she
says calmly, while I'm frozen like some kinda spell has been
put on me, and she gives them the address. "Yes, he's threatening me." She hangs up. "You'll never get Rose away from
me. The only way you'll get her is to kill me. Is that what
you want to do to Bianca? Get yourself put in jail for murder
and kidnapping so she'll be left all alone again? How's that
going to help the baby? You better leave, Roberto, before
they arrest you."

I don't say nothing to this snake woman, but I wave my
knife at her and she steps back, trying not to show her fear.
The baby twists in her arms, turning to look at me. When
she sees my knife glittering in the light she reaches for it.

"Shit!" I pull the knife away quickly. I don't want Bianca's
baby cutting herself 'cause of me.

"Get rid of that thing and get out of here before the cops
come, Roberto," the lady says quietly. "Go on, give yourself
a chance."

I fold up my knife, put it back in my pocket, and lean
against the wall. I ain't going nowhere without that baby. I
can already hear the police sirens but I ain't gonna let this
witch lady win out here, no matter what. "I'm only doing
what's right," I tell her. "They can arrest me if they want."

I hear the police car screech to a halt outside the door,
and I watch while the lady walks over and pushes the
buzzer. "At least get rid of the knife," she says, but I ain't
gonna budge. The cops bang at the door and when she
opens it, they stumble in and almost crash into me. Two of
them grab my arms.

"Don't you even ask if he's the right man?" the woman says. "He could be a friend, you know."

The cops look at her like she's crazy. "Is this the intruder, lady?"

She sighs and shifts the baby up her hip again. I see Rosalba staring at the cops in their blue hats and shining badges, kicking to get their attention. I guess she thinks they're some kinda clowns. "Yes," the reporter says, "but you don't have to be so rough. He's harmless." By now they've twisted my arms behind my back and it hurts, but I ain't gonna make a sound. They frisk me and find the knife.

"Okay, niggah, outta here," the cop says, shoving my hands into cuffs.

"We gotta take your statement," the other cop says to the lady. He pulls out his notebook.

The woman looks at me and I stare right back at her. Maybe my hood is knocked crooked, maybe I got a cop on each arm, maybe my hands are pinned behind my back like I'm nothing but a no-good criminal, but I'm still right. I give her this look I know goes down into her heart 'cause she says to the cops, "Look, he came in here and threatened me, but I know he wouldn't really hurt me. He's just a mixed-up kid here on personal business. Don't be too hard on him."

"Lady," says the cop slowly, like he's talking to a senile driver who just ran a red light, "you called 911, didn't you? Now do you wanna press charges or not?"

She pauses. "Yes, I do. I want him out of here. But I know about you cops. If you hurt him, the story'll be all over the papers. I'm a reporter."

"Look, you do your job, we do ours, okay? Now, tell me what happened."

The woman sighs but she begins to tell the story, and the cops spin me around and shove me out the door. The last thing I hear is the baby giggle.

Bianca

Roberto's uncle came round yesterday evening. I was real surprised 'cause none of his family's ever showed their face here before. He came all dressed up in his security guard uniform, looking proud and stiff, his tall, skinny legs like stilts under his blue pants, and his face old and serious. I woulda invited him in but Mami was out with Big Al making up their fight, and I didn't think he would come in anyhow 'cause he and his wife never liked me. He just stood there, his hat with its gold braids pulled down to his eyebrows like a soldier's, and he told me the cops came to his house the night before and said they got Roberto on charges of assault with a weapon and a bunch of other things. Roberto's in deep shit, his uncle said, and he gave me a look like it's all my fault. "I had nothing to do with it," I said. "That nephew of yours has always been crazy and you know it." He said the cops told him Roberto went to see Sarah Goldin and tried to take the baby away from her by force. Did that fool boy think he was gonna impress me with that crap? I don't hold with threatening women and babies with knives.

Listen, I know Roberto did this stupid thing 'cause he thought he'd win my love. But I woke up today after I cried all night, and I looked at my mother so worn out by her hard life, and I looked at myself and all my troubles and decided, hell, the last thing I need is to hook up with some boy who's in and out of jail for doing crazy things like that. I thought you were better'n that, Roberto, I thought you were serious, not dumb and fighting mad like the other boys on this block. I'm not impressed, I just think you're a fool.

When I woke up thinking about all this, I felt so bad I didn't even wanna move. It's the last day I can get my baby back, but I never heard a thing from that caseworker I called. When I got her on the phone she said she couldn't talk right then so could I call her back? I waited ten minutes at the phone booth, but when I started to call her again I got too scared to do it. I hung up in the middle of dialing. Now I don't know what to do. I could just go to school like it was any other day, and forget everything—let Roberto rot in jail and leave my baby alone with her new mother. Then I think, no, I can't even stand to think the words, her "new mother," it makes me feel so sick inside. I look over at Mami sitting there all quiet and sad, picking at her breakfast like it's made of sawdust, and I'm more confused than ever. Maybe if I get the baby back she wouldn't look so down anymore, like her heart's died inside of her and she's just dragging herself on for no reason. I want so bad for her to be proud of me again. She looks up while I'm thinking this and sees me staring at her, but insteada getting mad like she usually does, she says, "You okay now, mi hijita? I been worried about you. You been crying all night."

I shrug, "I guess."

"You wanna talk about it?" I stare at her face. Since when did she want me to talk about anything? Mosta the time she just be telling me to shut up. Maybe Big Al's teaching her to be nicer. "Is it something with Roberto, hunh?"

"Maybe." I look down at the table and start fiddling with the knife.

"What is happening with you and him, cuquita? Come on, you can tell me."

I don't wanna tell her—she'd be too mad—so I keep quiet and just scratch the table.

"Don't do that, Bianca, you know I can't stand that noise." I keep scratching. "Bianca!" I still keep scratching. Mami reaches out and slaps my hand. "I told you to stop that noise. Are you deaf?"

I cross my arms and kick under the table with my feet.

Mami gets up and begins pacing round our kitchen, which is hard to do since it's only about five feet wide. "Are you pregnant again, Bianca? Tell me the truth, now."

Pregnant! What's she think I am? I haven't let a boy touch me since that fucker Orlando. . . . not even Roberto. "You just think I'm trash, don't you?" I tell her. "You think I don't do nothing but sleep around with boys!"

"You not pregnant. Truly?" Mami looks so pleased I wanna smack her in the mouth.

"Is that all you care about?" I stand up, too, knocking my chair over, and grab my school things.

"Bianca, pick up that chair!"

"Sorry, Mami," I say, and I put the chair back on its legs 'cause I don't wanna be fighting with her no more. She's so surprised I did what she says she just stares at me.

"Biancita," she says at last, "I don't think mi hijita is trash. You know better'n that. I just get worried when I see you so unhappy."

"Mami?" I start to say, then I look at her standing there, her body skinny and hard like a tree that's been cut down, her face tired and wrinkling round the mouth with worry lines, and I don't know what to say. I wanna make her happy again, but just looking at her makes me feel so angry and weird inside I can't even talk. "I'm going," I say, and before she can answer a word, I'm out the door.

Downstairs I look around automatically for Roberto 'cause he always waits for me here, but then I remember why he's not there. I feel bad for a moment but I quickly put that feeling away. Fuck him, he got himself into trouble, he can get himself out of it. I begin walking to school, but when I see the bus come by on Broadway I find myself climbing onto it instead. I don't know why I'm doing this, but my feet, they seem to know where they wanna go. I sit down at the front and ignore the old lady standing in the aisle sending me dirty looks—nobody gave me a seat when I was pregnant, so it's their turn to suffer now. I look out the window; it's gray and depressing outside, everything looks dirty. Maybe I'll just stay on this bus forever, let it carry me away someplace where I don't have to try to figure out what's right or wrong. I close my eyes and rest my head on the windowpane, letting the bus rattle and bump my brain till I feel kinda dreamy and smooth. Yeah, I'm not gonna think anymore, it hurts too bad. I'm just gonna let my mind drift and my feet take me wherever they wanna go.

When the bus gets to Ninety-second Street my feet make me get off and push me down Broadway. I know they're taking me to Sarah Goldin's house but I don't know what I'm gonna say when I get there, so I keep walking, kinda curious about what I'm gonna do, like I'm watching somebody else. The air is cold and I wonder why I gotta be out here insteada being in school, where at least it's warm, but I guess my feet know something the rest of me doesn't. I see Sarah pushing Rosalba across Broadway at Ninety-first and I'm not even surprised. I just feel like fate's put me in a tunnel with only one direction to go.

I watch her get closer to me, register me, then try to walk on like she don't see me, but my feet make me stand in her way. "Oh, hi Bianca," she says, trying to cover up with this fake smile. "You're getting pretty good at hunting me out."

I shrug. "It's the last day," I say. "I came looking for you 'cause I wanna talk. I was gonna go to your house."

"Oh God, can't you leave me alone?" She stops and stares up at the sky, her gray eyes reflecting the clouds. Then she looks back at me. "You want to come to a café with me? I was just going to get a snack."

"Okay." I shrug again and walk beside her in silence. I don't wanna look at Rosalba, it's too painful, but I hear her babbling under her rain cover.

We get to a fancy coffee shop and Sarah finds us a table in a corner. She turns the stroller away from me, I notice, like she's afraid of what the baby'll do if she sees me, and she hands her a piece of melba toast to chew on. "You want some coffee?"

"Nah, I'll take Coke. A doughnut, too."

"I don't think they have doughnuts. How about a croissant?"

"Whatever."

She orders from this Arab-type waiter, then she says, "Listen Bianca, before we start on this I want to ask you a favor. Don't shout or raise your voice, okay? I don't want you scaring the baby."

"What you mean, scare her?"

"I mean she cries when she hears loud voices, remember?" She narrows her eyes at me like this is my fault. "Now, what did you come to see me for?"

"Well. . . ." I pick up a fork and start digging at this cigarette burn in the table. "I been thinking."

"How's your mother?" she asks all of a sudden, and I feel this idea come into my head like a motor starting.

"She feels bad," I say, real quiet and sad. "She's so unhappy since the baby's been gone, you wouldn't believe. I think she wants it back. That's what I came to see you about."

"I don't think so, Bianca. Your mother and I talked this over a lot, you know. She does love the baby, you're right, but she loves you more. She decided it was more important to keep you happy, and she couldn't do that with Rose— Rosalba in the house."

"She don't love me more. She hates me since the baby's been gone."

"She had a choice, Bianca, you know that. She could have kept Rosalba and had you sent away. But she chose to keep you instead. That's not an act of hatred. You should appreciate that."

I look down at the table 'cause her words are making me hurt inside. "But I miss the baby, too," I say. "I went through a hell of a lot to have it."

"I know you did," Sarah says quietly. "It must have been really hard." Then she reaches out and touches me with her hand, which makes me jump I'm so surprised, and I look up at her, kinda shocked. She's never acted like she remembers I'm the mother before—she's always treated me like I'm just some bratty kid in the way. "Bianca?" she says then. "I don't want you to think I don't appreciate what you're going through. It's very brave, and I'm sure it's very hard, even though it's for the best. I really admire what you're doing, do you know that? I haven't had my own baby but I did have a miscarriage once, so I know a little of what it must be like."

Bullshit, you don't know nothing about it, I think. But I do feel kinda glad she's trying to be nice. Maybe she isn't the bully I thought.

The waiter comes up with our coffee and Coke just then and Sarah spends some time putting in sugar and stirring and stuff. Rosalba is still sucking on her toast. I can hear her little slurps. "Are you back in school?" Sarah says suddenly in this cheery, ordinary voice like we're not talking about human lives.

"Yeah," I say, watching her face to see what she's up to. "My teacher says I'm a math whiz."

"Good for you!" She smiles. "Keep it up. Maybe you'll get to be a math teacher one day."

"Like hell I will." I pick up my pastry and bite into it. It isn't even sweet.

"It could happen, you know, if you work hard. I do stories for the paper sometimes on kids who win those national science prizes, and I'm sure you're as good as any of them." She takes a sip of her coffee. "Is it true that you're going to marry Roberto?"

"No way!" I stuff the croissant in my mouth and chew on it, hard. "He been hanging round talking that way for months, but I ain't interested." I think of Orlando and Mr. Jonas and Juan. "I don't like men."

"A pretty girl like you? Why not?"

"They're all shits." Sarah nods like she agrees with me. "Still," I say, "I kinda wish Roberto wasn't in jail."

"Yes, me too. He did pull a knife on me though. Did you know that?"

"I heard." I feel embarrassed for Roberto. Poor dummy. I know he meant to do good. "He's not like that mosta the time, y'know," I say, feeling like I gotta stand up for him. "He's never been in trouble before. He's like a daddy to his little brother and sisters. He's even got a job and he's gonna graduate high school this year."

"Really?" Sarah looks guilty. "I tried to get him to leave before the police came, but he wouldn't no matter what. He refused to try to save himself at all. It was strange."

I roll my eyes. "He's so dumb. Full of crazy romantic ideas. He listens to too much radio. He's like a walking love song! You know what he used to do? He used to stand outside my house staring at my window every day! And he wrote me these weird love letters. I coulda died of embarrassment." I chuckle and sip my Coke.

"What's going to happen to him? Have you seen him?"

"Nah. Not going to, neither."

"Why not? He probably needs to see a friendly face. How old is he?"

"Eighteen."

"That's too bad, it'll make things worse for him. Is he really that old? He looks sixteen to me."

"I know, he's kinda funny looking, but he is." Suddenly I feel sad again. I pick up the fork and go back to digging. "You really think I oughta go see him?"

"Yes. He probably needs you, Bianca. Does he have family you could go with?"

"His uncle and aunt hate me. They think I'm trying to get him to marry me. They don't know it's the other way round. His moms is dead, and his dad's in jail."

"What about your mother?"

"She won't go."

"That poor guy. He's really messed things up, hasn't he?" Sarah sighs and frowns, taking a deep breath like she's finally gonna spit out what's on her mind. "Okay, Bianca, how about this," she says at last. "If you go to school right now and agree not to bother me anymore, I will drop the charges against Roberto and get him out. I'll even get him a good lawyer if he needs one. Deal?"

I raise my eyebrows. What the hell is this lady talking about? What does she think we are, trading cards? "No deal," I tell her. "I ain't trading my baby for Roberto—you should know better'n that, lady! You oughta drop the charges anyhow, if you got any sense of right and wrong." She takes a deep breath, her big eyes narrowing, but I keep on talking 'cause her words have made me real mad. "Listen, I didn't come here for no small talk, and I didn't come here to make no deals, either. I'm getting the baby back. I already called the caseworker and she's gonna take you back to court like the judge said I could."

"Oh, Bianca!" She shakes her head sadly. "You don't have to do this. You and your mother will be much happier if you just stick to your decision."

"Don't gimme that bullshit! Mami made me give that baby up 'cause she thought it'd make me happy, and I gave it up 'cause I thought it'd make her happy, and now we both be so unhappy we can't hardly speak! It's dumb. She belongs with her family, with the people who made her. We made a big mistake, and now I'm gonna fix it and nobody's gonna stop me."

"But your mother can't afford to keep both of you, Bianca! How do you expect her to work and look after you and Rose with no help? Remember what happened before?"

"I'll get a job. We can take turns. People do it all the time, y'know. Mosta the girls in my school kept their babies and nobody's trying to tell them it's wrong!"

I notice her hand reach for Rosalba's stroller and grab it tight around the handle, like I'm gonna snatch it away. "Look," she says, "I understand why you feel bad. Giving up Rosalba was probably the hardest thing you've ever had to do in your life, and of course it's going to hurt for a while. But it's the strong thing, the right thing, Bianca. You and your mother will get over it. Why don't you just help her out and show her how much you appreciate her sacrifice? Then you'll see it was worth it."

"*Her* sacrifice! What about mine?"

Sarah sighs, still keeping her hand on the stroller. "Bianca, I don't think you've understood what happened. You proved yourself not only incapable of looking after this baby, but dangerous, too. Why did Rosalba end up in the hospital twice? Who was pinching her all over her legs? You think somebody who loves that baby would do such things to her? Goodness, Bianca, you even call her 'it' when you talk about her, do you realize that? Your mother told me that Rose flinches every time you walk in the room, and even I can see how she reacts to your voice. Babies don't forget when people have hurt them, you know. Your mother had to get her out of harm's way, you left her no choice."

"That's a lie! Anyhow, it's over now! I only did it a few times, and I ain't done it for months. I know it was bad, but Mami, she loves that baby much more'n you or anybody else can. It's killing her to give it up."

"Look," Sarah says, and she tries to make her voice kind, though I can hear she's desperate underneath, "it's sweet of you to do all this for your mother, but are you really so sure you'd be doing her a favor? Think of all the problems she had because of the baby before—you think those would be any different now? And what about Rose, Bianca? She's used to me now, and she's afraid of you. Anyway, you can't keep taking her in and throwing her out like a Ping-Pong ball. Don't you think of her feelings at all?"

"She don't know feelings yet. She's just a baby. Anyhow, she's only been with you a month—she been with us the whole rest of her life, so it's us she's used to, not you. And you broke your promise about a daddy for her, didn't you? And what about when she's older growing up with a white lady and knowing she's different every time she looks in the mirror! Have *you* thought about that?"

Sarah's face goes pale and she clenches her teeth together like a lioness. "That doesn't matter, Bianca, and you know it. All that matters is that she has a family she can depend on to be safe and loving."

"That's what I'm saying. Mami's the one who loves her. Me and Mami are her family, lady. Since she's been gone it's like somebody died in our house. You can get another baby, some baby nobody wants. We want our baby back and you can't stop us!" I get this burning in my eyes when I say this, my feelings so strong they sting like acid, but the inside of me feels like I'm not sure what I'm saying is true. Sarah just looks madder'n ever.

"You think the court is going to believe you after what you've done? If you take me back to court, I'm going to do everything I can to prove that I have a better home and a better life for that child than you can ever provide. You think you'll have a chance of beating that?"

That's all I need to hear. I know what kinda person she is now—I was right all along. I know I don't want nobody like that bringing up my child. I stand up, my chair falling over with a crash, which makes Rosalba cry, and I yell, "Roberto's right! You are just a racist thief, using your money and your power to steal my baby! I'll see you in court, bitch!" And with that, I run outta the café and into the rain.

PART FIVE

Teresa

Virgen, I don't even know if I should thank You or curse You for what You been putting me through. Bianca, she has changed so much these last weeks I hardly know my own daughter to look at her. Her whole life, she been sitting round thinking about her own sweet self, letting everybody else do the work and the deciding, just sitting there on her little butt like a guayaba waiting to be picked. And now she has taken charge for the first time in her short life, and mi Dios, that niña, she sure can shake things up.

She took us back to court, me and Miss Goldin, all them lawyers, the caseworkers—we all had to go just 'cause Bianca, she wanted it. "Mami," she says to me. "Mami, I made my mind up. I want that baby back. She is my flesh and blood, Mami, yours, too. I don't want no stranger white lady robbing me of my child."

I never heard her talk like that before, so I just shut my mouth up for a change and let her at it. "Mami, what you think?" she said, and her smooth brow wrinkled up all worried and sad.

"Bianca, pobrecita," I answered, "I don't wanna tell you

what to do no more. You never showed no interest in that baby before, was only me who loved her. You think you could love her, too? 'Cause I can't keep her for you if she comes back. I gotta stay in this job if we don't wanna end up homeless."

"I'll quit school, Mami. I'll quit and look after her. I can go back when she's older, right? Or get one of those GEDs? I heard of girls doing that."

I stood up then, put my arms round mi hijita, and kissed her silky head. "Mi muñeca," I said, "you too young to quit school. It is against the law. But you do what you think is right. If you think Rosalba, she can have a better life with us, if you can look after her good, I will stand behind you and I will go back on that night shift. But you gotta do it 'cause you want Rosalba home, not 'cause you don't like Miss Goldin or 'cause you wanna please me. And don't forget, mi chula, Miss Goldin loves that baby, too, and she's gone to a lotta trouble 'cause of us. She even lost her husband over Rosalba. It is gonna break her heart if we take that baby back."

Bianca stepped away from my hug then and looked at me. "It's you made her take the baby, Mami, not me or her. She can always get a baby someplace else."

"I did it to free you up, Bianca, and I did it to protect Rosalba from you," I said, my voice quiet 'cause I felt a little scared to be speaking this truth. Then I looked at mi hija, hard. "I know this is a tough question to answer, Biancita, and it is a tough question to ask, too, but are you gonna stop hurting her if she comes back? 'Cause if you don't, the whole mess is gonna start up all over again, but worse than ever and with no way out."

Bianca, she threw herself down on the kitchen chair when I said that, but her mouth was set and firm. "I don't know, Mami," she said, real quiet. "All I know is I don't want your heart breaking 'cause of me. I've given you enough trouble."

When I heard those words of love, my eyes they stung with tears. It was like my old Bianca, the little girl who used to hug her arms around her Mami, she was back again after a long trip away from home. "Bianca, mi cielito, you do what you think is right," I told her again. "I love you, child. You go ahead." The truth is, I didn't have the guts to stop her. I been waiting so long to hear that girl express some feeling for Rosalba or for me, some feeling that isn't about just her selfish little self, that when I heard her finally say those words of kindness my heart opened like a dying flower in the rain.

So she took us back to family court and, mi Dios, it was ugly. Miss Goldin was there, looking pale and worried, and I did feel bad for putting her through so much trouble and pain. She must be cursing the day she met me. She was holding Rosalba in her arms and it was good to see mi ángelita one more time, even though it hurt my heart. She has grown so much, her back straight and strong, her little legs slimming out with the crawling. And that face! Her eyes looking round at everything new to see, her cheeks so smooth you could die, her mouth red and round like she just sucked a cherry. Miss Goldin had her dressed in a green velvet party dress with white tights—she looked like an angel and a teddy bear all in one, and my arms, they ached to hug her next to my heart again. Miss Goldin was trying to hold her so she wouldn't see me, but I saw that little thing turn round and stare at me, her eyes big and curious like maybe she remembered me. Big Al, he had to hold me up it hurt so bad to see that baby looking at her abuelita from some stranger's arms.

Miss Goldin, she fought hard. She got the doctor from the hospital to come and say she found those bruises all over Rosalba, and to talk about the accidents on the bed and

in the high chair. She got some fancy blond woman in a silk
suit to say she was a good mother, and that Bianca and her
boyfriend had come around threatening everybody about
the baby, proving they weren't responsible adults—that was
a surprise to me and I stared at Bianca when I heard it. And
then she stood up and told herself about how Roberto, he
had come waving his knife at her and telling her he was
gonna take the baby away. So that's how that loco ended up
in jail, Bianca never would tell me. I just thank You, Virgencita, that Miss Goldin never found out about Miss Mandel
coming round to check up on us, but by the time that doña
and her witnesses were finished, she'd made my whole family sound like a bunch of malandros.

But we had a lawyer, too, although it was only some
tired-out guy from legal aid. Those bruises were nothing, he
said, they don't make proof of abuse, nobody at the hospital
reported anything about abuse, and the last two doctor ex-
aminations showed no more signs of any trouble. Bianca is
her birth mother, he said, and blood counts more'n what
kinda job you got or where you live. Roberto is not part of the
family, he went on, and his actions had nothing to do with
us. Even Big Al, he stood up in court and said I been working all my life, I never got in trouble, and I could give that
baby a good home. And for a while I believed it all and forgot myself why I worked so hard to give my Rosalba away.

After we were all done, we sat down and waited on the
judge, that same nice lady we had before, while she frowned
and leafed through some papers for what felt like ten years.
Once I saw her look up and stare over her glasses at Bianca,
but mi hijita was too busy kicking the floor to notice, her
smooth little face troubled and full of doubt. Big Al, he held
my hand so tight I could feel my pulse struggling under his
fingers like a mouse trying to escape. And me, well I was just
numb, numb from not knowing what to hope. If Rosalba
comes back to us, I was thinking, I will love to have her, but

our troubles, they will just begin all over again. Even if Bianca has grown outta hurting her, will she really be able to look after that little child, giving up all her hopes for herself? Won't that make her mad at the baby all over again, mad at me, too? And what about mi Rosita? Will she be able to forget her fear of her mother and live with her again? Señora Judge, I was thinking, I am so glad it is you that's gotta make this decision, and not my poor muddled self.

Finally, the judge, she slapped her hand down on the papers and barked out, "Mrs. Díaz, would you please stand?" Bianca jumped in her chair like she been pricked, then stood up quick. The judge stared at her over the top of her glasses. "This case has become unfortunately complicated," she said, and her voice was strict but not unkind. "You are the birth mother and I do not believe anyone but you should be making decisions over the fate of your child. However, I am seriously concerned for the safety of that child in your home, and I am not happy about the frequency with which you seem to change your mind. Therefore, I want you to answer a few questions. I want you to think hard before saying anything to the court, and to tell the complete truth. Are you ready?"

Bianca, she held her head up high when the judge said that, and she said in a shaking voice, "Yes, Your Honor," and my heart filled up with pride at this young lady who is my child. She has come so far, muchas gracias la Virgen, and now I am sure she is gonna go farther.

Then the judge said these words just like the ones outta my own mouth. "Now tell me, Bianca, do you honestly believe that you are no longer going to hurt that baby in any way?"

Bianca flinched at this like she was slapped, and she looked at me for a minute, her eyes wide and scared. I nodded at her. "Tell the truth, mi lechuza," I whispered. Her eyes dropped down to her hands. There was a long silence, everyone holding their breath.

"Bianca," the judge said. "Try hard to be honest. Put aside your anger, your feelings about yourself, and just think of the baby. Will she be safe with you?"

Bianca opened her mouth, then shut it. "I don't know," she finally said, just like she'd said to me, and her voice was shaking. She looked at me again. Once more I nodded, praying to You, Virgencita, to help her see into her own heart. "I feel like I got more control now," Bianca said at last, "but I can't swear it'll never happen again. That's the truth, Your Honor."

The judge nodded, the lights flashing on her glasses. "Good girl, that's an honest answer. I have another question. The report here from the caseworker suggests that your mother coerced you into signing the surrender papers. I want you to think about this carefully now. This is not a homework assignment, this is about the life of a child. Do you in all honesty feel that you were forced in any way to sign that surrender?"

Bianca looked down at me again, sitting next to her with the sweat soaking my armpits and the back of my dress, and I met her eyes for a second. My shame came up strong then and I realized how much I been pushing mi hija around on this to suit my own needs, and Rosalba's, too. That evil doubt, the one that hit me in the subway, it came back so hard I had to lean against Big Al just to take Bianca's eyes on me without falling over. I felt like her eyes were drilling through to my darkened soul. I thought I was doing the right thing, but sitting in that courtroom I didn't know anymore right from selfishness, wrong from sacrifice. I felt like I lost even which way is up, and I had no choice but to leave it to Bianca.

Finally I heard mi hijita take a deep breath, and I looked up again to see her lift her head to the judge. "Your Honor," she said, "my mother didn't make me do nothing against my will. She was just a step ahead of me knowing what I wanted."

"So you signed that surrender willingly? You did want to give up the baby?"

Bianca looked down at her fingers, twisting in each other like knitting yarn in a tangle. "Yes, Your Honor," she said so quiet the judge had to lean forward to hear her.

"And why, Mrs. Díaz, have you changed your mind now?"

Bianca glanced at me, and I saw her face was red and full of shame. "I . . . I wanted to do it for my mother. She misses the baby so bad."

"Dear," said the judge, while the tears came rolling hot and heavy down my cheeks, "that is all very well and fine, but it is the baby's welfare that counts here, not placating your mother. Do you understand the difference? I want you to think not of your mother, not of yourself, but of that little child over there." The judge pointed to Rosalba in Miss Goldin's arms, but I could not look for the pain in my soul. "I want you to tell the court, when you are ready, where you think the baby will best be served."

Bianca put her hands on the table in front of her like she might fall over, but she kept on her feet. She mumbled something but not even I could hear it and I was right next to her, crying in my chair like a child.

"What exactly are you saying, dear?" said the judge. "Try to make yourself as clear as possible. This is very important."

"I . . . I guess I'm not ready," Bianca said at last, the words coming out slow and painful. "I wanted it for my mother, but I see now that don't matter the most for the baby. I guess I think she'll do better with Sarah Goldin."

"You are certain now?" the judge said in this quiet, gentle voice. "Be careful. This has to be the final decision."

Bianca nodded, but I could see the words couldn't come outta her mouth no more. Then she looked over at Miss Goldin, whose face was dead white, her eyes pleading with

Bianca like a beggar dying for a last crumb. Miss Goldin was holding Rosalba tight on her lap and the baby was snuggled up next to her chest, asleep and peaceful. "You keep her, Sarah," Bianca said then. "I'm sorry for the trouble. I just had to work things out, y'know?"

Miss Goldin, she nodded, and this smile broke out all over her face like a curtain lifting to show the spring.

"You may sit down now, dear," the judge said, and she picked up that little hammer and slammed it down, and said the words I know will be haunting me the rest of my life. "The court sees no reason to disrupt the present arrangements. The infant will remain with her adoptive mother, with no further interference." Then she looked over her glasses at me. "Mrs. Rodríguez, may I suggest that you engage in some counseling for your daughter, and make sure that birth control is available to her?" I nodded, the blood rushing to my face. Then the judge looked again at Bianca, who was biting her lip, and said her final words.

"Mrs. Díaz, I congratulate you on your honesty. You just did a very difficult thing. Now go back to school, child, and let's have no more babies until you are fully grown, all right?"

"Yes, Your Honor," I heard Bianca mutter, and I looked over at her through my tears to see how she was taking it. And you know what, Virgencita? I saw this little smile at the corner of her mouth, just tickling there like a child taken with mischief. A little smile of relief.

So here I am at my altar, a sinner on my knees, praying to thank You, la Virgen de la Altagracia, for the lessons we learned. I know my heart it will always ache for Rosalba, but I am drowning my pain in giving attention to Bianca and to Big Al. Miss Goldin, she has got mi nieta for her own self now, maybe like You planned from the very first day You brought that woman into my life, and I know she is gonna give that sweet baby plenty of love. Give Rosalba a good life, Virgen, free of fear and bad memories about her mamá, and free of the Rodríguez curse. And if she grows up happy, I hope, one day, she will thank You in her prayers for this.

But most important is my Bianca. For a long time she seemed to be collecting troubles like other girls collect hair ribbons. She came up without me somehow, with a husband run back to la República and a boyfriend in jail and a baby in somebody else's home—already her life seemed as messed up as mine. But now she has lightened up so, laughing with her friends and acting normal like a kid insteada like some worn-down old lady at almost fifteen. I gotta thank You for steering my Bianca the right way up, Virgencita, and for teaching her to care about me and family and not just her own cute self. It has been a hard lesson but I know, at least for Bianca, we done the right thing. Maybe if we had money or family, if Bianca's papi had stayed around earning an income, if Bianca wasn't so young, maybe if all these things had been true I coulda kept mi nieta. But it wasn't like that so I guess it had to happen. I won't ever be all easy in my heart about giving away Rosalba, but I know I gotta accept life for what it gives me. It is Your way.

Thank You, la Virgen de la Altagracia, for listening to my prayers. Amen.

Bianca

Some things never change. I feel like I been to hell and back going through all that court shit, having to stand up there in fronta everyone and expose my most intimate feelings, but Roberto's come back acting like nothing's happened, as if the world stopped when he was gone. He's as crazy in love with me as ever. I don't know if I'll ever get rid of him.

He got outta jail 'cause Sarah Goldin dropped the charges against him. I don't know if it was 'cause of getting to keep Rosalba or just 'cause what I said to her made her face up to the shit she was doing—but anyhow, they had to let him go. He said the cops roughed him up a little but he's okay now, and he grinned at me like I was s'posed to congratulate him or something. I told him he wasn't gonna get no sympathy from me. "You loco, Roberto," I said to him. "The sooner you learn you can't take over my life and be doing violence and stupid things to impress me, the sooner we can be friends again. You look after your little sisters and brother, estúpido, and mind your own business. Whatever happened to you, you deserved it." Roberto looked real ashamed when I said that, his big eyes sad and droopy. I guess he thought he was being some kinda hero. That's what comes of listening to too many love songs, if you ask me.

So, him and Clara and me, we be hanging together like the old days before Juan or Rosalba or Sarah or anyone came along messing in my life. Clara got herself pregnant with that shady guy she been seeing, but she hustled off to a clinic for an abortion real quick after watching what I went through. Some days I think things woulda been a lot easier if I'd done that, too, but then I remember the baby's little red mouth and I can't think about that no more. Maybe Rosalba made me and Mami unhappy for a while, maybe she being born did make me do some things I'm ashamed of now, but I gave her up for a better life than I got, just like Mami made sacrifices for me, and that's how the Rodríguez family is gonna make it in the end. Maybe Rosalba won't even have to make sacrifices at all to make it, not for herself nor for her own kids if she has any. Maybe her life with Sarah will take care of all of that, and one of us, at least, will have it easy.

Sarah wrote us and said she and Rosalba moved back into her old apartment, that fancy one with the fans and the trees outside, 'cause she won it in the divorce when her husband never came back from Boston. She told us the baby is walking already, way ahead of her friends. She sent us a photo, too, showing the two of them cuddling on a couch, Rosalba laughing with her beautiful eyes all lit up and Sarah resting her lips on her head. It made me and Mami both cry. I guess all the shit I put Sarah through made her really know she wanted that baby. It's weird to think of, but maybe, in the end, that was my good angel at work after all.

School's going good most days, too, though I am sick and tired of those cranky pregnant girls. I'm gonna change to a regular high school next semester now I got no baby to worry about, and I'm really happy about that. Mr. Jonas says he don't want me in one of those zoos where the boys be

shooting each other up over a pair of Reeboks, so he's looking into a good place for me where I can get to without being stuck on the subway an hour every day. I been doing
that tutoring thing with him, and he says he's real pleased
with my progress. I'm gonna miss him and his sexy voice,
and the little bit of flirting we do to make each other smile,
but I'm so excited about a new school my heart jumps at the
thought. Maybe I'll find me a decent boyfriend there, and get
myself into college. I wanna go into science and work in a
lab in a white coat, or maybe accounting and make a lotta
money. Mr. Jonas says, "Keep on working, Bianca, and you
might make it happen." Roberto just grumbles and kicks the
ground when I talk about it. He's jealous.

The thing I feel best about, though, is Mami. She and Big
Al are getting so tight I feel squeezed outta the house sometimes, but it's so good to see Mami happy again I can't stay
mad too long. They go off to work in the morning, dressed
like twins in their sweatpants and rubber boots and lumpy
jackets. He is so ugly in his thick glasses and that mustache
like a wire brush, and Mami looks so tiny and skinny in all
them clothes—I laugh every morning I see them go off.
They look like the elephant and the mouse. But Big Al's
okay. He's got these three daughters live with their mother
who come over sometimes, and all but one of them is pretty
cool. The oldest, Rahel, is seventeen, finishing up high
school; the middle one, Naimah, is my age, almost fifteen;
and the little one, Tiffany, is younger, maybe thirteen. I don't
like the little one so much, but the other two and me have a
good time together. Last night they came over for dinner,
and I looked round the table Mami had set up so nice, and
there was me and her and Big Al and Rahel and Naimah and
Tiffany all laughing and screeching and making noise, and I
thought, wow, I got a family again.

Listen, there's just this one other thing I gotta say. It's to
the baby. Little Rosalba, I'm sorry I couldn't keep you. I

know it wasn't your fault. You kinda got born in the wrong place at the wrong time, y'know? But I think we've fixed that now, least I hope so. Be happy, little girl, and I'll make a special wish for you every one of your birthdays. Maybe one day we'll meet on the street. I'll be a grown-up married woman in a suit, going off to work, and you'll be a pretty little girl going off to school, and we'll smile at each other.

"Say hello to the lady," Sarah will tell you (she'll be looking all worn-out and old from being a mom).

"Hi," you'll say, and you'll smile that dimply smile you got. "My name is Rose."

"Yes," I'll say, "I know." And I'll watch you go off down the street, holding hands with your moms, and no one but me and her and Mami will ever know your secret.

As Mami likes to say, "This family, it has been through a storm and a whole lotta troubled waters, but all is calm now, all is peace. Dios que está en el cielo, please keep it that way."

Amen.

· A NOTE ON THE TYPE ·

The typeface used in this book is one of many versions of Garamond, a modern homage to—rather than, stricltly speaking,
a revival of—the celebrated fonts of Claude Garamond
(C. 1480–1561), the first founder to produce type on a large
scale. Garamond's type was inspired by Francesco Griffo's
De Ætna type (cut in the 1490s for Venetian printer Aldus
Manutius and revived in the 1920s as Bembo), but its letter
forms were cleaner and the fit between pieces of type im-
proved. It therefore gave text a more harmonious overall ap-
pearance than its predecessors had, becoming the basis of all
romans created on the continent for the next two hundred
years; it was itself still in use through the eighteenth century.
Besides the many "Garamonds" in use today, other typefaces
derived from his fonts are Granjon and Sabon (despite their being named after other printers).